PRAISE FOR *UNPARDONABL*

"A rousing murder mystery that's also an absorbing inquiry into sin, guilt, sexuality, violence, and responsibility, *Unpardonable Sins* features a host of memorable characters, most notably John Reimer, the earnestly, vulnerably inquisitive Mennonite preacher-turned-sleuth. This entertaining, provocative novel immerses us in the streets and politics of Chicago, and the mysteries of family, faith, and action in this lovely, brutal world."

—JEFF GUNDY, AUTHOR OF *WITHOUT A PLEA* AND *SOMEWHERE NEAR DEFIANCE*

"The history of detective mystery novels is littered with tough cops and boozed-out private sleuths who track down bad guys and bring them to justice. But until I picked up *Unpardonable Sins*, I never came across anything like the exploits of a Mennonite minister in pursuit of a ruthless killer on the North Side of Chicago. John Reimer is a middle-aged, semi-burned-out pastor of a dwindling congregation who finds himself trying to solve a young man's murder.... *Unpardonable Sins* crackles with fascinating characters, clever dialogue, and surprising twists and turns."

—AL GINI, AUTHOR OF *THE IMPORTANCE OF BEING FUNNY* AND *WHY WE NEED MORE JOKES IN OUR LIVES*

"Mennonite pastor John Reimer is the gritty protagonist I've been waiting for—secure in the soil of deep roots, resolute about justice and truth, unafraid to confront his flaws and theological vagaries, and confident that holiness has no coin if not fleshed out in action."

—WALLY KROEKER, RETIRED EDITOR OF *THE MARKETPLACE* MAGAZINE

"A gripping narrative that intertwines Chicago history and weather, politics and police, with Mennonite potlucks, church politics, and Karl Barth. *Unpardonable Sins* … undercuts simplistic explanations of why and how human beings live and find meaning. This mystery novel by an astute observer of Chicago street life and a master wordsmith will introduce you to a Mennonite pastor you will not soon forget."

—JOHN KAMPEN, DISTINGUISHED RESEARCH PROFESSOR, METHODIST THEOLOGICAL SCHOOL IN OHIO

Unpardonable Sins

Unpardonable Sins

DAVID SAUL BERGMAN

RESOURCE *Publications* · Eugene, Oregon

UNPARDONABLE SINS

Resource Publications
An Imprint of Wipf and Stock Publishers
199 W. 8th Ave., Suite 3
Eugene, OR 97401

www.wipfandstock.com

PAPERBACK ISBN: 978-1-7252-8973-4
HARDCOVER ISBN: 978-1-7252-8974-1
EBOOK ISBN: 978-1-7252-8975-8

02/02/21

for George Classen and Howard Moody

If any man see his brother sin a sin which is not unto death, he shall ask, and he shall give him life for them that sin not unto death. There is a sin unto death; I do not say that he shall pray for it.

—1 JOHN 5:16

Chapter 1

DAWN CAME LIKE MOCHA latte, seeping slowly into a cup of black sky. Then the sky turned the color of plums. This was not the true light. This came before the light. As it was becoming real, all the electric stars shining in the streets and buildings of the vast city began to fade. Then the first *real* light played across Lake Michigan, picking up the flat surfaces of Gold Coast high rises in bursts of pink and fire. The city shrugged off its sleep and began to rouse itself into the morning.

Near the Lincoln Park Boat House a young man took repeated blows to his head. His face had turned into a sopping, bloody mash, but he still managed to land a solid kick to his assailant's groin. The assailant bent over. But it wasn't good enough. The young man expelled a surprised grunt, and then received another blow from the butt-end of a pistol, and a swing and a miss with a piece of lead pipe. When the lead pipe made contact on the second try, its harm couldn't be undone.

Falling, his eyes open, the young man started to choke on his own blood. He reached for his assailant's legs in a fading tackle. But all his voluntary movements had stopped, his will ended, by the time he hit the ground.

The assailant watched a final twitch in the body when he turned it over and ripped open the young man's shirt. Across the corpse's chest, the tip of a hunting knife swiftly moved to inscribe hieroglyphs. Then with a different motion, a single efficient slash, the assailant's knife opened the body further to the indignities of the cold March air. He lifted a hot mass away from the body and wrapped it in a couple of steaming loops around the dead man's neck. The killer straightened up and looked north and south along the running path. He dragged the corpse off the path and rolled it with his feet under some bushes, then adjusted his jacket and jogged off.

❖ ❖ ❖

Chris stepped back from the tree where he had urinated and tripped over a bicycle. He shook his head. He could make out individual trees as they began to appear in the light. The lake lapped quietly against the breakwater.

Chris glanced at the overturned bike and decided to take a closer look. He tested the handle grips, the durable black foam, tight and easy under his hands, and he tentatively swung his leg over the seat.

As he rode past the body rolled under the bushes, he shrugged at the dark shape long on the ground. He looked again and shifted gears. There were often such shapes of men under the bushes at this hour, especially on this stretch of the lake. He didn't see that the blood leaking from the dead man's torso had begun to congeal. It was not important, and whatever he saw in those bushes began to fade.

Above his head the sky began to change, half-and-half cutting through French roast. He didn't stop. As he pedaled faster, whatever he had seen, that darkness, fell away into an abyss. *Oh, I can go places on this bike all right,* he thought.

Chapter 2

NORTH ON BROADWAY THE halfway houses and deteriorating SROs had begun their retreat before the onslaught of prosperity: shiny BMWs and Volvos, newly sandblasted greystones, neat black iron fencing in the high Victorian Gothic style behind which patches of manicured grass lay in repose. The Caribbean and Filipino nannies had begun their days by walking the little ones off to school or taking the strollers and their precious white cargo out for the morning promenade.

Nearby, transients pushed shopping carts piled high with their precious possessions and carried plastic drawstring bags over their wrists like purses. There was always an untied belt trailing from their stained and frayed coat, those coats that never looked quite warm enough for this balmy—by Chicago standards—morning at the end of March.

John Reimer, just turned fifty-nine years old, ran south on Broadway. He took this in as he negotiated curbs and lights. Bold print, posted on the back of a bus-stop bench, blazed at him: 1–800-GOOD-DOG. 1–800-DI-VORCE. There had to be a connection. He ran with the stride of a toiler. He was not a natural and had not found the cure for his wasted vertical motion. Reimer's bushy white mane exaggerated the size of his head, already large given the size of his torso. When he ran, he looked like a brother of Mark Twain. His hair flared out under the 1970s-style green terry-cloth headband. A tattered black sweatshirt and baggy gray gym shorts, fluorescent green Asics, completed his getup. He had old-man socks that his daughter Sarah always mocked; they clung halfway up his calves. On this morning he didn't care; in this kind of weather one didn't want to face the outdoors half-naked.

He passed two evicted women who sat side by side on a torn couch, trying to sell off their possessions before the trash collector took them away.

A broken chest of drawers lay nearby on its side. Shoes and bedding were strewn about the sidewalk. These were large women with big breasts and close-cropped hair, and they sat together like forlorn twins. "The fuck it is cold," one of them said. The other shook out a Kool from a pack and nodded to John as he passed. While he waited for the signal to change, he said, "You need any help?"

The smoker smiled at him as she lit up and then waved out her match. She squinted through the smoke. "Thanks for asking. We'll be okay."

He nodded and kept going. Running like this helped him get back some of the rhythm that he had lost five years earlier when he signed his wife, Viola, into the nursing home in downstate Meadows. Packing the suitcases with her the night before—that had thrown him into a maelstrom of depression. As always, though, she had been perfectly composed and gave him directions on what to pack and what to leave behind.

"I don't want to go," she said. "But I understand."

Keeping his grief bottled up in that moment nearly killed him.

Yes, he had agreed, as the counselor pattered on about a full continuum of care, it was the best thing, the only thing he could reasonably do, and so forth and so on.

His physician Crenshaw had told him, "Look. Denial works until it doesn't work anymore. The next time she falls down a flight of stairs at home, she might not be smiling afterwards. If she breaks her neck, what are you going to say to me then?"

Crenshaw didn't let up. "Oh, I know, you're a hero for giving her the Heimlich. So you learned it from watching TV. Whatever. I have to step in before you start to think you're some kind of fucking MacGyver. Vi's condition is only going to get worse. You can't take care of her and do your job. I know you want to, but you can't. I know you learned the virtues of perseverance and faith on that little Mennonite homestead in Kansas. But when you're dealing with HD, faith and perseverance will take you only so far."

John listened mutely.

"Notions of grandeur are never healthy, especially for a man of the cloth. You Mennonites mix it up with your goddamn martyrdom and that's a toxic blend I will not tolerate." Crenshaw knew he could go rough on the reverend. "Look, hard as you try, you're not Iron John, okay? The default here is for me to prescribe pills. I can do that, and I know you're depressed from everything you've told me and everything I see. But before we do that, why don't you give these a try?"

Crenshaw's gift was a pair of high-end running shoes and a chunky stopwatch.

All these thoughts churned in John's head as he continued his run. Farther south on Broadway the Faith Tabernacle Church, a cool concrete cube topped by a titanium cross, sat in the middle of a new asphalt parking lot, made possible by the demolition of a block and a half of dwellings. On the corner stood a drive-through teller machine. John wondered if the message was "Drive a Car" or "Jesus Saves." He hadn't met the minister yet and thought it was about time to pay a collegial visit.

This morning John had pushed himself past his normal limits: six miles, a slow jog south that seemed to turn into a marathon somewhere back on the cinder path connecting Waveland Golf Course and the softball diamonds laid out between the lake and Lake Shore Drive. Without breaking his stride, he blew his nose into a red bandanna and kept going.

His nose could be taken for that of a Roman consul, or maybe just a wheat farmer. At least that's what his older brothers had intended for him. But he told them he was through with Meade and planned to rent his sections west of Dodge City before going away to seminary—before getting away. John stuck around for his mother's burial and then fled the path of his brothers, escaped especially his oldest brother Andrew's pieties—always well intentioned—and the whole lot of them. Their black, plain-suited authority dressed up in biblical intonations. Andrew had said his farewell: "You can choose the community of faith or you can choose the world."

Now at the Melrose, John asked permission to take a chair to the sidewalk. It was a brazen request, but in a month the outdoor customers would equal those on the inside, and the glorious sunshine today promised spring. It sustained the necessary courage. A busboy lugged a two-top outdoors, set it down, and then brought out a chair. Another brought a glass of ice water. A skateboarder flew past and John caught a flash of purple mohawk. The sun was just warm enough to take the edge off the March wind.

"What will you have, Reverend?"

John turned in his chair to see the waitress put bottles of ketchup and cayenne pepper sauce on the table. Alex flashed him her familiar smile. He was never quite sure how to smile back. Her lithe motion in a pair of black Nikes and white ankle socks contradicted her graying hair. She was descended from Icelanders who had settled Washington Island off the tip of Door County, John knew, and she reminded him of some of his cousins in northern Montana. Pretty enough to turn heads, strong enough to buck bales onto a flatbed trailer.

"The usual?" she said. She looked at the busboy, who was hauling another table outside for two other customers. "You've started something out here, Reverend. We weren't planning to set up outside for another month and a half."

"I'm sorry."

"Don't be. You're entirely justified."

She pulled out her order pad and waited.

"I'll have the omelet. Make that with Swiss cheese, not the mozzarella. And more onions," he said. "Home fries, not the hash browns. And a large tomato juice, please."

She tucked her order pad and both of her hands into her apron pockets and hunched a little against the wind. "How is Vi doing?"

Alex always made a point of asking. She never offered comfort; she just listened; only once, about six months after Vi's move to Meadows, Alex had said to John, "Look, I know what you are going through, and I am so sorry." And she had covered his hand quickly with one of her own. John never asked her about that allusion to her own life. The busboy passed her the coffee, and she poured John a cup and set down a stainless-steel creamer full of half-and-half.

"Vi is about the same, just a little worse," John said. "She still says my name. She recognizes my face. She wants to keep walking but with all the falls . . ."

"Liability issues, I'll bet."

"Yes. They want to strap her into a wheelchair."

Alex paused and looked away. "I'm sorry, John." She looked right at him. "There's something I want to talk with you about. Actually, Annie wants to talk to you," Alex said, gesturing back toward the inside of the diner. Here, it's in the local section. She put the *Sun-Times* on the table and pointed to the headline:

Lincoln Park Murder Victim Still Unidentified: 23rd Precinct Task Force Organized

The body of an unidentified man in his early twenties was discovered yesterday morning around 7 a.m. by a jogger in the wooded area at the edge of the North Pond, adjacent to the Lincoln Park Boat Club. The Coroner's Office listed the cause of death as stabbing.

Detectives from the 23rd Precinct are seeking the public's help in identifying the victim and the perpetrator of the crime. They describe the victim as 5'11", 165 pounds, Caucasian. He wore black spandex cycling pants, a T-shirt, and a navy-blue windbreaker. Any information should be directed to the Chicago Police Department or the Cook County Coroner.

Authorities have declined to comment on whether this incident can be linked to the unsolved deaths of three other young men on the North Side since November. Officials have signaled that the evidence might point to a serial or spree killer targeting gay men. Two of the victims have been African American.

Police Commissioner Warren DeMello denied allegations from leaders in Chicago's gay community that the investigation has been slowed because of police bias. One officer recently stated that the killings were "merely faggot bashings."

Alderman Edward Fitzsimmons, under pressure from citizens in the 44th Ward to upgrade street patrols, strongly concurred with DeMello and insisted that his office has made the safety of all Lincoln Park and Lakeview residents a "top priority." He condemned the violence as "an outrage in our community that will be stopped."

Fitzsimmons declined to comment on whether the investigation will proceed as hate crime. "Until evidence is in from the forensics unit and precinct officers," he said yesterday afternoon, "it would be premature to make such a judgment."

Community leaders are indignant. Doug Campanis, of Chicago's Gay Task Force, accused both the alderman and the Chicago Police Department of "stonewalling on hate crimes." Campanis said that Chicago was "the number one faggot-bashing capital in America," according to data from a recent national survey. McLeary Thomson, head of the Pink Angels Anti-Violence Project based on Halsted Street, said his volunteer organization would be stepping up patrols along the lakefront and would continue to consult with 23rd Precinct police officers. But, he added, "They have given us lukewarm support in the past. We have learned that if we want protection, we're going to have to provide it ourselves."

Another Pink Angels source shared that many of the organization's civilian patrol members already carried a firearm or were planning to arm themselves in light of this most recent death.

John wondered what the story had to do with him. He recollected what his friend Wiebe had said about murders in the 44th Ward: they made the front page, but murder on the South Side or the West Side was so common it wasn't worth writing about. He contemplated the eggs as Alex set them down in front of him and flipped to the sports section to catch up on the Bulls.

A few minutes later, a woman in a Pendleton flannel shirt and impossibly tight Levi's walked out of the Melrose entrance. Her reddish-blonde hair hung in a recent pageboy cut, and a big leather purse slung over her shoulder, together with her laced-up army boots, made her look overwhelmed with gear. She was clearly making an effort to maintain composure, but it wasn't working. She walked straight to John's table.

"I feel really stupid, Reverend . . . Reimer, right? But Alex said I should talk to you. I need to, I need to—"

"Here's a chair," John said. "Sit down. Talk to me."

"Like, I'm totally messed up, excuse me, I'm sorry." She blew her nose into a wadded-up Kleenex. John wondered if she had been doing coke. "Alex said I could trust you. You don't look like any preachers I know. Or any Mennonite, for that matter, and I've seen a few in my part of Ohio." Her voice was underlaid with an Appalachian lilt.

"Thanks for not asking me where my buggy is. Look, Anne—may I call you that?"

"My friends call me Annie."

"Annie, John." He extended his hand.

He noticed her chewed-down nails. She blew her nose again. He wiped ketchup from the side of his plate with a napkin corner and tapped the newspaper. "You wanted me to read this. Do you want to talk about it?"

"Not here. Someplace else, if that's okay?" John noticed she had done a careful job with her makeup but her mascara was in trouble.

"My office is close to Wrigley," John said.

Alex came back to the table and John paid the bill. When he rose to his feet the tendons creaked in his knees. Alex watched him and said, "Now as Annie's people might say, she *needs counseled*, okay?"

"Your people?" John asked, as he scrutinized Annie once more. "Ohio Valley, West Virginia border?"

"Right," she said. "Or as some would have it, Ohio below Columbus. How did you know?"

He didn't want to bore her with his meandering history of unfinished graduate degrees. "I have a noon appointment. Should we go to my office?"

Gray clouds unrolled above them and a seagull cried. A single drop of rain slapped down hard upon the table.

John looked at Annie, and she was crying still. With a proprietary gesture she took the newspaper from him and put it in her purse. They walked to the corner and she hailed a taxi.

"We can walk," John said. "It's not that far."

"I'm very tired," Annie said. "And I don't have an umbrella."

John's knees creaked again when he got in the taxi and sat beside Annie. He sensed she was a recent mourner. *A fine friend of the suffering*, John thought. He hated to admit it, but he had a nose for funerals.

Chapter 3

IN THE CAB SHE asked him if he ever missed Kansas. *What else has Alex told her about me?* "What else do you know about me?" he smiled, but neither of them could muster a laugh. He carefully changed the subject to her work. John had never been very good with polite talk. The ride was mercifully short so he didn't have to endure too much of it.

Inside his study at home—which doubled as his office—he motioned her to the oak chair on the other side of his cluttered desk. She held her body carefully, as if relaxing could cause breakage. Her eyes were too quick to look away when he turned on the lamp beside his desk. She examined the contents of his stacked bookcases, at once curious and dismissive, and John guessed she was wondering why she had even come. She motioned as if to leave.

"You have something to tell me. Please stay." John threw his sweatshirt on a hat rack in the corner and pulled a wool sweater over his T-shirt. He loosened the collar around his throat. Annie watched John nervously run his fingers through his ruffled mane. Wiebe had once told him that in his most thoughtful moments he resembled either an ancient cockatoo in a fusty den—or a damaged, more cerebral Norman Mailer. Neither analogy had struck John as a compliment. He didn't care for tropical pets, or pets of any kind, and he didn't think much of Mailer, especially the man's take on Egyptology. Now John felt rather plain and foolish as he sat before this rather striking young woman, who, if he was honest with himself, made him slightly aroused.

He wondered what he was supposed to do next. Every episode of pastoral counseling, at least in his experience, turned into some kind of adventure.

She spoke. "I'm afraid it's him." John had to think twice to register her meaning. She pointed to the newspaper, hugged her purse to her belly, and bit her lower lip. She rocked back and forth as she struggled to control her tears. "I'm sorry, excuse me. Again, I've been wondering since early this morning . . . The description . . ."

John nudged a box of tissues in her direction and waited.

"You see, it makes absolutely no sense, him being out there, and there is no way, no way . . ."

John waited for her to finish. When she didn't, he asked, "No way what?"

She spoke in a rush. "I don't even know for sure if it's him. But there was no way he was gay."

"I don't think they're saying that, are they?"

"The news story is implying it. I hate that."

"I don't think we should get ahead of ourselves. They haven't identified the victim yet, have they?"

"No. But I swear he isn't gay. Wasn't gay. Oh, shit . . . I'm sorry I didn't mean to say that—I'm just scared. Can you help me?"

John spoke. "Tell me what I can do. Do you want some tea or something?"

"No, that's fine, thanks. I'm afraid, that's all." The young woman gripped her knees and rocked in her chair. "I've been calling. All I get is the answering machine with his and Trophy's message."

"Trophy?"

"His roommate."

"Okay, Trophy and—what is your friend's name?"

"David."

"All you have heard is David and Trophy's answering machine. You haven't talked with David since . . ."

"Since two days ago."

"And Trophy is unavailable," John finished.

She nodded mutely. John looked at her and said, "Okay, I can help you. The first thing you need to do is get some facts. This is all supposition right now, am I right? Make a phone call to the police, or the coroner, before we go any further. You will have no peace till you know some things for sure. If you'd like, I can make the call."

She shook her head no even before he finished speaking. Her gesture made him think momentarily of his own daughter, the way she would skip ahead on the sidewalk on the way to Washington School when she was small, make him feel like the slow competitor.

"Listen to me," John said. "The call is hard, but not knowing is even harder. Not knowing can be the worst thing."

"Oh, I don't think so," Annie said. "Not the worst thing."

"You can do this. You owe it to yourself. And if it is your friend David, well, they'll need someone to identify the body"—she went pale—"and let them know. They'll need information to solve this." John paused. "You owe them this call if you think it's him."

"I can't call the police," she said.

"You can't?"

"No." She rubber-banded her hair into a ponytail and continued, "This is very hard to explain."

"Look," John said, "you can make this more difficult. If it is him, they will speak to everybody he knew. They will get to you eventually anyhow. They will come and speak with you."

"But they claim it's a fag killing. I know. I can't talk with them. There's no point."

"Let's find out if David's alive first and worry about his sexuality later, okay? You don't know if it's him. There's no point jumping to conclusions before you call."

"Ruth Ann said they said it was a fag killing."

"Ruth Ann who?"

"Jimenez. We share an apartment. She does data entry part-time at the 23rd Precinct. She called me this morning."

"Here's the number," John said. He flipped through the phone book and tried not to look impatient. "Here's the phone. In the next few minutes I expect you'll gather your courage and call. I can help you but you have to help yourself." John circled the number with a ballpoint pen. "Tell them about David and everything you know about him. In the meantime, I am going to the kitchen to make a fresh pot of coffee. Cream? Sugar?"

Annie looked up at him and John wondered if David got looks like this from her. "Just two-percent it you have it."

"When you're through speaking with the coroner's office I will be in the kitchen. Come talk to me then."

Annie Casper's eyes streamed anew. "Reverend, you are a very hard man. Alex told me you were a tough son of a bitch."

"And you chose to talk to me. Maybe you should be more careful." John handed her the phone across the desk. She looked at it in front of her. "Look," he continued, "I know how it is. You want to know, and you also don't want to know. But you know you should make this call."

He closed the study door behind him and left Annie to figure it out. He had given her enough directions. No more intervention from him would make any difference. She would either do as he suggested or sling her huge mystery purse over her shoulder and abscond.

He unlaced his running shoes, threw them into the bedroom, and padded in his stocking feet through the dining room into the kitchen. He was surrounded by an unrelenting atrium of white walls in his railroad flat. The only walls his daughter Sarah had left alone, in her fit of decorating enthusiasm, were in the study. *At least she had had the good sense not to cross that line*, John thought.

Sarah had told him that in a week or two he would come to like the bright space and that he was depressed because the grim colors of his pastoral predecessor were "killing his spirit." Right. She said nothing about Viola's absence. Just a lot of commentary on the color of his walls.

Now here he was grinding some coffee for a kid from Appalachia who reminded him of his daughter. The young woman was clearly hiding mountains of information. Most likely she couldn't deal with her boyfriend's predilections. But John didn't dwell on it. She needed human compassion now; other experts would take over with the story's details.

The residue of latex paint, that new-paint smell, hovered in the kitchen. The church moderator, Nancy Huefflinger, had admired Sarah's work and informed John that it inspired the church council to order new kitchen cabinets for the parsonage's apartment. Nancy made a point to personally oversee installation of the butcher-block countertops. She said that no matter how good the cabinetmakers, it's always wise to stay on top of the details.

All these women telling me what I need to be happy, John thought, as he leaned on the coffee grinder. Often, they were right. He held down the plastic top of the Krups grinder and felt the beans thud into powder as the blade whirled them to dust.

He looked up at the kitchen skylight, a miniature house of chicken-wire-reinforced glass that opened to the sky in his twelve-foot ceiling. He glanced down the hallway.

Ten minutes later Annie came out of the study as the coffee maker stopped its gurgle.

"I need just a little more of your time, Reverend."

"You can call me John."

"John, they want me to come to the coroner's office," she said. She wasn't crying now. Dry, her eyes seemed more violet. "I had a bad feeling about this ever since I read the fucking paper—I mean, the paper—this morning. Pardon me."

"You need somebody to go along."

"Yes."

"Here, drink some of this first."

He handed her the mug. She told him he looked like somebody she knew in Fly, Ohio.

"Your dad or your grandfather?" he asked.

Her smile, her first that day, lit up the kitchen, and she drank deeply from the mug that she cradled in both hands. "That's good coffee, John. Thank you."

Pastoral counseling, indeed, he thought. The day was just beginning.

Chapter 4

By early afternoon National Public Radio was reporting winds of forty to fifty miles an hour, plummeting temperatures, and delays at O'Hare. Lake Michigan had begun to wash across Lake Shore Drive.

John looked out his study's window, watching pieces of paper impale themselves on fences, crushing flat against buildings and parked cars. Barefoot and shirtless in his running shorts, he checked his watch. He resembled an aging jockey in a paddock, arms slumped listless at his sides. He wished he were sixteen again in Kansas, breaking horses east of Meade with Andrew keeping watch. Not this. Anything but a visit to the Cook County Medical Examiner's Office.

After he took a shower, he got out his ironing board and an iron and plugged in the appliance. Outside, rain was turning to ice pellets that rattled the windows. He looked at the elements battering the glass. Chicago is a place where the cold kills the weak, then the heat kills off the others, and in spring the wind sorts and tests what remains. "But the one who endures to the end will be saved." He ironed his white Oxford, starting with the collar, and then the sleeves, as Viola had taught him. He listened to the steam hiss on the shirt and thought of one of the difficult sayings: "For to all those who have, more will be given . . . but from those who have nothing, even what they have will be taken away." For some time he had been entertaining a sermon series on the Jesus of Little Comfort.

He finished the shirt and went into the bedroom to get dressed. He slipped on an old tweed sport coat, threadbare at the sleeves, then a rumpled raincoat. He pulled on a pair of Sporto rubber boots. On the landing above the staircase, he listened to the wind and abandoned the idea of an umbrella, instead tugging on a battered fisherman's cap.

Outside the sleet hurled fury in his face. By the time he reached the car he was drenched. When he double-parked outside Annie's building, she stood under the awning and looked twice before recognizing him. He had to honk.

"You ought to dry out," she said, when she opened the passenger door and looked in. "I shall call you Captain Ahab."

John didn't respond, simply smiled. She got in and he pulled away from the curb.

He turned left onto Ashland, with wipers and defroster both set on high. This was not the time for small talk. Annie sat shivering in a light wool jacket, her jaw set. She had ditched the big purse and was carrying a small beaded clutch and a compact pop-up umbrella.

"Captain Ahab says you need a parka and a pair of mittens." She smiled. He sounded paternal, he knew, but how could he not see her as an orphan entrusted to his safekeeping, at least for the rest of this day? Her hair was gathered up under a blue beret and she had restored her makeup since he last saw her. As they drove south, John could tell she was comfortable with the silence. Out the window were ragged blocks of bodegas, used-car lots, cheapening storefronts.

"Do you want to tell me more about David?"

"No."

West on Harrison the buildings thinned out. They drove by the crawling, yellowed façade of Cook County Hospital, with its garish, ornately designed pillars partly covered with scaffolding—another last-ditch effort at renovation. The place was certain to be condemned. Then on through the futuristic complex of Rush Presbyterian, elevated walkways snaking between orderly heaps of concrete and glass. And the endpoint of this road trip was perfect in its logic: the Cook County Institute of Forensic Medicine, marked in block letters above the entrance, a slit cut in the polished granite. It was some designer's brutalist dream of a twenty-first-century pillbox. Long on stone, short on windows, form met function. A fortress for the dead.

Annie stepped out of the car and opened her umbrella, but the wind nearly ripped it out of her hand, dislocating its ribs upward. They snapped back down with a painful pop as she aimed the handle into the wind. John helped her grip the handle and ran beside Annie into the morgue.

The receptionist behind the glass window looked up from a paperback. Annie spoke through a small round hole in the glass. "My name is Anne Casper. I called a couple of hours ago."

The receptionist's shoulder-grazing gold earrings swiveled in her ears as she consulted a clipboard, and she raised a pair of painted-on eyebrows to consider her client.

"I'm here to make an identification," Annie said.

John sat down next to a pay phone. A crippled palm tree was lean-ing askew, bandaged with duct tape to a steel pipe hastily jammed into the planter. The ventilation system made low creaks and rattles overhead, like a spaceship freighter.

A group of people emerged from a hallway. John was reminded of his own whiteness. At the head of the group walked a man clad in a forest-green sweat suit and festooned in gold: Rolex, bracelet, chains around his neck. He had a plastic name tag clipped to the pocket of his zip-up top, and the dome of his shaven head picked up the fluorescents above. He looked like an or-namented Christmas tree as he listened to the commentary from the group.

"Pooky didn't make it," an older man in the party said.

"The rest of them just ran," said a woman in a long red coat and high boots.

John pretended to be reading.

"Yeah, one shot to the chest. Bro didn't even have time to think about leaving the car. Got stuck in the front seat."

Another voice in the group: "They don't know if he died instantly, but it was pretty quick."

After Pooky's family exited, the man in green returned. John stood up and extended a hand.

"Lucius Robinson, intake specialist," said the man. He ignored John and looked directly at Annie. "You're the one who called? About making an identification?"

"Yes," Annie said.

"And this is?" Lucius said, looking back at John.

"John Reimer, minister of Lakeview Mennonite Church."

"Pleased to meet you, Reverend." He extended a hand studded with rings and a heavy bracelet. "This way, folks."

He led them down a polished hallway filled with closed doors. Further down trapezoids of white light spilled onto the shine where doors had been left open.

Lucius led them into a windowless room with two brown sofas and a low square table. In the corner a TV set was bolted to the wall with a metal bracket. Lucius went out of the room and came back. "You going to be okay, miss?" he asked Annie. "You just let me know if you recognize him."

She looked at him and then looked at the blank screen. "You are fuck-ing kidding me, right?"

"Ma'am, we recommend the viewing on the screen here. This will only take a moment. Now take your time, he is a little bruised."

"No, not on TV. This is unacceptable." She walked out of the room as a badly color-tuned image appeared on the set. John thought Cook County could have done a little better job with the tint. He told Lucius: "She wants to see him. No television, please. I think it would best."

Lucius put up his hands in resignation. "If she loses it, are you the responsible party? I have seen how this can go. This is our standard protocol."

"Brother," John said, "if you recommend a straitjacket, I know how to put one on, okay?"

In another room down the hallway a camera mounted on an overhead metal track stared down like a silvery eye at dead David Talbot's face. He lay zipped up to his neck in black plastic; a heavier vinyl cover draped over the body bag that held him. His face and head were not in good condition.

Lucius and John stood in the doorway and watched Annie lean over the long metal tray that held the corpse. She touched the battered, torn lips with her finger.

She said, "David? Is this you? David?" And they all waited as if the sound of her voice would bring the corpse to life.

Some minutes later, Lucius looked at her and at his clipboard. "Any identifying marks?"

Annie said, "His left thigh, a birthmark. And right above it, a tattoo."

Lucius took her beside the table on the other side and lifted the vinyl canopy. The sound of the zipper ripped through the silence. Lucius partially rolled the corpse over on the metal table. John turned away. He was sick with the smell of medicine and disinfectant and death, and he was cold now and bile burned in his throat. He wanted to get back to his car.

"Yes. It's him."

Lucius told Annie: "If you sign and you're not next of kin we have to hold him four more days. If you want a release now, we need next of kin."

"His aunt lives on Orchard Street in Lincoln Park. I think I have her number here." Annie dug in her clutch. "Or it's a great-aunt, I'm not sure." She scrabbled through a tiny red address book.

John wondered what other pertinent information she had withheld. "You didn't tell me about an aunt," he observed.

"John, I haven't told you much of anything. I'm sorry. I meet a lot of people. David introduced me to her once, okay?" Her anger was carrying her through the tide of grief, John thought, and that was fine, that was necessary, let it be.

Annie made a call by the bandaged palm tree and they sat down to wait for Helen Talbot-Smith to arrive.

While they waited, Lucius regaled them with stories of his days as a personal bodyguard for Muhammad Ali. He said he had been at the Rumble in the Jungle. John listened to Lucius describe how Foreman hit the canvas while Annie looked at herself in a compact mirror and checked her eyeliner. The humming machinery in the ceiling rattled and sighed.

Chapter 5

THE CLOUDS BOILED COBALT gray for Helen Talbot-Smith's arrival by cab but withheld further rain, as if in deference to her blue-haired royalty.

She entered the waiting area bearing her inlaid ivory cane more like a field marshal's baton than a walking instrument. She waited a moment beside the receptionist's cubicle before tapping twice on the glass with her stick. "Excuse me," Helen told the receptionist, "I am a relative of the deceased. May I speak with the examiner?"

The receptionist's eyebrows rose with pencil-line precision. "Ma'am, he will be right with you."

"I am David's great-aunt. Now where is he?" She turned with a start toward John and Annie. Her head trembled on her neck like a ruined heavy flower on a fragile stalk. She stood just over five feet tall, swathed in a mink coat and leather flats that twinkled with tiny rhinestone bows.

John inhaled Chanel as she reached her hand forward to shake his. The grip was strong in the palsied way of the ancient ones.

"You must be the preacher. Reverend Reimer?" Her smile was full of money and good dentistry, and her left hand gripped the ivory cane. One look at her and John realized this was a woman who hated very much being old. Monstrous and charming, she was like some kind of fossilized flapper.

"Call me John. Pleased to meet you. Mrs. Talbot-Smith?"

"Helen, thank you."

The cane bobbed on Helen's wrist as she turned to Annie. Annie looked at her hand clutched between the great-aunt's two gnarled ones.

"Why didn't you call me right away?" Helen said. Her voice shook.

"I didn't know, Helen. I didn't know for sure until an hour ago."

"Sweet, merciful God in heaven," Helen said. "Who could do such a thing to our David?" Her voice sought a new beginning. The ductwork in the ceiling pinged. "Now what am I supposed to do? What do they want from me? What are we to do?"

"I told you—they need next of kin to sign papers," Annie said.

Helen looked at her watch and stared at the lobby as if lost. "How did he die?" she asked John.

"He was jumped—assaulted in the park at North Pond." John did not think it was his place to offer a forensic report. "They didn't give us any other details."

Julius took Helen into the TV room to look at the picture of the dead man's face while Annie went to wait outside. When Helen and Julius came back into the lobby a few minutes later, Helen was holding her silver wire-rimmed glasses and hanging onto Julius's arm. She walked unsteadily into John's arms and her shoulders heaved. John sensed she was a woman who had spent a lifetime asking directly for what she wanted, and at this moment that would be comfort.

When he thought she was ready, John helped her into a chair and asked, "Does the boy have parents? They need to be notified."

"David called me only two months ago," Helen began. "He said he was working as a bike messenger. He didn't want my help. Look, you need to understand he was the kind of boy who never wanted anyone's help. He talked about starting classes at DePaul. He was getting over his mother."

"Getting over his mother?"

"She died in San Diego a year ago."

John waited for more.

"Of a long illness."

"I'm very sorry," John said. "And his . . . ?"

"Oh, of course it is his father you want to know about, don't you? Let us simply say he was most irresponsible, disappeared before David's birth. He renewed my belief in the necessity of hell. May that piece of shit rot there." She took out a pack of Wrigley's spearmint gum. Her polished nails worked the tinfoil wrapper off a stick, and for a moment, as her teeth found the gum, the image of a patrician woman in furs blended with something early Jurassic. "Pardon me, Reverend. I get carried away. I know this sounds a tad harsh, am I right?"

"Tell me about his father."

"We don't speak of him. He left Elinor twenty years ago and moved west. The boy never knew his father. Forgive me for getting carried away. You're not Anglican, are you?" Her eyes twinkled.

"No. How could you tell?"

She glanced at his clothing, head to toe, in the briefest kind of appraisal. "Perhaps the Germanic name. Look, more than one clergyman has told me I have an anger problem. Especially when I talk about *him*. But we must be practical first. There are funeral arrangements to consider. Where is Annie? Where is that girl?"

John read her motion to leave and extended his hand. She looked at him as he helped her to her feet. She dusted off the back of her coat and wrinkled her nose. "Would it be rude to say this place has a smell?"

In the waiting room, Annie took a moment to respond to Helen's query. "I confess I have no idea. I've never done this before." When she recovered her voice, she said, "I don't think David would want a church."

John suggested a private service at the chapel in Kerdigan's mortuary on Lincoln Avenue. He arranged it by phone on the spot. It wasn't the first time; he could count on Kerdigan in a pinch. Helen signed more forms on the clipboard. John told the receptionist that Kerdigan's car would pick up the body.

Julius reemerged from the hallway. "Some gentlemen from the police department are on the way, and they wish to speak to you," he said to Annie.

Annie looked at her watch. "I have been here nearly two hours. If they are so anxious to speak with me, they can reach me at home. You have my address. It's on your clipboard, sir."

"I must insist, ma'am, that you wait."

"And I must insist on going. Thank you for your concern."

John spoke. "These ladies have been through quite enough, don't you think?" He gave Julius his card. "Tell the officers that Anne and I will meet with them. That's my number."

Back in the northbound traffic of Lake Shore Drive, John wondered whether it was the time to ask Helen more questions about David's parents. He decided it could wait. Annie sat in the back seat, silent, and made occasional eye contact with John in the rearview mirror.

The wind still battered the city with staccato bursts and the three of them found little to say. John dropped Helen off first. Her old woman's voice came out gravelly: "We will talk soon, I expect. Let us have tea sometime after the funeral. When we can think straight." She turned to Annie in the back. "You are a sweet girl and I am so, so sorry."

At Annie's stop she left the car with a quick goodbye. As John drove home, he thought about his sermon notes, about the way Helen hobbled to the landing of her Orchard Street row house, the rhinestone flats twinkling on her feet.

He thought about Annie Casper, who had hijacked his day.

Most of all he thought about the body on the stainless-steel table, a young man whose story John wanted to know. But the story there would require others to tell it. Both of the women, he was certain, had much more to tell. He wondered whether their ancient and modern testimonies would corroborate each other. This would require considerable study.

Chapter 6

WHEN HE WAS ALONE, those who were around him along with the twelve asked him about the parables. And he said to them, "To you has been given the secret of the kingdom of God, but for those outside, everything comes in parables; in order that

> 'they may indeed look, but not perceive,
> and may indeed listen, but not understand;
> so that they may not turn again and be forgiven.'"
> And he said to them, "Do you not understand this parable?
> Then how will you understand all the parables?"
> —The Gospel of Mark 4:10–13

It was a Sunday John would rather forget. There had been a spectacular flute solo, Jean-Pierre Rampal, by a graduate student from Northwestern new in attendance and promising to return. But not enough of a congregation had been there that morning to appreciate the music, too many empty pews. Even the singing of 606 didn't quite lift off.

After the service, during coffee hour, the church moderator Nancy Huefflinger shrugged her broad shoulders and gave John one of her dark-eyed looks, which continually annoyed him, and said that most of the young adult group had gone to the Michigan dunes for a nature walk.

"I wish I had known," John said. "I seem to be out of the loop. Isn't it a little too early in the season for that?"

"Don't take it personally. It's springtime. We've lots of free spirits in this place. You wanted an urban congregation and you got one."

"Yes, but what about being informed?"

"Lighten up. With as many ex-fundamentalists as we have here, they don't always want to tell Daddy what they're doing."

Nancy had the reputation in the wider Mennonite conference of being an Amazon to watch out for. The patriarchs found her style threatening. In her high heels she stood almost six feet tall, and at formal gatherings she made sure to wear heels. She liked to look men in the eye, preferably at a slightly downward angle.

John had once overheard a conversation by fellow ministers deeply engaged in the subject of her wardrobe. It had been during intermission at a national church convention on the subject of sexuality. A lefty woman minister from San Francisco had married a lesbian couple, and now there was talk of expelling Tenderloin Mennonite, as it was nicknamed, from the national fellowship. But the conversation in the men's room that afternoon during the convention's first break, where the real caucusing at these events tends to happen, had been all about Nancy. Even district ministers weren't above occasional lewdness, especially if it could be conveyed in the earthy wholesomeness of Low German, an otherwise vanishing dialect.

John wanted to tell Nancy later, but the conversation was not exactly translatable. He was certain that he would keep his private laughter in that moment to himself.

The patriarchs of the conference had some reason to fear Nancy. John knew how deftly she could wield her unique combination of finesse and brute will. An attorney in her early forties who had just made partner in a South Loop firm, single, and more administratively driven than devout, she ran the Lakeview Mennonite church council the way she drove her Chevy Blazer: steady and firm but with a deep understanding of its limitations. She had insisted on the renewal of John's contract when his wife entered the nursing home half a decade earlier, held the line with the older membership who viewed a pastor without the proper pastor's wife as a kind of spiritual amputee. Nancy was a good listener—not only did the older membership stay, John did too.

He noticed that she didn't say anything about the morning's sermon. He wondered lately whether close exegetical reading of biblical texts was an anachronistic practice, whether he wouldn't be wiser to pick up the newspapers and gloss current events.

But John was stubborn about some things; modernity hadn't completely corrupted him. He still wanted to keep the pulpit separate from the pundit. Nancy from time to time assured him that his exegetical habits were fine, but then she admitted that in her line of work, intellectual property rights and patent law, the game of close reading was still appreciated. John wasn't sure she represented the general pulse on this.

Out of the blue Nancy announced, "Mark's Jesus certainly presents more of a problem than Luke's, doesn't he?"

"Are you saying I'd do better with Luke?" John asked. "Jesus the Great Physician?"

"Not at all." She pointed in the direction of the coffee makers and said, "Why don't you go ask him?"

A leathery man with a graying ponytail, dressed in black jeans, lizard boots, and a turquoise bolo tie over a western shirt from Sheplers stood by the urn maniacally stirring four spoons of sugar into his brew. This was Alan Wiebe, head of the worship committee and distinguished professor of New Testament and intertestamental studies at a seminary in Hyde Park.

Wiebe had authored a slim monograph on apocalyptic source literature that made him famous in scholarly circles when he was just a kid at Vanderbilt in the early 1960s. He quickly parlayed that fame into a reputation on the Dead Sea Scrolls dispute. He had branched out some since then, making a habitual practice of scandalizing academic gatherings with his views about the apostate, compromised condition of the American church, in language that ranged anywhere from moderately salty to downright profane and even blasphemous, by some accounts and depending on the audience.

He came from the same Russian Mennonite roots that John did, though not the Kleine Gemeinde. In other words, his people were also rigid, but rigid in different ways. Wiebe knew the plains of Kansas farther east, a place called Hillsboro to be exact, a tiny concentration of devout Brethren most recently marketing itself as the Sausage Capital of America. The town had spawned an unlikely hodgepodge of scholars, theologians, artists, and feeble ethnic jokes. "You know what the Russian Mennonites coming over from Molotschna said when they sailed into New York Harbor and first saw the Statue of Liberty?" Wiebe liked to ask, thin lips expressionless. "If this is New York, what must *Hillsboro* be like?" Ba-dum-tssch.

"Tell me, Alan," John asked him, "is exegesis dead? I've been debating whether to preach from Mark at all. Do the youth go on nature walks because they seek more uplift and comfort?"

"Too many damn Mennonites turning into warmed-over Romantics as far as I can tell. Fucking tree huggers." Alan slurped his coffee loudly, and spilled a little down his shirt front. He brushed at the spill. "John, we must decide if we are the church of Jesus or of that pissant William Wordsworth, and I think it's high time somebody clarify the difference."

"Wordsworth?" John asked. "English Romantics?"

"Well, yes, actually. If we stuck to Blake, we wouldn't be too bad off. 'The vision of Christ that thou dost see / Is my vision's greatest enemy.' You were asking about the gospel of Mark. Actually, I think Blake totally got Mark's gospel."

"Did you know about this nature walk to the dunes? Was I the only one left out of the loop?"

"Yeah, I heard about it. Not interested. Actually, I think this urban professional crowd you're so good at cultivating is worse than their parents."

"Yes? How is that?" Nancy sidled into the conversation.

"Okay, listen. One reason is that unlike their parents, they didn't freeze their asses off in the middle of winter in a dirt house in Wolf Point or Corn, Oklahoma. Or like their grandparents getting cut down by fucking Cossacks in the Ukraine. Without a proper grasp of suffering, and I'm not just talking about watching CNN here, we've turned the gospel into a bloody self-esteem clinic. I've always said, John, that theology is as much geography as anything else. We underestimate geography. The Jewish people, of course, have a much more realistic sense of this than we do. We think it's all ideas, all *spirituality*. Bullshit!"

Wiebe was just starting to get going now. "But as far as more sweetness and comfort and uplift, John, I don't think so, if you're fishing for advice. Are you? You are, aren't you?" He laughed again, heartily, and wiped some coffee from his mustache with the back of his hand. John found himself looking into the eyes of this man and wondering, as he always did, *What is it that I like so much about the crazy people of this world?*

Nancy spoke. "Yes, Alan, but if you had your way, we'd simply turn Menno Simons into Lenny Bruce. Some of us are still looking for an occasional hint of redemption, you know?" She had a rumbling alto laugh and wasn't afraid to mock her colleagues, especially the scholars.

John always listened with amazement when Alan spoke. He conversed as if in front of a classroom, a perpetually seething core of conviction laced with barbed irony. His students affectionately called him The Ranter. His classes were packed out, not only with Protestants but increasingly with Jews and Catholics. The more he mocked the pope's debilities, the more they came. He took potshots at Orthodox rabbis and got away with it because his mastery of midrash had earned him respect. He shook off the praise with more insults. He excoriated liberals, fundamentalists, divinity students who let slip that they shopped at Benetton. He was an equal opportunity ranter.

Wiebe sometimes preyed on John's nerves, but like Nancy, he had the right instincts for this congregation and John often relied on his advice.

"Alan is partly right," Nancy conceded. "Sure, we want uplift. But we also want more than that."

"If you want uplift, join the choir and drink the blasted coffee," Alan said. "We have the best damn coffee hour on the North Side. It's positively evangelical. Or if you're weak of will, there's always our New Age herbal teas.

Here's to uplift." He hoisted a mug emblazoned with "Duke University Press: Post-Contemporary Interventions."

He got in jabs against the New Agers at every opportunity. He'd almost resigned his congregation membership a year earlier when one of the young mothers, who believed in something she called holistic faith—"If I hear the word *holistic* one more time, I'm going to fucking hurt somebody," Wiebe liked to say—stored the placenta from her first home birth in the freezer and requested that it be planted with a young tree at an ecumenical Earth Day celebration. Wiebe had gone ballistic in council, pounding the table in a performance reminiscent of Khrushchev at the United Nations.

Now he reloaded the mug with Mennonite fair-trade Colombian roast, and resumed. John and Nancy listened intently.

"Look, John, and I'm absolutely serious, let me tell you something about Mennonite urban professionals, and I've told you this before. We not only need to be tweaked with a little guilt now and then. We require it for our mental health, because that's the authentic Mennonite experience. Without a good solid base in guilt, we're spiritually dead. Hell, John, you know this. You're Kleine Gemeinde. Do I need to explain this? I'm being redundant for you. When it comes to guilt, we kick Jewish and Catholic ass combined. And you know it. I'm doing a scientific survey, figuring out a way to crunch this paradigm. I think it actually has basis in statistical reality. I'm keeping track. So keep throwing us those hard sayings. Throw us Mark in all his prickly impossibility. We need you to help us cut through—"

"To cut through our knowingness, right, Alan?" Nancy finished for him. "The price we pay for having escaped suburban religion and Melmac dinnerware." She took John's elbow and steered him through the crowd, away from Wiebe's voice, which was already on to reaching new listeners.

"I'm hungry," Nancy said. John saw the destination: a plate of apple *plautz* pastries in the kitchen adjacent to the social hall.

A stout matriarch stood at the counter replenishing a platter with ginger snaps, and she smiled, slightly gap-toothed. Her round face was homey with love. She gave John a hug with one arm while continuing her task with the free hand.

"Good morning, Mildred," John said. He dreaded her fifteen volunteer hours a week in the church office, although he had to admit her secretarial skills were useful. She brought him around to agreement on most things by bringing in plates of pastries, the recipes of which she claimed had originated in Vi's cookbook, published by the Zoar Church Sewing Circle in 1964. Talk about guilt. Every time he bit into one of those sour cream twists, one of those rhubarb yard-pie *prishki*, he thought of his dear dead mother and his sick vegetating wife and all the pious godly women like Mildred Unruh who made the world a place worthy of habitation—and then his objections to her trailed off in a euphoria of finely rolled pastry, butter, sugar, and God knows what else melting exquisitely on his tongue. This too was of the kingdom of God, as he understood it.

Then Mildred would usually say something like, "Don't you think more time with parishioners and less with just anybody who wants your time would be wise? Should I get you a bigger appointment book?" And John would have to remind her that his ministry was a welcoming one. To keep her friendly concern at a proper distance was one of his distinctive challenges.

On more than one occasion he'd overheard her on the phone telling a member of the congregation, "That poor man, his wife in a nursing home. I don't know how he does it. He's lonely, but he doesn't admit it. Reminds me of when my Arthur was sick the last year."

Mildred and Nancy exchanged nods. Mildred hurried out with the plate of cookies to the social hall.

Nancy said to John, "There's another AA group that requests use of our facilities. This one's mostly gay, lots of HIV positive, and they're asking permission to smoke in the basement. Peters think we should say yes, but I think we have to move carefully. I think we'll run into trouble on council. We should have had that meeting yesterday."

John bit into a piece of the apple *plautz*. "I'm sorry I had to cancel," he said as he chewed. "I may get us deeper into hot water, you know. I'm doing a funeral on Tuesday at Kerdigan's."

"Why is that a problem?" Nancy asked.

"This one could be different. You read about the murder in Lincoln Park?"

Nancy stopped. "You're kidding."

"No. The lady companion of the deceased and a great-aunt agree he wouldn't want anything too religious. I seem to fit the bill for agnostic funerals. I spent half of yesterday ferrying people in and out of Cook County morgue. You ever been down there?"

"No."

"I'll keep you informed. I expect there could be publicity."

"I wish you had let me know sooner."

"Ah, but must we tell Mother everything that we are doing?" John grinned. "Look, I had no idea at ten yesterday morning that any of this would develop. I'm as surprised as you are."

"How did they get hold of you? I mean, why are you involved?"

"It's one of the perils of being a regular at the Melrose. Talking with my favorite waitress leads to trouble. Then there's pastoral counseling. Always perilous."

The lids of Nancy's eyes closed slowly and opened. She looked at the kitchen floor and then straight at him, through him. She leaned back slightly against the cabinet by the sink. She had told him once that she was capable of throwing a javelin a hundred thirty feet as an undergraduate. He had been duly impressed.

There was an edge to her voice as she said, "We need to communicate better, John. Canceling on an hour's notice doesn't quite work for me."

He didn't try to explain. Strong women, like strong men, could sometimes be rigid. Later he would wonder whether this were a matter of church polity or simply their first domestic quarrel.

Chapter 7

Sᴜɴᴅᴀʏ ᴀꜰᴛᴇʀɴᴏᴏɴ Jᴏʜɴ ᴅᴏᴢᴇᴅ in his BarcaLounger. He woke up and kept himself company with the *Tribune* and *Sun-Times*. When his eyes tired, he half-heartedly channel surfed a while, volume set at absolute zero. He switched off the set and went to the kitchen to pour a glass of sparkling water. He traipsed back with it through the dining room, where several piles of moldering theological journals and newspaper clippings cluttered the walnut table. He didn't entertain much around that table any more. He was a little surprised Sarah had been kind enough to leave it alone during her frenzy of interior decorating.

He went to his study and spent two hours with René Girard and Jürgen Moltmann, covering fifty pages in each and scribbling annotations down the margins. There were a dozen different books stacked at the left upper corner of his desk, his current reading pile. A little later, in a separate yellow notepad he wrote, "Reconsidering the Scapegoat." Further down, he wrote several words in a list: Jews, women, blacks, and homosexuals. He pondered and then added "smokers" and "Palestinians." He thought about it a little more and added "fat people." He imagined what his daughter would say about the list, so he crossed out "smokers" and set his pen down.

He dozed off in his chair. His older brother Andrew, in a plain suit, and still smelling of the dairy barn on Sunday morning, looked over his shoulder.

"Johanne, was macht es bedeuten?"

As soon as he awoke, another face swam in front of him: David Talbot. The crumpled crown of the skull, staved in, when Julius had tipped the body on its side, the jagged lacerations and bruises. John considered the multiple translations of the Bible and commentaries in the middle of his desk. He looked at the old family pictures under the glass writing surface.

Kerdigan once told him that, after an autopsy, you never know who did what damage.

John decided to get dressed to go running on the cinder path in Lincoln Park. He didn't usually run on Sunday, but today felt different.

He thought about Wiebe's problem with theological "uplift," the man's objection to Romanticism. And then he looked at the picture of a young and lovely Viola, there under the glass by his left hand. The picture had been taken in 1954, shortly after their wedding and the move to Philadelphia, where John did his alternate service in the Byberry state mental hospital. John took out the yellow notepad, tore out a sheet, and wrote another heading: "Anabaptism and Romanticism." He pulled a battered Oxford paperback anthology, *Romantic Poetry and Prose*, from a high, seldom-visited shelf and added it to his current reading stack.

He found himself praying for the souls of the dead, like a Catholic, for some kind of peace. Viola's face haunted him. What was that line from Keats about living a posthumous existence? He wanted to call his wife in Meadows, but it was no good because she wasn't there anymore. Existing, but not there. That was one problem the young man in the morgue didn't have to face.

Chapter 8

ON MONDAY MORNING JOHN awoke at six. He wrapped himself in a robe and made coffee, then flipped on the TV to catch the early news. There was no update on North Pond. Killings, even those in the 44th Ward, had to be extraordinary to get any play. John wondered when the cops would call him for their interview. They'd probably be irate that he had skipped out of the morgue with the women.

John toasted a garlic bagel, spread it thick with cream cheese, and downed it with a glass of orange juice. After his scalding shower, he padded out of the bathroom, dripping, a towel knotted around his middle.

He went back to the study and lifted the blinds. A new dumpster sat across the street. Above it, a plastic chute ran out of a third-floor window. Puffs of dust rose methodically as debris rolled down the pipe and slammed into the dumpster bed.

Annie Casper called him at seven-thirty when he had nearly finished the pot of coffee and gave him an address. "I have one more favor to ask of you. You can say no if you want, I'll manage somehow. I'm on my way to work."

"Yes, but in exchange for these favors I would appreciate if you would shed a little light on my ignorance."

"Trophy called me. He wants David's things out of his apartment. He said the cops went through it all and it's a mess, and he wants it out now."

"I take it you'd rather not see Trophy?"

"Actually he said he would rather not see me."

"Okay, I get it."

Annie hesitated on the other end of the line. "Could you go? You've been so kind already and I don't want to use you."

"What's the address?"

Annie gave John the information and said, "I'll tell him you're coming."

John was firm. "Annie. You recall I am taking care of a memorial service tomorrow, at your request. There are arrangements to make."

"Yes, I know."

"We can talk after the service about picking up David's things."

"Look, you have good reasons to be pissed off. I wanted to tell you the cops already paid their visit, so you won't have to set up an appointment for me. They came here last night. Two guys."

"Did you get their names?"

"They left a card. It's here somewhere."

"Did you learn anything? Or maybe I should ask, did they?"

Annie laughed. "You're asking me if I was reassured. The answer is no. They seemed clueless, I mean in the worst sense of the word. I don't know if they have any leads, any suspects, anything. They talked to me, they talked at me. They jerked me around, if you really want to know."

"Unfortunately that's how a lot of people feel when the cops get done with them," John said. He found an appointment book amid the debris atop his desk. "I can work this in tomorrow afternoon, three o'clock. Does that suit you? Do you want to go along? There may be things David wanted you to have that you would want."

"No, I mean, yes, that works, but . . ."

"We can make arrangements with Trophy at the memorial service in the morning. He will be there, right?"

"I don't know. I wouldn't count on it."

"Were he and David on good terms?"

John could hear her thinking about how to answer.

"I don't know," she said.

"At least call him for me, and tell him a friend will come by for David's things, three o'clock tomorrow. Tell him a guy named Reimer, a benevolent old man with white hair. If you're not along, he needs to know who to let in."

"This is super awkward."

"Yes, it is," John said. "Do what you need to do. Thanks."

After she hung up, John was exasperated. He thought, *I need to have dinner with her, find a way to force an extended conversation. She's cagey. I've got to get her to talk.* He wondered if that's how detectives worked. Sources, chitchat, this and that, all justification of the method. Set up the right situation to get the needed information. But he couldn't very well sit her down in a precinct office and show a badge.

Trophy might have some answers. But that name, and its troubling combination of glittering metal and sharp wooden edges. John thought such a name presaged trouble.

Before he could get too worked up, another call came, this one from Kerdigan Junior, the son and partner of his undertaker friend on Lincoln Avenue.

There had been "a change of venue" for the funeral, Junior told him, and John's services wouldn't be needed after all. "Dad's got more details," Junior said. "But you need to come over here today. I'll fill you in on what I know."

Louis Kerdigan had eyelids sloped down at the outsides and a habit of almost never blinking. This, combined with his six-foot-four frame, gave the impression of a praying mantis at rest after mealtime, or an aging but still dangerous collegiate point guard. The predator look was deceptive. If anyone had ever built a business on kindness, it was Kerdigan. He ran his mortuary on Lincoln Avenue in a neighborhood that had been prosperous and then declined and now was returning to full prosperity once again. He had seen the years, the decades. He had staying power, what his wife, Eva, referred to as "a steady keel." Louis was more modest and had a different version. "Eva's the keel," he liked to say. "I'm just the kielbasa."

When John had moved to the city years earlier, a minister in a struggling neighborhood, he found himself conducting many funerals for those headed to the potter's field. John and Kerdigan became frequent companions. At these events, the mourners numbered anywhere between one and a half dozen, and the suit in the coffin was likely to be one of Kerdigan or John's own, donated for the occasion.

John couldn't quite say what Kerdigan believed in. It had something to do with proper ritual and dignity, and the wisdom of Yogi Berra. Kerdigan was fond of reciting the master before he and John went into the parlor with the open casket—for the chance straggler or stranger. "Always go to other people's funerals; otherwise they won't come to yours." He said it as if he were reminding himself.

Louis sat, eyes droopier than usual, behind his teak desk in the back office. A white ceiling fan turned slowly overhead. John could see a triangular patch of gray stubble on his lean chin that he'd missed shaving. Louis put a Life Saver mint in his mouth. He always had several rolls available under the green-shaded banker's desk lamp.

"Okay, goodbye," he said into the phone, and with a flap of a big hand motioned John into a chair.

"Change of venue?" John said. "Excuse me?"

"Strange events," Kerdigan said. "It seems the boy had a father after all, and one of some prominence. There were investigators here early this morning with an affidavit."

"Two guys from Area 3?"

"Yeah, how did you know?" Kerdigan, bemused, wrinkled his brow. "Anyhow, they had the paperwork. Spit and polish. These tactical officers were dressed up. The works. Suits from Neiman's. More FBI than Chicago PD. Not the usual cowboys. They had the body yanked out of here before I could barely get the doors unlocked."

John spoke. "Doesn't your brother work out of Area 3? That's at Belmont and Western, right?"

"As a matter of fact, yes, he does. So, John, you seem a little edgy. What's with all the questions? You on a mission or an inquisition?"

"A man of the cloth is always on a mission. I wondered if Bill might have some answers."

"To my knowledge, Bill is not covering this case."

"I'm just saying he may have some answers."

"What the fuck, John? You're a Mennonite preacher, for Chrissake, not Inspector Clouseau. Just wait until you have the whole story. It gets even more exotic. Here, let's catch the news."

He opened his desk drawer, removed the remote, and aimed it at a small set bolted in the upper corner of the room. John remembered the cameras in the morgue. The 4 p.m. news break came on.

"Excellent," Louis said. "They do have their timing down. That's what this phone call was just about. Check it out."

The faces in the crowd were sharp on Louis's set. There was a carefully preserved blonde with inelastic lips in the foreground. She had an affected Barbara Walters, a honeyed contralto overlaid with a whisky burr, except for her raised vowels that came from somewhere north of Oshkosh. Gray clouds scudded in the background, behind the faces lining up to get on camera.

"Good morning, Bob. I'm standing in front of the 44th Ward headquarters on Belmont Avenue where Alderman Edward Fitzsimmons is about to hold a press conference that has drawn community leaders and law enforcement officials from around the city. We are told that he will announce the identity of the body found just a few days ago in Lincoln Park. Sources say it is stunning news. Back to you, Bob."

"Come in, Terry. We're on the air."

The wind crackled and jostled in the microphone as the camera panned over the crowd. The reporter in her tan trench coat returned to the screen.

"Bob—pardon these technical difficulties. Alderman Fitzsimmons is about to make his announcement." She looked at the camera: "We're live at 44th Ward headquarters on Belmont Avenue and this is Channel 7 Eyewitness News."

The alderman came into focus behind a bank of microphones, a stout, heavy head with curly steel-gray hair and bifocals sliding down the prow of his well-built nose. The white shirt and green silk tie, the cardigan sweater, the suit coat, the overcoat, the layers of clothing all bespoke preparedness for any crisis. Fitzsimmons took the measure of his audience. He gripped the podium. He wiped his eye, as if the wind irritated him.

"My friends and citizens of the 44th Ward, in Lincoln Park and Lakeview, and the City of Chicago, it is with great sadness that I speak to you today. Police officers in the 23rd Precinct and Area 3 detectives have learned the identity of the victim in last week's vicious attack in Lincoln Park. A crime committed in the early hours of Friday left a young man dead and his family mourning."

He wiped his eye again. "We are here to announce to the perpetrators that these crimes will not stand. We are here to announce that the murderer will be arrested. We are here to declare that justice will be served. I vow to do everything within my power to make this kind of horror impossible in our neighborhoods and in our streets.

"I speak to you today out of a great sense of personal grief, of grief for that young man who died in the park, as well as for his family. That young man . . . that young man is, was, my son."

John motioned for Louis to turn up the volume. The wind whipped across the microphones again.

"He and I had not spoken for some time . . . We had been estranged. We did not see—we did not see eye to eye on many matters." A spattering of rain began to fall on the alderman and the bank of grim faces behind him. An aide held an open umbrella over his head. "But David Talbot was my son, and I loved him. And I vow that his killer, and other perpetrators, will be brought to justice."

Fitzsimmons folded up the notes in front of him as the rain fell harder. He spoke directly to the cameras, his voice choking. "This is very personal. Pray for David, and pray for me. Thank you."

The camera cut from Fitzsimmons as he removed his glasses and worked at his eyes with a handkerchief. The crowd began to clap slowly and then with more fervor. It was reverential clapping that grew into boisterous applause and a chant of "No more hate! No more hate!" Fitzsimmons waved a hand and disappeared, ringed by colleagues and staffers. The camera returned to the reporter. She spoke loudly over the chanting crowd.

"A funeral has been announced for Our Lady of Mount Carmel tomorrow morning," she said. "Again, for viewers just joining us, Alderman Edward Fitzsimmons of the city's 44th Ward announced moments ago that his own son, David Talbot, died in the Lincoln Park attack Friday night. This is the fourth murder of a young man on Chicago's North Side since last November.

"Officials say they are trying to determine whether the murders can be attributed to one killer or to random acts of violence carried out by anti-homosexual hate groups that have been operating in Chicago and the northern suburbs over the past year. Some law enforcement officials have referred to these groups as 'spree killers.' Alderman Fitzsimmons today expressed his grief and declared war against the perpetrators of these murders rocking Chicago's North Side.

"According to a news brief issued by Area 3 police, David Talbot, Alderman Fitzsimmons's twenty-two-year-old son, had moved to Chicago from the San Francisco Bay Area late last fall. He worked as a bicycle messenger for the Cannonball agency in the Loop.

"We'll have more news on this story as it becomes available. Back to you, Bob."

Kerdigan clicked the set off.

"The prodigal son, with a botched ending," John said.

"It's one hell of a story," Kerdigan said. He chewed on a fresh Life Saver.

"I have a question," John said. "This business about not seeing eye to eye. Are we all assuming he was homosexual?" He recalled Annie's vehemence that David was not.

"What, are you dense? We have maniacs out there who have settled on a final solution for every gay man on the North Side."

John rose to his feet.

"Look," Kerdigan continued, "and this is in absolute confidence. I saw how they carved his chest. Someone has a clear agenda. They're very eager to make examples of boys caught over by North Pond after midnight."

Chapter 9

JOHN WALKED HOME FROM Kerdigan's. Across from his apartment he paused to watch the progress of the gut rehab. The interior of the building's shell emitted clouds of dust and the roar and squeal of power tools. John waved at a couple of Mexican construction workers busy shoveling broken plaster into the street dumpster. Then he turned the key in the double lock to his apartment and went upstairs to consult the phone book.

He played back his messages and was not disappointed. The voice of David's aunt Helen was clipped and precise. "I am sorry, John, about the unlisted number; no doubt you tried to call me. Please blame telemarketing. You're probably wondering by now why I did not contact the alderman on Saturday. There is much to tell you, but not by phone. Please meet me at David's service tomorrow at Our Lady of Mount Carmel at quarter till, in front of the church. You and I will talk later, over tea. Goodbye."

John was beginning to feel like an errand boy, but the tasks that lay ahead began to arrange themselves into a discernible shape. He changed into his running clothes.

The proper course of action would be to phone her beforehand, but intuition told him to just go there.

He knocked, waited, and knocked again before the lock turned. She tugged the door open several inches and stared at him through the chain security then closed the door to unlatch it. He looked at her as she swung the door open. She wore a heavy gray leotard and a crop top that read "Mountaineers." She turned unsteadily on her feet and said, "Come in."

The dark interior was several notches above college-student decor. A lamp with a square rice paper shade stood in the corner. One wall was covered with ghostly black-and-white photographs of barges, a river, aluminum mobile homes scattered like lozenges on the side of a mountain. An arrangement of these framed pictures bearing the initials *AC* hovered on the wall above a black leather midcentury modern sofa. The adjacent wall held books from floor to ceiling in cheap Scandinavian-style stacked shelves.

The room smelled of cold pizza. John looked out the window into the courtyard, where there was a slipshod gazebo with warped shake shingles, someone's idea of rehab in the early 1970s. The gazebo roof festered under a layer of pigeon droppings.

"There's a lot you haven't told me." John found the switch on another lamp beside her chair. The room's brightness doubled.

Annie picked up a tumbler of clear liquid with ice and squashed lemon slices. On the end table a handle of gin showed an inch left at the bottom. She took her glass and drank from it so quickly that the gin splashed on her shirt. She started to brush it away with an awkward backhand as it rolled down in little beads onto her belly. Then her shoulders began to move and she leaned forward without a sound hugging her knees to her face. The tumbler in her hand spilled onto the sofa.

John took the glass away from her and set it down. Leaning over her, he looked at her more closely. He put his hand under her wet chin and lifted it for the benefit of the light.

"Who did this?" he asked.

"I'm a mess," she said. "I'm a terrible mess. You should always call before you drop in on a girl like this."

"I had a feeling," John said.

Hers was a beautiful face that was coarsening early from pain and liquor. John wondered what she would look like in twenty years, even in ten. "Who did this?" he repeated. He tilted her face toward the light and she did not resist. His thumb touched purple and yellow bruises along her jaw. There was swelling under the edge of her cheek. She flinched away and he could see her tongue moving on the inside of her cheek, searching for the broken edges of flesh.

Her crying came from a place outside the usual human range. John had heard women and men cry like this before, mostly in the psych ward in Philadelphia. He had never hardened himself to the sound, and he wouldn't start to now.

He said quietly, again, "Who did this? Tell me." She didn't hear him. He leaned forward and got to one knee. Her eyes weren't focused. He needed to get her attention. He grasped her shoulders and tried not to shout. "Annie!"

He looked at the gin bottle and for a moment wanted to slap her. He saw the bruises again in the light. There were some on her arms, as well.

She'd been somebody's punching bag. She fell forward onto him and her arms closed around his neck. Her weight was light and her breasts pressed in on his neck and face but she reeked of gin and this cured him of any arousal. He helped her get to her feet.

She hit him feebly with her fists. "He's dead, he's dead, goddammit, he's dead. But he would never lie to me, they said he lied to me and he would never lie to me. Don't you ever believe that—and then those fuckers called me a fag hag!"

Her face was blotched. John began to walk her toward the bathroom as she confessed, "I think I'm going to be sick."

She knelt in front of the toilet and with hunched back vomited repeatedly into the bowl. When he was sure she wouldn't pass out, he rinsed a washcloth under the cold water tap and gave it to her. Then he left her alone and closed the bathroom door behind him.

He entered her kitchen. He threw the crumpled napkins into the pizza box, folded it up, and stuffed it into the overflowing trash. He ran hot water into the sink and squirted soap into it, then wiped down the table with a sponge. He did the dirty glasses and plates and rinsed them under the warm tap. He stacked them in the rack. He went into the living room and collected more scattered plates and glasses and threw them in the sink. When he was finished, he returned to the living room, drying his hands on a tea towel.

He picked up the gin bottle. He heard water run in the bathroom and the sound of teeth being brushed. He emptied the gin into the kitchen sink and stepped on the plastic bottle until it flattened. He added it to the trash bag, which he knotted. He found the porch off the back of the kitchen and walked the bag down to the alley.

These tasks accomplished, he returned to Annie's living room and looked at her books. A lot of photography, a sprinkling of literary theory, mostly French feminism. She returned and stood in the doorway. She wore a heavy shapeless sweatshirt and had tied her hair up in a handkerchief.

She said, "I'm sorry."

"Annie, who hit you? Don't tell me it was the cops."

She shook her head. "No, of course not. It's nothing. I don't want to talk about it."

"Whoever hit you told you to be silent. Listen to me. I know someone you could stay with. You can trust her." He hadn't called Nancy yet but could see that he would soon have to.

Annie shook her head vigorously. "No, please." She hesitated. "Ruth Ann wanted me to change the locks anyway. I'm going to be fine."

"Ruth Ann?"

"My roommate? I told you."

"Look, about David, I know it must be hard, there are things sometimes we don't know or cannot understand even about those we trust . . ."

"No, John, you don't understand. He was my lover, okay? We were close. And he never lied to me." She wiped away tears that were starting up again. "I need to be alone. Ruth Ann will be home soon. I need to pull myself together."

"Your roommate? I hope you are sure it's your roommate coming back. Not someone using your face for a punching bag."

She turned her head and looked into the kitchen. "Thanks for doing the dishes. You're very kind."

"Listen, I still plan to visit Trophy tomorrow afternoon."

"What day is today?"

"Today is Monday. You remember the funeral is at Our Lady of Mount Carmel tomorrow morning, right? It got switched to the church. This is out of my hands now."

She nodded mutely.

"Okay, I'll pick you up and we can go there together and meet Helen."

"Thanks. I'll be better."

"Yes, good. Lay off the gin. I killed that bottle for you, by the way."

"Oh."

"One other question. Do you know the alderman?"

"No, I've never met him. I had no idea."

"So David didn't lie, but there were a few things he chose not to tell you. Like about his father."

John stood up. He didn't know whether to give the girl a goodnight hug and a teddy bear or a lecture about growing up. She stood aloof, finding her composure, and said, "I need to sleep."

He left full of frustration. She wanted a lover and she wanted a daddy but she needed a bodyguard right then and he couldn't deliver on any of those. This was no job for a man of the cloth. He was radically unequipped.

He decided not to go home yet and set off in a slow jog toward the lakefront. Some way down the running path later, near Lincoln Park Zoo, he stopped, dizzy. He had forgotten to set the stopwatch for the usual stretch between Belmont Harbor and the Fullerton underpass. How was it already getting dark?

He thought of what else he could have done. He should have found her liquor cabinet and emptied the works into her sink.

Stop it, he told himself.

Chapter 10

JOHN REIMER AND ANNIE Casper stood together on the sidewalk outside the black iron fence fronting Our Lady of Mount Carmel and watched the mourners climb the steps to the arched stone entrance.

The church was newly refurbished, cream limestone. No city soot stained it. The fence's scrollwork protected the manicured yard within from the shabby SRO hotels and neon-lit gay bars in the vicinity. Several empty pools and fountains dotted the grounds toward the rectory, which stretched east from the soaring spire that abutted the sidewalk on Belmont.

John could still remember this one from before it had shed its immigrant kitsch inside, to make way for the murmurings of power and taste of its newly rich and Americanized parishioners. The economics of an old Chicago church can be judged by its exterior work; once St. Peter's Episcopal had perfectly clean masonry, but the wealth in Lakeview had been shifting from the Episcopalians to the Catholics for some time now.

Of course the low churches, Methodists and Baptists, have almost no past to maintain or conceal, John thought. Like the Mennonites, they were hardly players at all. His own church had no real heritage in this city, just a good real estate deal from a Congregationalist group that was transplanted to the suburbs after World War II.

These were thoughts John could have shared with his daughter or with Nancy, but he figured Annie wouldn't make the same receptive audience for his pitter-patter about sociology and ecclesiology. Standing so close to her on the sidewalk, he didn't look at her directly, but he did notice that she was shifting around on her long legs, moving with restless energy on the sidewalk, like a young foal, her ankles crossing and uncrossing.

She had metamorphosed since yesterday's drunken crying jag. Then she had resembled the detritus of a biker bar. Now she looked ready for a trip to Marshall Field's, dressed stylishly in black dress, hose, pumps. Most astonishing was that she showed no signs of yesterday's collapse. It struck John as a miracle of youthful resilience. He glanced at her jaw. Makeup and dark glasses did wonders. *Great cover-up job,* he thought, *splendid.*

She wore her hair down, only the golden tresses on top pulled back beneath an opal clip. In her ears were opal posts. The sun flashed off of her and the rustling tall trees by the corner at Orchard Street.

She smiled with an air of unreality. John had seen it before in mourners. But looking at Annie, he realized his thoughts were not entirely on death either.

"Let's find Helen," John said. An entourage of suits attached to ornamented women entered the church, accompanied by hefty men in unbuttoned blue blazers. The alderman walked at the center of one of these clusters, and a steely redhead in a tightly disciplined jacket accompanied him, her arm in his. The hefty men moved deliberately, their eyes roaming the crowd. John looked at each bodyguard. Uniformed police officers were posted on either side of the iron gate, and then more were stationed by the tall wooden doors of the cathedral—they scanned every individual who entered. The clusters of people began to metamorphose into a crowd. The street became clogged with long white and black parked cars, and the chauffeurs got busy opening and closing doors.

Other groups of men gathered on the sidewalk and watched the entourages; some of them made little effort to mask the rakish flamboyance. "Gorgeous!" one of them exclaimed as a flash of pearls moved past.

The final contingent arrived on bicycles, wending their way in and out of traffic as they came up Belmont. John recalled Talbot's employer: the Cannonball messenger agency. Some of David Talbot's fellow workers arrived in a haze of sweat and spandex. They carried webbed green mail pouches, wore bulging fanny packs and backpacks.

They glided in like shiny insects wearing helmets, hair plastered down under plastic and Styrofoam, and with practiced nonchalance bumped their bikes up the curb onto the sidewalk. They deftly dodged the pedestrians and in a whir of spokes moved against the fence. One of them wore what looked like body armor and had a jet-black helmet to match. A single word in white capital letters was emblazoned across his chest: velocity.

"You recognize any of these people?" John asked Annie.

"Not really. David didn't talk much about work." She nudged John with an elbow and pointed toward the body-armored one. "Him I know. David pointed him out to me once before he became a picture on the Express Mail ad. Remember? Super Jim Conroy. David thought he was a total jerk."

The church bells began to ring out the hour when John spotted Helen Talbot-Smith slowly extricate herself from the back seat of a cab stuck between two limos.

"You'll be sitting with the next of kin at the front?" John asked her as they entered the church. The big church was three-quarters full.

"No, absolutely not," Helen said, staring at him with reproach. "Didn't I tell you? I am not on speaking terms with the alderman. I had planned to sit with you and Annie. May I have the pleasure?"

They accepted programs from two pasty-faced adolescent ushers. The heavy bronzed casket sat in the center aisle on a catafalque, banked with impossible quantities of flowers.

The church smelled of incense and a garden, of money and tradition. Light fell in broad patches through the newly restored stained glass. The organ stopped to clear the air for the austere, tender symmetry of the opening notes of Chopin's funeral march. A shudder went through Helen when the piano began to play. Anne sat like a stone.

The notes washed through the space of the white vaulted chamber above them and the small noises of pain began in the audience, as much in response to the terrible beauty of the composition as to the body encased in bronze and oak before them. *After all,* John wondered, *how many of these people knew David Talbot?*

They stood at a distance on the sidewalk and watched the casket loaded into the hearse, but they did not go to the interment. John asked Annie if Trophy had been at the service. She shook her head. He had noticed her body go rigid when the Lakeview Gay Men's Choir sang "Abide with Me," and her hand had slid over to grip John's forearm. She left nail marks.

A good funeral allows mourners the opportunity to grieve openly—and only when that process is complete should the assurances of the Psalmist be wheeled out. *"Miserable comforters are you all" was a lesson more clergy needed to comprehend,* John thought.

John relaxed in his BarcaLounger. The young priest at David's service had impressed him: precisely because he had refused the temptation of premature optimism. As the notes of the Chopin had died, the priest had spoken, almost brutally: "We are here to mourn. And we are here also to express the depth of our anger and our pain. For grief is all we have when our questions to the Maker surpass any of His answers."

Then the priest had recited a Psalm, but not the Disney psalm.

John levered himself out of the chair and went to his study. He found the passage, Chapter 88. He wondered why he had never used it before in a funeral. He wondered about doing the predictable thing. He wondered about the funeral sermon he would never give for the young man he had never met.

The passage burned into him. More Ecclesiastes and Job, really, than the maudlin shepherd of green pastures and still waters:

> Hear my cries for help;
> For my soul is all troubled,
> My life is on the brink of Sheol;
> I am numbered among those who go down to the Pit,
> A man bereft of strength:
> A man alone, down among the dead,
> Among the slaughtered in their graves,
> Among those you have forgotten,
> Those deprived of your protecting hand.
> You have plunged me to the bottom of the Pit,
> To its deepest, darkest place.

After the reading by the young priest, John knew that any comfort still lay around a very distant corner. He considered Helen's refusal to speak to the alderman: what had happened between them? The physical beating of Annie, her silence, and her refusal to speak of it, her refusal to speak of David's roommate Trophy: why? John looked down at the nail marks, still visible on his arm.

And where was the dead man's roommate, this Trophy, in all of this? John wondered if he should talk with Louis Kerdigan's brother Bill, the detective. In the mortuary Louis had seemed reluctant to talk about his brother. *Undertakers and cops—quite a world I'm entering*, John thought.

The more he thought of it, the more irritated he became. All these people, unwilling to talk. Louis would likely tell him to let it go, leave it alone, move on.

But there had been an oddness, an abruptness to that removal of David's body from the parlor on Lincoln Avenue. Even Louis had dared to comment on it. And then there was the elaborate production of the funeral.

The alderman and the bike messenger, the father and the son . . .

John got to pondering a more mundane question: What tie to wear to Helen's? He put on a red silk one with black diagonal stripes. His daughter, Sarah, often reminded him that his best sermon, preached fourteen years earlier in Kansas City, had opened, "Life is too short to wear neckties I don't like."

John didn't hold back in his tie choice. And he looked forward to visiting Helen. She had mentioned tea, and that always meant the slight possibility of scones with strawberries and clotted cream.

Chapter 11

By the time he arrived at her front door, he had dialed down his hopes. He recalled similar visitations in moneyed neighborhoods where he'd been overwhelmed by the smell of cat piss in the front hall and then the enthusiastic attention of a full-blown cat lady.

As soon as she opened the door, the felines were there all right, three of them moving surreally, as if by occult timetable, from one room to the next. Helen, standing atop a Persian runner the length of the front hall, wore an angora sweater and silk pants. A balustrade rose behind her, guarded at its base by a potted fern.

"Reverend Reimer, I am so pleased to see you." When she smiled, a shred of tobacco showed near her gum. Reading bifocals sat low on her nose. She appraised him head to toe, and he had a moment of misgiving, a flash of the first time he had gotten dressed up to eat with Vi at Dodge City's finest steak house. Going into town from the farm. How the waiter's eyes mocked him as he stumbled through a thicket of unfamiliar menu items, his tongue mangled with the accents of the Kleine Gemeinde's Low German. That was the evening he had vowed to leave home and go to college.

Helen took John's coat and seemed to admire the knot of his tie. The room assaulted him in its Victorian splendor. He took in the cavernous entrance hall, the black walnut wainscoting, the dark flowered wallpaper that climbed to a scrolled picture rail above. In the gallery of gilt mirrors and paintings some of the landscapes contained grazing cows, and peasants bent over, in attitudes of spiritual bliss, harvesting grain under the sun. Helen sat him down in a wing chair beside a cherry bookcase with leaded glass. She crossed her shrunken shanks and folded her hands as she reposed in an easy chair.

"You're a country boy, aren't you, Reverend?" Her smile was wicked. She did not waste any time.

"Yes, I am. Kansas, as a matter of fact."

"I should have guessed. Did you ranch? My family was in meatpacking. Father built this house after we moved from the South Side. Where in Kansas?"

"Meade, near Dodge."

"My goodness, Reverend Reimer, my awe of you grows and grows." John watched her with dread and fascination. When coming on to him, she shed twenty years. "We're practically related. Imagine your daddy selling to mine!" She let her bifocals fall on their chain from her nose to her flat chest. "Would you like tea?"

"Thank you. Please."

"Come with me to the kitchen. I will tell you what I know about David."

They traveled through a generous but dimly lit formal dining room, apparently converted over several decades into a permanent storage space. The cat smell got stronger as they moved deeper into the house. A mahogany table for twelve held the repository of a library's periodicals room.

"You didn't want the alderman to know about his son," John began, when they reached the kitchen. "And you didn't want me to know about David's father. Excuse me, but things don't quite fit."

"I meant what I said about having no communication with him. Fitzsimmons abandoned my niece, David's mother, when she was a very young woman. This has not endeared him to me."

She set the kettle to heat on a crusted stove. John wanted to go to work on it with a Brillo pad. She took a tea infuser out of a drawer, unscrewed the halves, and filled the metal ball with loose tea from a canister.

"Fitzsimmons is the most unscrupulous man I have ever met. And I have known my share." She smiled and a row of vertical lines above her lips tightened like a miniature accordion.

"The alderman stopped being family twenty-five years ago." Her hands trembled as she screwed tight the infuser's hemispheres. She lowered it into a porcelain china pot and proceeded to pour herself a drink from a crystal snifter beside the stove. "Peach brandy," she smiled. "A weakness of mine. Would you care for some?"

"Thanks, I'll just have tea. You were saying?"

"The marriage was a mistake. Elinor married the bastard without telling anyone. Not exactly eloped but did not let us know until it was done. A sorry cliché of a story that certainly a man in your line of work knows all too well."

Helen drank from the snifter. "He was just out of Notre Dame, on scholarship, his family didn't have a dime. Elinor had a trust fund—modest by today's standards—which he offered to invest for her. Oh, he invested it all right. He might have the money to collect antiques now, but back then she worked as a secretary to help support him."

John said, "A lot of wives back then were secretaries."

"Elinor and her parents—my sister Alice and her husband, Buddy— were naïve people. They tried to believe in the situation, make it work. You know how it is. He told Elinor that once he finished law school, he would make believers out of us all. The baby . . ."

"David?"

"Yes, he wasn't quite walking yet. Ten months old. It was incomprehensible. Elinor left Fitzsimmons without explanation. She never talked about it, just 'things aren't quite working out.' She took the baby to California."

The kettle whistled and Helen poured boiling water into the pot. A cat nudged John's ankles.

"At the time Fitzsimmons was using his contacts to work for the city. Mostly he did electioneering. He also understood putting in time at the right charity events and fundraisers. He told people Elinor was in California for health reasons. She'd come back for short visits. He was finishing law school. Et cetera.

"Then Elinor called me and said she needed money. The trust fund was empty—thanks to him. I was on a fixed income, and I couldn't do much. That sick bastard robbed her blind."

"What did Alice and Buddy say about all of it?"

"That's the strange part. They blamed their daughter for leaving a rising young politician. They couldn't understand. It turns out that Edward was still paying them off for loans he'd taken from them when he started law school."

"They didn't feel about the alderman the way you do."

"No, not quite. Although they didn't live to see him elected."

Helen took another shot of brandy and replenished her glass. "Everyone always acted like Buddy and Alice were the salt of the earth. Alice resented me for saying once that Buddy's business sense wasn't as good as Father's. Buddy despised me for having an opinion. I suggested an accountant look at the trust fund, and they both accused me of meddling. Alice said that with age I was growing more inappropriate."

Helen eyed the level of brandy in the decanter and looked at John. "It was hard to hear such things from my own sister. I told Alice that Buddy was making stupid investments and that Edward had been the worst of them. What can you say to a family like that? Maybe I was inappropriate, but I

was telling the truth! They saw Edward's monthly money envelope as promises, but I knew it was guilt money. The little weasel was bailing out. They
thought he was operating out of some sense of principle." Helen cleared her
throat. "Even after he paid off his loans to them, Edward kept sending them
money every month."

"So what about David during all of this?" John asked.

"I saw the boy a few times. Adorable. He spent part of each summer
with Edward, and the two of them would come here for tea exactly once a
year."

"Once a year?"

"Yes. Then when David was fourteen, or maybe thirteen, I've lost track,
he called and asked if he could stay a few weeks with me instead of his father.
I was unable to do that at the time. He never explained, and he never came
back to Chicago again, as far as I knew, until late last year."

Helen put an unlit cigarette into a carved bone holder, then lay the
holder down on the counter. "Things came to a head when Buddy and Alice
approached me for financial help. Young Edward's rising career had carried neither their daughter nor them along with it. And I could never get
a straight answer about the trust fund. They refused to talk about it. When
they came to me for help, I could tell Buddy was humiliated."

"So what did you do?" One of the cats was rubbing itself against John's
shoe. He gently nudged it away.

Helen finished off the peach brandy in her snifter again. "I told them I
was on a fixed income and there were limits to my means. My circumstances
forced me to say no. And that is the truth."

"So they wanted more help from you than you were able to give."

"Precisely." Helen lifted the infuser from the pot and poured the tea,
a little unsteadily, into two Wedgwood cups. These and a plate of covered
pastries she arranged on top of a silver tray and asked John to carry it back
into the living room.

"It's funny. The longer she stayed in California, the more the family
turned me into the Wicked Witch of the Midwest. I understood from Alice
that Elinor had grown quite addicted to prescription pills. She stopped writing. The whole family was busy cutting me off."

The store-bought strawberry tarts were slightly dry and not up to
John's peasant standards. They certainly weren't the scones with strawberries and cream he had imagined. He chewed on one and sipped the tea.

"They took to hanging up the phone when they heard my voice. Coin-
cidentally, this was after I had to say no to their financial requests. It was as
though they blamed me for Elinor's problems as well as their own. Buddy
spoke to me only once after that, about four or five years before their car

accident. He told me, 'So at least Edward repaid his loans, came through when we needed him. More than I can say for you, bitch.'"

John watched the face of the old woman work at these utterances in the fading afternoon light. "I am sorry," he said. "You must be saddened by all this." The trouble with so much emotional scarring was that the truth very often fell apart like rust in your hands if you tried to grasp it and figure out its shape. All that remained were broken shards of rage.

John poured himself more tea. "It must have been quite a surprise to see your great-nephew last year."

"It was a total shock. I had no idea who the young man was. He stood on my porch and I almost didn't let him in. I opened the door just a crack and he said in a man's voice that I'd never even heard, 'Aunt Helen? Great-aunt Helen?' Oh God, he had Elinor's eyes. You don't know what family means until you've lost all of them."

"I know a little bit about loss," John said.

Her trembling hands took one of his. He set down the teacup and she spoke steadily through the tears: "It seems impossible that they are all gone now. But they are. And I am left. And now this, for something like this to happen to David, it is beyond . . ."

John waited to resume. "Did David ever speak about his father?"

"David and I rarely spoke about Edward. He mentioned him once, indirectly, when he told me about his new stepdad in California. He said, 'You know, Aunt Helen, Mom's second choice of a husband is as bad as the first.' What do you say to a boy like that? Elinor had remarried five years before she died, when David was a teenager."

"Were you surprised that David was in Lincoln Park at that hour?"

"You don't have to speak in euphemisms with me, John. You are asking whether I knew David was gay? Look, I'm Anglican. We stopped asking that question a long time ago."

"But what was his relationship to Annie Casper? Do you know?"

Helen said, "I thought they were very close. They had shared artistic interests. Annie seems like a good person."

"You do know that he was living with a man named Trophy."

"David didn't talk with me much about his domestic arrangements. And I didn't think of asking."

John found himself in a place where he couldn't stop asking questions. And that made him feel even more sorry for Helen, an old woman who sat with her legs curled up beneath her. "Did Fitzsimmons ever remarry?"

"You keep asking about him, don't you? No, he didn't, though he has a reputation for young things on his arm. There's an anorexic redhead now, one of his office staffers. Rumors were that he was quite disappointed when Hefner closed the Playboy mansion.

"Listen, John. He is a toad, a slug. With a charming smile. A ruthless climber who has mastered the art of Midwestern nice. This city is full of them. And I know what he did to his wife and child and how he climbed. He could always simulate sincerity. That is why I am so incensed to this day. This sudden appearance as the estranged but loving father is a complete fraud. The fucker!"

John said, "Yes. I understand that even more exasperating is that your niece Elinor, and your own sister, chose not to see it that way. And that makes you furious."

Helen looked at him strangely. He continued. "And now Fitzsimmons took even David's funeral away from you."

Walking away from her house, John hoped the long cry on his shoulder had done Helen some good. All that fury against the alderman, all that peach brandy, the excess flow of her own thrumming conscience. John knew alcohol was no truth serum, and turning over the fragments of the woman's words, he doubted whether much truth of any kind could be salvaged from the ruin.

John wanted to know how much money Elinor had asked for, just how fixed was Helen's fixed income. How much trust got lost in the trust fund? *Schuld*, debt, guilt—all the same.

Maybe Karl Marx was right, John thought. *These questions of the human heart run to capital after all.* He brushed strands of cat hair off the bottom of his pants as the handsome homes stared down on him. A nanny pushed a stroller past, and two fair-haired twins poked their heads out of the canopy like furry animals.

Rich people . . . he told himself.

Chapter 12

JOHN KNEW HELEN'S STORY had given him a lot to think about. By the time he reached his car, he was certain it wasn't simple. But he was running late for his appointment with Trophy.

He lead-footed it to Bucktown, sweaty, exhausted, a vague sour stomach from the pastry. He should have used the bathroom. He had consumed too much tea.

Trophy. The heavy edges of that name brought back the picture of Annie's face, the knuckle wounds along her jaw. Helen had provided a sordid account of family breakdown but precious little information about David or Annie. Annie doubted the official story of David's murder and seemed bent on proving his heterosexual prowess.

Somehow the two accounts had to mesh, but it was turning out to be harder to crack than a parable. *Maybe Trophy will give me some answers*, thought John.

He wondered exactly why he was getting involved. No doubt Mildred Unruh would soon comment on his erratic office hours this week, and Nancy had already registered her discontent. Eventually, he knew she would require a full explanation.

With his bladder on fire, John parked illegally in a fire hydrant's yellow painted zone. He rang the bell on the three-story brick house and stepped back on the stone porch to survey the neighborhood: two more brick buildings, garbage bags piled high on the neighbors' adjacent landing, a rat scurrying away. Across the street was a dirt parking lot surrounded by a mesh fence topped with razor wire so spanking new it looked like it was clipped from mirrors. An empty warehouse on the next block down showed high banks of broken windows but a recently painted sign announced "Lofts to Lease" and a phone number. Just beyond, John knew, was a string of independent coffee shops and zine stores and on the corner a neon sign for Rapido's Bikes.

John buzzed again. The typed label by the button inside the entrance read "Trophy Gallante" and underneath, inked neatly with ballpoint, "David Talbot." When no one came to the door, John thought he must have missed Trophy, so he walked up the block and got a coffee so he could use the restroom. A tattooed barista with a nose ring served him politely, but the look told John he had no place with hipsters.

He drove home and checked for messages and phoned Trophy to apologize for being late. He took a run by the lake and after a shower ate supper alone in his study at his desk, a plate of microwaved enchilada casserole. Mildred had reminded him to please return the Pyrex baking dish the following Sunday.

He meditated again on the problem of getting information out of reluctant human beings. He remembered his older brother Andrew's gift for extracting confessions. How had he done it? There was a lot to dislike about Andrew, but he had had a gentle way of prying the truth out of wayward Brethren. Indeed, there had been an impressive catalog of sins that members of the brotherhood had admitted to in the waning days of the Kleine Gemeinde. A veritable litany of unspeakable acts, which Andrew had methodically discovered—adultery, fornication, sodomy, lust of many kinds, things with animals, for which there was no vocabulary. It wasn't *bestiality*; it always had to do with sex. Some of these details had never been recorded in the official histories, long after the demise of Andrew's community. People in Meade were reluctant to reminisce about these periodic upheavals of confession and absolution, and John suspected that if Andrew were still alive, he too would keep silence. The confessions had been . . . overdetermined. After all these years, John no longer knew what to believe of that era. Perhaps it had been collective hysteria, or a hangover from the Great Depression and the terror of still speaking German during both world wars.

Andrew's weapon, his instrument, had been gentleness: a voice that told you he cared, a voice he claimed was not his own but God's voice speaking through him. Few penitents could say no to that voice. It induced ecstasies of guilt and repentance. John remembered the spectacle of an entire community on their knees in a plain, varnished-wood church shouting the truth of their transgression to the heavens.

Andrew had been an elder to reckon with. John wondered whether any of that talent lay buried in him. Kerdigan had asked at the mortuary earlier, "On a mission or an inquisition?" Well, John had to admit, there was no avoiding making a few inquiries. The problem was that getting to the truth so often clashed with making people feel better. It was the conundrum of his gospel calling: the sword that divides; the balm that heals.

Chapter 13

JOHN'S LOFTY THOUGHTS WERE disturbed by the sound of his doorbell. He went to open the door.

It was Annie. *Maybe she's here to talk of her own accord*, John thought. *I can hope.*

"May I come in?"

"Of course."

She followed him up the stairs.

"Did you hear the news?"

"This afternoon? No. I was drinking tea with Helen."

She threw her leather bag on his sofa and stuffed her hands in her jeans pockets. She began to walk back and forth in his living room.

"Well, they've made it official," she announced. "The police have declared it a hate crime. The alderman has said he was estranged from his son because as a practicing Catholic he found the lifestyle unacceptable."

"Okay, he more or less said that yesterday. Is he a Stone Age Catholic?"

"No. That's the thing. He's a big booster of the John Howard Society, prison reform. Swears by AA. As far as I know, a devout Catholic but very progressive. He said that whatever his personal convictions, as a public servant he is not going to tolerate the murder of homosexuals."

John interrupted. "And your point is?"

"I'm telling you something is very rotten here. Something's not right."

John's face must have shown impatience, because she held up a hand and stopped him from speaking.

"Look, I know you think I'm a totally fucked-up kid from Ohio who is deluded and silly and drinks too much—

"Let me finish. And you think I'm probably a slut besides, the way I cried all over you. I'm sorry. You're maybe right. But I came to you because

56

Alex said you were trustworthy and you would keep confidence. Okay? I know I wasn't very responsible the other night. But listen to me, please. Let me be very clear. David and I were lovers. He wasn't gay. He wasn't bi. He wasn't socially constructing his goddamn sexuality. I don't know what he was doing in the park that night, but I know he wasn't cruising."

"Annie, he could have been mistaken for gay . . . I'm sorry. Let me start again. Whoever they are, whoever is doing this, whether it's some gang or some militants from Michigan, they probably aren't that careful about who they decide to kill. They're maybe not particular."

"You're full of theories, aren't you?" she said, and contemplated him as if for the first time. He ruffled his hands through his mop of white hair, perplexed, and looked back at her. She flatly stated, "I need you to help me find out what really happened."

"You can talk to the police as well as I can."

"We went over that already. I don't want to talk with the police. They have already made up their mind what happened. They're no help."

John pondered his next words. "Annie, I've listened patiently to you. Now you listen to me. If you want my help, then you start by telling me everything you know. Everything. And stop withholding."

She didn't reply, and he pressed forward. "Let's try this again. Who hit you?"

"That's not relevant."

"Let me be the judge of what is relevant. I may look like a *schlüntz*, a little slow at times, but I might also surprise you. So just one more time, who hit you?"

He realized while he spoke that she was sitting in his BarcaLounger and he was hovering over her in a somewhat threatening position. He backed away from the chair. He could hear the blood pounding in his temple.

"In my youth I was a cowboy and I could slow my pulse, which is obviously what I need to do right now. Coffee?" He remembered now that one thing Andrew did was slow down his speech patterns whenever there was stress.

"That would be good."

He settled his nerves in the kitchen and brought out the coffee. She poured two-percent into her cup and the coffee marbled beige when she stirred it. She took a swallow and spoke.

"My husband," she said.

"Your husband?" John said.

"My husband hit me. We have been separated for two years. He still insists—he insists—on visiting sometimes. I'm trying to get a divorce. He is not cooperating. He says with therapy we can save our marriage."

"Did he really say that?" John's eyes danced.

"He says we can still work things out."

"I'll bet he does. Did you report him?"

"Listen, I thought I made it clear. Let's leave the police out of this."

"What is his name, your husband?"

"His name is not important, please."

"He has a name, and I need to know it. I know he was at your place after the detectives' interview the other night. Correct me wherever necessary, okay? And then he hit you." John looked at Annie. She wasn't drinking coffee now. "And he told you that if you ever uttered a word about him he would kill you."

John waited for her to respond. After a while, she said, "Alex told me you were intuitive. That is exactly what my husband told me. That if I ever say a word to the police about him he will kill me. What else do you want to know?"

John looked at his running shoes, on his feet but still unlaced, and wondered how fast he could run. A sudden image flashed of a smiling, towering mountain man in a wifebeater and camo pants, wielding a hunting knife. John tried to regroup.

"Your husband hated David. Did he hate him enough to want to kill him?"

"Look, he likes to threaten, he talks a lot of trash, but he would never do something like that."

"But he had no problem using your jaw for practice. He could have easily broken it. You're lucky. You just told me he's threatened to kill you. And that's why you can't, or won't, talk to the police. Look, I know someone whom I trust. He is an acquaintance and a professional. His brother is one of my best personal friends in this city. His name is Bill Kerdigan."

"And what do you want me to do?"

"I want you to go with me to Area 3 at Belmont and Western and tell Detective Kerdigan the whole, complete, unedited tale. And if you won't, I think you're being irresponsible. You have to understand. This isn't my normal line of work."

"John, Preacher Man, Alex said you can be trusted. Alex said you're not a quitter."

"Oh, that's very good, Annie, you know how to make an appeal, don't you?"

"Don't you get it? I can't go to the cops. He'll kill me. I beg you, please, don't talk to your friend, or any of them. He'll kill me. He will. Look, I'm afraid he'll kill me, but that doesn't mean I think he would kill David, okay?"

The girl was incoherent, but John couldn't blame her. Was it any wonder? Who wouldn't be tired or incoherent in her circumstances? Still, as John carried the coffee mugs into the kitchen, he felt his empathy drain away. He put them in the sink and turned to see that Annie had followed him. She stood framed in the doorway. The young woman had some kind of grip on him.

"All right, I won't talk with the police. As far as I'm concerned, there is only one more item for us to take care of, and that is to visit Trophy and get David's things. Then I'm finished. You need to help me find Trophy at work. I want to get this done. Let's go."

"You understand I despise him. He's less likely to talk with me there."

"Annie, I don't care at this point whether he talks or not."

Annie stood, picked up her bag, and slung it over her shoulder. She put on her dark sunglasses.

"Can we walk?" John asked.

"Yes," she said. "I'm taking you to the Berlin. Have you eaten supper yet?"

"Trophy now, maybe a piece of pie later. Am I dressed okay?"

Annie appraised him. "How about a pair of khakis and a nice button-down. That old tweed thing you wear. You know, your uniform."

John was a little angry. He wanted to keep the distance between them chilled, but he could feel it melting away.

Chapter 14

JOHN PUT A KNIT stocking cap over his head and snugged it around his ears. He found himself huffing a bit to keep up with Annie and thought that he should have put on an extra layer. She moved fast in her long heavy sweater and tight jeans, taking gloves out of her purse as they turned the corner from Racine onto Belmont. Her stride was a long, easy lope. She pulled on the gloves and gave John a nervous smile.

They passed a pizzeria, a tattoo parlor, and a new shop at the corner with a glittery sign that read "International House of Condoms." Beneath it ran an ad for the daily special: "For Microsoft Lovers: The Laptop." Further on down the street smells took over: the heavy, spiced aroma of marinara and moussaka wafting out of one of John's favorite diners, a place run by a Greek Albanian who said things like, "Makin' some money, boss?" or "Good day at the races?" After five years as a regular there, John still didn't know whether Stephanopoulos had any idea what those phrases meant.

The nightclub Berlin stood a block away. John had never been inside, and he paused to look up at the club's stainless-steel letters bolted beneath a shiny hooded light.

Inside, Annie led him to the end of a thirty-foot bar. Two mohawks and a shaved head, the only other customers, were sitting in a booth. The slow, pounding rhythm of house music overlaid with low Egyptian wailing filtered through the space. Three fans slowly spun under the flat black ceiling above an empty dance floor. Silent moving images played on the wall, old clips of Dietrich, Monroe, Hayworth. There was Leni Riefenstahl, John noticed, bosomy and youthful, on the alpine set of one of her early productions. Then Jackie appeared in one of her signature hats and elegant suits. JFK delivered without the soundtrack his "Ich bin ein Berliner" speech. Topless models in Barbarella getups striding down a fashion runway.

John turned his attention back to Annie. "Is this place always deserted?" he asked.

"No," she said. "It gets going after your bedtime. Usually around eleven o'clock."

"Is this where Trophy works?" John asked.

"Be patient."

"Please order me a seltzer with lemon," John said, excusing himself.

In the bathroom he emptied his bladder and glanced at a poster for "Degeneration." "10 pm–2 am alternative saturday. Come cast off those workweek, kissin'-the-bossman's-butt blues. degenerate."

Back at the bar Annie introduced John to a barrel-chested man behind the counter with two silver rings in his ear and a bronze barbell in his eyebrow. He wore generous amounts of black eyeliner, which clashed with his peroxide hair, until John saw his dark roots.

"Nice to meet you," Trophy said. He rattled some ice into a glass and looked at John. "I waited at the apartment until three-fifteen. Had to get to work." When he spoke, a pink carnation bobbed on his black T-shirt pocket. He lisped slightly, which struck John as an affectation. Annie wasn't smiling. Trophy poured seltzer into the glass and dropped a wedge of lemon on top. He pushed the glass toward John and wiped the counter with a rag.

"My apologies. I was caught up at another appointment."

"Busy man," Trophy said. "Reimer, right?" He extended a chubby hand and went on. "Queen Anne here tells me you're a counselor."

"I do some of that, yes."

"Did she tell you how much I miss her David?"

"I gather you all miss David," John said neutrally. "When is a convenient time for us to pick up David's things?"

"It's pretty much packed up, although the fuzz made a mess of things when they searched." The carnation bobbed and trembled. "I don't know what they were looking for. Bastards."

"Jackbooted thugs, huh?" John asked.

"Yeah."

"Did the alderman want to claim any of David's possessions?"

"No."

"They were pretty distant from each other, weren't they? I mean David and his father."

"Yeah, they were distant," Trophy said. "Why so many questions?"

He didn't wait for John's answer but walked down to the other end of the bar and angled a glass under the tap for Annie, filling a fourteen-ounce beer glass to the brim. He waddled back like an athlete gone to fat and set the drink down in front of her on a pewter-colored bar napkin. Some of the foam ran over the edge of the glass, and Annie sipped quickly, leaving herself a little mustache on her usually winsome upper lip.

John resumed. "My point is to figure out how just how estranged father and son were."

"God, you therapists. Let me guess your specialty. Grief adjustment?"

"There's no need to be hostile."

The stubble on Trophy's chin was beginning to go gray though he looked barely thirty, and John thought his face to be a cross between the cartoon Bluto and Truman Capote. John turned his attention to the mural behind the bar above the neatly arranged bottles. It was in the art-deco style, three Aryan men thrusting toward a nude blonde whose head was tilted back from her shoulders at an impossible angle. She exposed swollen and upturned nipples to the gaze not of the seeming marching Gestapo but rather two fully clothed women outfitted in the starched getup of crossing guards. The blonde was about to collapse backward into their waiting hands.

John didn't want to linger much longer. "When can I pick up David's things?" he asked.

"I work late tonight," Trophy said. "Tomorrow morning, ten?"

"Good."

"Try to be on time, okay? Is she coming along?" Trophy gestured at Annie.

"You're such a prick," she said. "John, come on, let's go." She threw a dollar on the counter and headed for the door. Half her beer was still in the glass. John wheeled on the barstool to leave and a pudgy hand gripped his arm.

"Look, I'm sorry. She doesn't understand. I cared about him, you see? I cared about him a lot." Abject, Trophy still stooped down to retrieve the dollar. The Capote mouth with the little underbite quivered. "And that threatened her, you know?"

"I can see that," John said. "You shouldn't let the decor rub off on your manners, though. We can talk more tomorrow."

John caught another glimpse of the promotion "Degenerate" on his way out. He thought of lamb kebab, swimming in spices, baklava. Stephanopoulos maybe spoke little English, but it didn't matter, he knew the comfort food John needed.

John told Annie he preferred to eat alone and she didn't argue. It would be dark soon, and he walked into the diner, grabbed the *Trib*, and chose a booth. The fading sunlight was warm and bright on the red vinyl. Walkers passed swiftly on the sidewalk outside the window. At the back of the diner a waitress cleaned crusts off the ketchup bottles.

Stephanopoulos was waiting on John personally. "Good day at the races?" At the back of his mouth a molar flashed gold.

"Wonderful day. Great day at the races." John lifted a forkful of moussaka to his mouth. "But not this good."

"You going to make some money, boss." Stephanopoulos returned to the cash register, where he rearranged the bowl of mints on the Astroturf pad beside the toothpick dispensers.

John read the newspaper in a bliss of forgetfulness. He had seconds on the moussaka. So many interviews after a funeral made a man hungry.

Chapter 15

GERTRUDE, MANAGER OF THE Speed Queen near Roscoe, squirted soap out of a squeeze bottle onto shirt collars, one at a time, spreading the fabric beneath her nicotine-stained fingers as if trimming filets. She was sixty-five years old, lean but with a potbelly. Her lower lip protruded from her ravaged face like a miniature shelf upon which a lit cigarette rested in patent defiance of the laundromat's "No Smoking" signs.

She looked at John drop his dirty laundry, stuffed in two pillowcases, on a plastic chair by the dryers. "Little early for you, isn't it?"

"The older I get, the less I sleep," John said.

"Isn't that right." Her laugh turned into a cough, the sound of wet shammies snapping in a high wind. John winced.

She took his laundry to a cage in the back and returned. "Ready by six tonight. You want your shirts starched?"

"The usual, go a little easy on the starch."

"Righto."

John did five knee bends on the sidewalk outside and started his morning run.

At Wrigley Field he turned east, passing the 7-Eleven. At Lake Shore Drive he crossed over at the Irving Park underpass, by the Kwanusila totem pole, its base shrouded in fog rolling in from the lake. A wooden deity crouched at the top, a carved thunderbird who presided fiercely over the green park.

Cars on Lake Shore Drive shushed by like ghosts, strangely quiet in the white mist. A single pigeon sat on the traffic light at Irving Park, a fellow sentry to the carved predator atop the post across the road. In the middle of the totem pole a whale bore on its back a man brandishing a harpoon, and the bottom of the carved column showed the sea monster, Leviathan. *Not to be drawn out with a fishhook,* John thought. At the base of the monument, a man lay snoring on a bench under a rancid blanket, his head at rest on a bulging shopping bag. His open mouth showed a row of sparkling, widely spaced front teeth that looked like clean white pegs stuck in a rotting yard.

South from the monument the running path angled toward the lake. John passed the bird sanctuary, a stand of beech and oak; to the right of the sanctuary lay the northern end of the boat harbor, still empty this early in the season. The dirt trail widened. He inhaled the cold air and picked up his pace. He looked at his watch and pressed the button. Past the archery range by the harbor the trees thinned out and showed the rocky granite slabs along the waterfront, barely discernible in the fog. The softball diamonds and the golf course stretched away in the whiteness. John picked up his moderate pace into a full run, heading south along the lake on the concrete walkway. Only the very tip of the Hancock showed itself above the high collar of fog. He pushed himself until the pain mounted and he slowed when he drew even with Diversey. A gleam of light struggled through the fog onto the surface of the lake.

He jogged slowly on a trail through Lincoln Park that passed by the North Pond. He wondered where the police line had been set up. Two young men in pink berets nodded at him when he passed, but he looked down quickly to his watch. He noticed the slope of the ground, steep into the water's edge. Above loomed the façade of Columbus Hospital. His final sprint carried him to Fullerton, where he stopped and consulted his watch. He decided to turn back toward Belmont. The cinnamon rolls at Ann Sather would be coming out of the oven just about now. He would get a light snack before his council meeting at nine.

He was not alone in his fondness for Ann Sather's. At the entrance, he knocked on the plate-glass window of the restaurant. Two familiar faces looked up from the table inside: Rabbi Kaufmann, from the Reformed congregation in Lincoln Park, and across from him, Arthur Modeski, a freelance writer and columnist. John had once introduced Alan Wiebe to Modeski at Ann Sather's; later, Wiebe said the man was a cross between Mike Royko, Herbert Marcuse, and Oscar Wilde. The conversation had run on high octane and was one of those rare occasions when John actually saw Wiebe short on words.

Modeski wore a scruffy, fraying Cubs baseball cap pulled down low over horn-rimmed glasses. Arguably the most famous Cubs cap on the

North Side, known by literati and paparazzi alike, its brim now obscured a large chunk of cinnamon roll leaving the man's hand and entering his mouth.

John joined them at their table. Modeski nodded a quick hello and continued to concentrate on dismantling, with delicate but filthy fingers, the finely constructed edifice of a cinnamon roll four inches in diameter. John waved over a waitress, pointed at Modeski's plate and tall tomato juice, and said, "I'll have the same."

The rabbi spooned salsa on a plateful of scrambled eggs and carefully laid two slabs of sable over a toasted poppyseed bagel.

John looked at them. "Am I interrupting something?"

The rabbi said, "No. Well, actually, let me revise. Arthur was beginning to wear me down."

Modeski grinned mordantly. "You notice how this early in the morning the cinnamon roll is not quite baked through to the innermost layers. It is still slightly on the verge of doughiness. Like an unfinished self, it attains its final completeness, its full identity, only by merging with the Other." His mouth opened and engulfed the roll.

"Let's leave Martin Buber out of this," the rabbi said.

"Actually, I was referring to Bakhtin," said Modeski.

Kaufmann replied through a mouthful of eggs, "This is a generational gap."

John bit into his cinnamon roll. "I still think they would be better with raisins."

"Why would that make them better?" Kaufmann asked.

"Because that is how my mother made them."

Their attention turned to Modeski, who pushed the final fragments of dough rings into his mouth and busily licked his fingers. Kaufmann watched with disgust. He was a diminutive figure, and his yarmulke seemed to enlarge his gnarly head. No one John knew could ascertain his exact age. John thought, *In twenty years I'm going to look just like that. Or maybe I'm already there—I have hair growing out of my nose and ears.*

The rabbi caught him staring. "So what wisdom does the Mennonite bring this morning? What is new in your corner of the world?"

"I do not keep track of my corner any more. It's so bad that I've started to ignore my mail." The waitress refilled his coffee. "We are quite distracted by the local news."

"You mean the Talbot boy?" Modeski said. He wiped his hands on a napkin.

John nodded.

Kaufmann spoke. "Strange, but maybe not the strangest."

"If he were a fashion designer and not a bike messenger it would be a bigger story," said Modeski.

"If he were a fashion designer we would have known sooner about his father," said Kaufmann.

John said to Arthur, "Did you know the alderman had a son?"

"No, not until this happened."

"I thought if anyone would know, it would be you."

Modeski grew a little defensive. "My knowledge is vast and my files extensive, but I don't keep tabs on every politician in the metropolis."

"I thought you might," John said. "And this is our alderman, after all. You usually have the sources."

"Yes," added Kaufmann caustically. "Mr. I Told You So."

"You think too highly of my sources," Modeski said. "Look, if you want to know a secret, I guess a lot of the time. Some of my guesses are accurate. Hence my well-publicized powers of divination. Like weather reporting, the people forget what you said last week."

The rabbi interrupted. "I heard the funeral was large."

"Very," said John. "Three, maybe four hundred people."

Both men looked at him.

"I didn't know you were a friend of the alderman's," the rabbi said.

"I'm not," John said. There was no point in explaining anything. He shook pepper into his tomato juice and tore off a piece of roll with his hand. He continued, "I thought all the Lakeview clergy received an invitation." He looked at Kaufmann. "You didn't?"

"And you thought our alderman was completely ecumenical. Perhaps you overestimate the man."

"I know almost nothing about him. He's a name to me, little else. The Methodist guy, what's his name from the Near North?"

"Smith?"

"Yes, Smith, he introduced me to the alderman at a Rotary social a couple of years ago. He made a lame joke about the Amish. You have no idea how tired I am of Amish jokes. And just as tired explaining the difference between the Swiss and Russian branches of my people."

Modeski and Kaufmann nodded wearily and rolled their eyes.

"Smith told the joke, or the alderman?" Kaufmann asked.

"The alderman. Fitzsimmons."

"You always insist your people don't become politically involved. Just like you to stay clear of any kind of violence. Of course, why would you have reason to know the alderman?" Kaufmann asked.

"Property tax abatements, maybe?" Modeski asked. He quirked a little smile.

"In the world, but not of it," John said, "unless you call this worldly." He pointed to his plate and spoke through a mouthful of cinnamon roll.

"Some call it decadence," said Modeski. "But I say there are no moral or immoral cinnamon rolls. Only those properly or improperly baked." He had taken off his cap, exposing a few long strands of hair plastered over his bald skull. "I think pagans and Christians have common ground calling this gluttony. Of this sin I pronounce you guilty."

"This is a deadly sin?" John asked. "No way. This is the bounty of God. One of the waitresses told me."

"I have noticed that, too," the old rabbi said. He shook a steady finger in John's direction. "I see how the Mennonite looks upon young waitresses and listens with eager attention."

"Look, I am no match for a pagan and a Jew. Show a little kindness," John said, waving his fork. "Leave a humble farm boy to his peasant repast."

They watched him eat. He continued, though: "It is interesting, Arthur, that you should raise the question of the deadly sins. Lately I have been thinking again about the unpardonable sin."

"Speak, son of Menno," said Modeski. "Though I thought that you liberal mainliners, starting with Schleiermacher, abandoned the whole concept around 1805. Then Hawthorne, earnest but wayward Puritan, gnawed the idea to death in the New World."

"Whatever makes you think I'm a liberal Protestant?" John said. "About the same time Schleiermacher rhapsodized on the religion of the heart, my people in Russia were rejecting the elders for going too soft on depravity. I'll take Hawthorne and the Puritans, thank you very much."

"The unpardonable sin," Kaufmann said. He had finished the eggs on his plate. "For your people that would be militarism, joining the Marines. Don't you shun that?"

"You might be surprised. Lots of us have caved on the military question," said John. "Did you know Dwight Eisenhower's parents were Anabaptist? River Brethren who settled near the Flint Hills. One of our best-kept secrets. But that is not the unpardonable sin."

Kaufmann smiled broadly now. "Maybe the wayward Mennonite did us all a favor, no? Some of us believe D-Day was a blessing."

Modeski waved impatiently. "Come on, it's not complicated. Isn't there a standard seminar reply on this one? That the unpardonable sin is simply a refusal of God's grace?"

John nodded. "For a pagan, you know an awful lot of Christian theology."

"Thank God for Jesuits."

Kaufmann followed up quickly. "And if it is the amazing grace you people always sing about—please understand that I mean no disrespect—technically, then, wouldn't real grace be an offer you cannot refuse?"

John thought a moment. "If it can be refused, it seems like a lightweight offer, doesn't it, and if it cannot be refused, well, it's coercion. Is God basically Don Corleone? I admit this poses an awkward dilemma."

Modeski interjected: "Listen. I've read the scriptures that both of you holy men lay claim to, and putting God in a dark suit with a toothpick in his mouth sounds about right to me. A lot more in character than Charlton Heston. A touch of Brooklyn, a touch of the pope. A soft-talking bully who saves his roaring for the special occasions."

The Mennonite and the Jew looked at each other and waited for the diatribe to end.

Modeski went on. "That's why I broke my mother's heart. When I told her I was keeping the Roman but dropping the Catholic."

"You broke your mother's heart?" John said.

"I did. When I was fourteen. I broke my Polish mother's heart."

"Did she forgive you?" the rabbi asked.

"Eventually."

John said, "I want to hear more about your mother, but may I change the subject?"

"Does anyone ever stop you?"

"Help me with something, Arthur. You know the classics. Is there anything like the unpardonable sin in Socrates or Plato?"

"Not really. Plato's argument, of course, is that error and ignorance account for acts of evil in the world. This became the standard Enlightenment view."

"Right," John said. "A sweet liberal sentiment blown apart by World War I. That was when most thinking people figured out it was more than a head problem, wouldn't you agree?" John looked at Kaufmann. "I think our rabbinical brother knows of what I speak."

Kaufmann nodded and motioned for a coffee refill. "Yes. But as for the unpardonable sin, there are some acts in our time that have achieved such magnitude. Some acts for which we have no utterance. Of course you know what I speak of. To speak of them, well, we do not know yet how to speak . . ."

He gesticulated, but the words weren't there. His hands dropped in his lap. "Maybe this is as hard a paradox as your understanding of grace. I don't know. We still do not understand what has happened to us."

"More than a head problem, though?" John pressed.

"Most definitely more than a head problem."

Modeski scoured the curve of his plate for any icing that remained. "I admire your tenacity, John, for wanting to bring sin back into late twentieth-century ways of talking. I can see that it is a vital part of your job. And I admit that for his historical moment, after the Great War, Karl Barth made a lot of sense.

"It's just that I think all this talk of sin, whichever way you package it, has done far greater damage in the world than good. Those who talk most loudly of sin are always talking of everybody else's problem. Doing no harm strikes me as a safer proposition than rooting out sin and saving the lost."

"You're a modest man," Kaufmann said to Modeski.

"For me, the best pagans at least exhibit the virtue of modest aims. Don't get me wrong," he said, looking at John, "I think you're among the most modest men I have known."

"Keep guessing," John said. "I have a heart of darkness. Even the pagans knew that to live authentically we must exceed ourselves. Modesty goes only so far."

"You sound like a man ready for Nietzsche," said Modeski.

"Do you ever wonder why so many of our conversations come back to Germany and things German?" John said.

Kaufmann responded, "I wonder about that all the time."

The meeting ended with Modeski slipping away in a hurry. He had an editorial meeting on Rush Street, and he took his leather book bag, stained with ink and bulging with papers, off the back of his chair.

Yet only when the waitress brought the bills did his two companions notice that he was gone. They looked at each other, amazed.

"The pagan knows how to walk a check," Kaufmann said. "Is he human or is he a dybbuk?"

John looked at the pile of crumbs around Modeski's empty plate. "Don't give him too much credit. I would say a *schlöb*."

Chapter 16

He barely had time to go home and shower and change for his morning meeting with Nancy Huefflinger and the church council.

As usual, the group convened at a pancake house near the Chicago Historical Society. This morning it was business as usual until Nancy read a letter from an AA group wishing to use the church's social hall. At that moment, Wesley Unger, one of the congregation's old-timers, picked up his newspaper and leafed through it in full passive-aggressive mode. The youngest council member, Rachel Swartzendruber, piped up in her sweet voice to ask about the group's smoking policy. She was a fellow in public health at the University of Chicago. She added that, given her personal experience with AA groups, smoking policies were "quite often problematic."

John wondered whether he had always disliked graduate students so much or whether he was simply growing old and gnarly. He had been a graduate student himself but lately was finding the type rather tiresome. He looked around the table and said he thought it a sign of health when churches let community groups share their space, especially when their goals were mutual. "I think we might keep in mind the bigger picture," he added.

Swartzendruber's rejoinder came without hesitation: "Well, perhaps keeping Lakeview Mennonite smoke-free is part of the big picture."

Nancy intervened. "Might we try," she said, looking at Rachel, "a probationary period? I would propose giving them a three-month trial run, and then we can revisit the decision. And if need be, we can put in a no-smoking policy at that point."

Unger laid his paper on the table. John looked at him and saw him as a potential source of a church split down the road. He had expressed various dissatisfactions of late—about the excessive formality of services, the process for choosing conference delegates, the slack attention to updating

71

the membership roll, the budget committee. Not the least of his concerns was John's sabbatical-style summer break from preaching. Unger ran a commercial print shop and he liked to get value for his money.

Directly to Unger's left sat Dennis Hoover, a man in a blue suit with a benign and self-satisfied glow. He handled church polity like he managed his fast-growing portfolio of ethical mutual funds. He didn't ruffle, and one never knew when he bluffed. He spoke: "Could we know a little more, Nancy, about this group's—uh—general demographic profile? Mind you, I'm not worried about our congregation's response per se, I'm thinking more about the district leadership. We might anticipate their concerns." He smiled wanly.

Unger responded, "Can we speak plain English here? 'Demographic profile'? I'm afraid I don't have enough letters after my name to translate."

Nancy looked at him, held up a finger, and said, "I'll get to that." Then she said to Hoover, "Dennis, it's true. The members of this particular AA group are mostly gay. Some are HIV-positive. Many are retired or near retirement. They're from Lakeview and West Lakeview. And pardon me for sounding callous, but I suspect some of them would be most interested in information on your ethical investing funds. I don't think that would constitute a conflict of interest, and I believe many of these individuals are worth meeting. We might extend the invitation to them to attend on Sunday morning." Turning to Unger, she said, "I think that may also answer your question about the demographic."

Hoover straightened a jacket cuff and Unger nodded, a little shell-shocked.

Nancy looked around the table. "I think it appropriate to raise these concerns, but why imagine the worst if we are doing this on a trial basis?" If I don't hear any objections to a three-month probationary period, I'd like to hear a motion." Rachel so moved and Hoover seconded, and there were ayes and an absence of nays, with Unger offering the lone abstention.

The rest of the meeting lacked drama, and when it adjourned, John exchanged a few pleasantries and went to the men's room. When he exited, Nancy was alone at the front cashier, paying her bill. She took him by the elbow and steered him out through the doors onto the sidewalk. "Look, there's something else we have to talk about, John, but I didn't want to bring it up with the entire council."

They walked in the cold sunlight.

"What is going on with you and this Talbot murder?" she said. "You're holding out on me, and I want to know why."

He motioned with his chin toward his car. She walked with him and got in on the passenger side. When they were both seated, he said, "What do you know?"

"He's dead and buried, and you're involved somehow. Would you mind telling me exactly what your involvement is, and what is going on?"

John thought of Annie's request for confidentiality. He knew anything he said now he might be sorry for later.

"It seems his girlfriend is convinced it wasn't a gay-bashing at all. She thinks something else happened. She has asked me to keep confidence. That's about all I can say right now."

"Oh, his girlfriend. Did she put you on her payroll? What is this, Gumshoe Mennonite? Let me remind you that you are already gainfully employed. Tell the damsel in distress you have a job."

Nancy swung her handsome face toward him. Flashing dark eyes and dramatic eyebrows, the smallest of dimples at the corners of her strong mouth, amber pendants in silver settings swung in her ears. He saw the little muscle below her temple flex and he imagined her heaving a javelin at the center of his chest.

"Nancy, there is no need to get harsh. Give me a few days. This is sensitive. I know I've been hard to reach lately."

"That's right. You seem distracted. I should come over and cook dinner for you. I could chop some nuts on those new countertops I had installed. You might tell me things."

"Great, then we'll really give Unger something to talk about."

"Not to mention the banker," Nancy said. "Hoover is our real problem. He's the smart one."

"I know," John attempted to joke. "You attorneys tend to run scared from the accountants." When Nancy got out of the car to go to her office, she wasn't smiling.

Chapter 17

THIS TIME, JOHN MADE his appointment with Trophy on schedule. He pulled up outside the address in Bucktown promptly at ten. In his own home, the bartender from the Berlin was actually civil. This left John momentarily disarmed. The woodwork on the porch landing seemed recently scrubbed and varnished. The apartment inside was stylish and clean, smelling slightly of joss sticks. There were bleached oak floors and an absence of clutter. It was a serene space, John thought, and Trophy showed no trace of yesterday's hostilities.

They sat down across from each other in the living room. Next to a mission-style futon sofa stood a large aquarium occupied by a single blue and green striped tropical fish. Its inquisitive eyes swiveled in its head as it hovered, big as a grapefruit, in the middle of the tank. The gills fluttered in tiny vibrato.

"That's Omar," Trophy said. "He was David's."

"A big guy, isn't he?" John said.

"Yeah."

John looked around the room. "Was David the decorator, or you?"

"We collaborated. Although I think he would have admitted the best ideas were mine. We were a good team. He added and I subtracted." Trophy laughed at some unspoken memory.

"Impressive results," John said.

Trophy went into the kitchen and brought out two mugs and a metal carafe. He poured coffee for John and said, "Sumatran blend. David's favorite. He left several bags in the freezer. It's sort of a reliquary now, I guess you could say."

"Thank you," John said. "That's very good." He put the cup down. "You said the police were here and made a mess."

"Yeah."

"You keep a clean house. That's something I'm working on."

"David always called me a neat freak."

"Did the detectives find what they wanted?"

Trophy brought a bureau drawer into the living room and lifted out small cardboard boxes. He dumped one of them out on the sofa. A mélange of mostly bicycle and travel magazines. A couple of notebooks with graffiti in ballpoint on the covers, the kind kids do when they're bored in junior high. Store receipts, movie ticket stubs.

"What else?" John said. Trophy emptied another box. A jar with a screw-top lid, full of pennies and matchbooks. A scarred copy of *Zen and the Art of Motorcycle Maintenance*. A couple of Ayn Rand paperbacks. More magazines, *Outside* and *Granta*. John picked up one of the paperbacks.

"The cops saw all this stuff?"

"Yeah. They spent about five minutes in here tossing things out of drawers and destroying a closet. Then one of them looked at me and said, 'Let's let the fruitcake lover boy rest in peace. Fitzsimmons's little faggot boy.' Then he said, 'It figures.' That's what the cop said." Trophy paused. "I didn't hear all their conversation, but the alderman's name came up. It was weird."

"What do you mean, 'It figures'?"

"I don't know." Trophy shrugged.

"What were they after?"

"I think they were looking for jack-off novels or coke spoons. Maybe some chaps and leather harnesses."

"Were they successful?"

"That wasn't David's style."

"Did David ever talk about his father?"

"Not with me. Come on in here. There's more if you want to take a look. But there's really not much to see."

"I'll take more of that Sumatran if you have any." John sat on a single bed in what had been David's room. They looked at the last of David's personal effects, held by a Johnnie Walker double-walled cardboard box. Three boxes like it that bore the imprimaturs of Absolut and Bacardi were stacked by the door.

"Good for packing," John said.

"The best. One of the bonuses of my job."

The remainder of the effects struck John as increasingly poignant, though they offered no clues: a CD collection that filled four shoeboxes; a Sony Walkman; a small stack of letters and postcards from scattered California addresses; an old army-green nylon backpack with more inked graffiti on it; a couple of nice pinpoint oxford shirts and a stack of T-shirts and jeans; more paperbacks, including *The Portable Thoreau* and some Calvin and Hobbes cartoon collections. John picked up a trophy from a memento box. It bore the inscription "Lake Conahee Best Camper Award 1980." A cigar box contained some foreign coins and a few Mexican peso bills.

"Did he have any pictures of his mother?"

Trophy rifled through the box and retrieved a plastic binder. "Here."

The picture of the woman had been airbrushed in the way of a successful small-town studio photographer. The shag haircut from the early 1970s looked cleaned up, touchingly innocent. The woman's olive skin was smooth on high cheekbones, and her eyes seemed older than her face, but the airbrushing made these things hard to judge.

"David told me that was taken before he was born. While his mom was still in Illinois. Here, there are a couple of his baby pictures, too." The boy looked a lot like his mother, John decided, though the curly hair showed traces of Fitzsimmons.

"Any pictures going back further? Other family photos?"

"No, that's it."

"Any pictures of Annie?"

"Queen Anne? The Bitch?" Trophy's face went through a dark transformation at mention of her name. "None that I know of."

John slipped the photos back into the binder. "So this is it?"

Trophy hesitated. "There is one other thing. It's in here. Follow me."

In the kitchen, the apartment's biggest room, a beat-up Schwinn bicycle leaned against the windowsill.

"This was the bike he used for work," Trophy said, gripping the handlebars. "An old three-speed." The bike's tires were slicks, and the frame looked as though it had been modified for mountain riding. The seat was wrapped in several layers of worn duct tape. The oversized red reflector mounted behind the seat still had mud splattered up through the middle.

"The work bike you say. You mean he had another one?"

"Yeah. He had a racing bike he rode on weekends. The pleasure bike. That one's gone. It was a really nice bike, too. You know anything about bikes?"

"Next to nothing. Where I grew up, we rode horses."

"He paid good money for the one he was on the night he was killed. Twenty-four speed Shimano grip shifts, triathlon rims. He'd wanted Bullseye hubs, but I told him they were overrated, rusted out pretty fast."

"Were you also in the messenger business?"

"Yeah, before I bulked out. I know, I know—looking at me, who would ever guess, right?" Trophy laughed. "That was before I started the catering and liquor trade and put on the fat. You wouldn't believe it, but at David's age I was positively svelte. Anyway, he must have been riding the Slingshot. The cops are probably holding the bike as evidence."

"Evidence for what?"

"Well, who knows? Or he parked it somewhere and it got ripped off before, you know. I told him to be careful. Bikes like that have a way of disappearing."

"You saw David the day it happened," John said. "I mean, the day before the evening it happened."

"No. He and I kept different schedules. I work a lot of nights so I often sleep part of the day. I thought he was at Annie's. Sometimes he'd stay over there."

"I'm still trying to understand this triangle of you and David and Annie. Can you explain it to me? I am living in a land of riddles with Annie about this."

"Look, John, you're asking a lot of questions, and for all I know, you could be some sort of investigator yourself. I'm taking Annie's word for it that you're okay. I don't know what the hell I'm doing showing you David's stuff. What are you, anyway? I'm not buying the therapist line anymore."

"I'm not an investigator."

"You act like a fucking investigator."

"I'm a preacher."

"You're kidding."

"No, I'm a preacher. A Mennonite preacher."

"Yeah, right. And I'm the Dalai Lama. You mean like the Amish and such? How do they allow you to drive?"

"I'm not putting you on. And yes, some of us drive. Cars. I was driving a tractor when I was six."

"Why are you involved in this? Shouldn't you be working for world peace or something?"

"Let's talk about David now and I can tell you all about peace studies later. Annie tells me David was not a homosexual, he was not cruising the park the night he was murdered, and she believes the cops—and I guess also the alderman—have it all wrong."

Trophy folded his arms. "What are you getting at?"

"Annie asked me to make informal inquiries. Believe me, I am not used to doing this. But you and I have to talk, despite getting off on the wrong foot. My point is to ask whether you think she's right."

Trophy sat at the foot of the bed and looked down. John continued, "Look, I need to know, and you can trust me with absolute confidence. David lived here. What was your relationship? Something else, which I hope you can keep in confidence: I know you hate Annie. Maybe you know it, maybe you don't—she's married and her estranged husband interrogated her the night after the cops asked her questions. The guy nearly took her head off. You know about him?"

"No, not really."

"Not really?"

Trophy was starting to wear his resentful dog look again. "I mean I don't know his name. David and Annie never spoke about him. I knew she had been in a relationship before David. That's all I knew."

"So David seems to have made more than one man very angry. How did he meet Annie?"

"We met at a club. The Vortex," Trophy said.

"The Vortex?"

"Yeah, can you stop repeating me? It was a gay industrial dance club. It's closed now."

"That sounds like a complicated place. So what was your relationship with David?"

"Look, we never had sex, okay? Any kind of sex. Are you happy? Are you happy now?"

"But you wanted to." John said it gently, a declaration.

"Yes." Trophy looked down, miserably. They both stood behind the Schwinn bike. "We were companions. We were extremely good friends. He said he wanted to keep it that way."

"And when the cops interrogated you, you made sure to mince. You did affectations. You lisped as outrageously as possible. That's clearly one of your habits when you're angry."

"No one has ever told me that."

"It's pretty obvious."

"Thanks for telling me." Trophy sprawled in a kitchen chair and lit a cigarette, his thick hands quick and graceful with the lighter.

"Listen, I want you to do something for me."

"I'm listening." Trophy blew a smoke ring.

"I need to know about the detectives who visited you here. If you didn't write their names down, can you find out? And second, I need the name of Annie's husband. Can you check around?"

"Yeah, I'll do that." Trophy inhaled some smoke.

"Be careful," John said. "He's a maniac."

"You don't sound awfully concerned sending me after this madman. Do you think he could have done it?"

"I said check around, don't seek him out. But yes, I think he could have. Annie doesn't think so. And she's refusing to report him to the cops because he's threatened to kill her."

"Jesus. Excuse me, I mean . . ."

"What I'm telling you is in absolute confidence. Here, help me carry this stuff out. I need to be going." John hoisted one of the liquor boxes on his shoulder and started for the door.

Trophy moved with a sumo's grace and carried the other boxes in one trip. Outside by the car, John asked, "You're not going to fight Annie for David's possessions?" He slammed the trunk shut.

"No. I'm keeping the bike, though. Annie said she didn't want it."

"We might do some peacemaking here yet," John said. He got into the car.

"Please don't invite me to get your religion."

"I never coerce," John said, and put the stick shift into first. "All things in due time. Feed your fish."

He watched the thick, sad figure at the curb recede in his rearview mirror. He wondered what Annie would do with David's possessions, with his best camper award. John shook his head and drove out of Bucktown toward Lakeview.

Chapter 18

John surveyed the crockery and pans covering one of the fold-up tables in the social hall. Somebody was playing Andean folk music. Half a dozen women and a man rushed around, setting out stacks of plates and bowls and cutlery. A multitude of smells filled the room, a pleasing clash of east and west, of curry and barbecue, of village and city.

The younger parishioners hauled in salads that brimmed in carved wooden bowls, vegetarian casseroles, complicated Tex-Mex variations. The More-With-Less crowd had graduated to nouvelle American cuisine, John decided.

He looked in vain for the generous plates of *vareniki* that Mildred Unruh usually put on the table: cheese dumplings boiled and then fried until the edges went golden brown, waiting to be anointed by her famous ham gravy. Mildred understood the old ways her people had brought from the Ukraine when the virtuous life was less complicated. He thought of a simpler time in Meade and Zoar and Gnadenau, the repasts of baked ham and *prishki*, homemade chicken-noodle soup, zwieback spread with freshly churned butter and rhubarb preserves. *Pluma mous, plautz*. The long board tables in the church basements, heavy with food. The days when simple faith and *faspa* were virtually indistinguishable.

Mildred wore a polka-dotted scarf around her head that made her look Hutterite. Breathing hard, she bore a heavy shopping bag in each hand and muscled her way in through the back door. Once inside, she backed her posterior against the door to close it against the traffic and cold. John went to greet her. She smelled of baked bread.

John worried sometimes that she didn't always know when to quit. He could see that the handles of the shopping bags were cutting into the palms of her hands. *This,* he thought, *is the genuine Mennonite stigmata: crucifixion by one's own potluck.*

He thought of his mother in the early morning, her hair coiled up in a tight bun under a wool scarf, leaning in against a cow and squirting milk straight from the Holstein's tit into the open mouth of a waiting cat. He remembered her powerful hands, farmer's hands, and the rich smell of hay and cattle in his nose, the switch of a cow tail, the sting on his cheek.

"Here, help me with these, I still have a casserole dish in the car," Mildred said.

John took the bags. "Bread?"

"Yes. Some of that is still in the car, too. Leave these bags on the counter, I'll be right back."

A heavy jar of dark red preserves lay at the bottom of one of the bags. John lugged the booty to the kitchen counter and strained to twist the lid off the jar. Alan Wiebe joined him, and they tore off a couple of warm crusty ends of the bread and began to spread jam. Mildred returned and caught them. She set down an enormous casserole dish on the counter and, standing on thick babushka legs and mopping her brow with the back of her forearm, glanced with disgust as John and Wiebe gnawed shamelessly on the bread.

"Men," she said. "You are not much better than animals. Go, sit down, or pray and get us started. Or at least make yourself useful and slice the bread for the table!"

Men in the kitchen violated Mildred's sense of the creation order. She lifted tinfoil off the top of the voluminous Pyrex tray and the primal aroma of *vareniki* rose into the air. John imagined it must have been for something like this that Esau gave up his birthright. The onions, the cheese, the pastry. *Ah, the pastry,* John thought, so like the blintz and the pierogi, yet superior to either one. This was one area in which he would not apologize for rank ethnocentric bias.

Viola had never taught him how to make *vareniki,* although she had suggested once, toward the end of her days of clear thinking, that it would be a skill worth acquiring. Always eminently practical she had been, even in the terrible period of diagnosis. "When I am really ill, John, you will wish you had learned." The small tremor and brave smile as she spoke. She had handled the crisis so much better than he. As to cooking, he was an old dog unwilling to learn new tricks.

He took Mildred's orders meekly. He stood in the middle of the hall and looked around. The people noticed his body language, and it took only a few moments for them to grow quiet. He said a short prayer. The people gathered in a circle. A child whined, and his mother comforted him with a container of Cheerios.

In the midst of this horn of plenty, the people forgot their differences. Two lines formed along the serving table for the biweekly Lakeview potluck. John glanced at Mildred behind the serving counter, stooped over an open oven door. Man does not live by bread alone, John had once observed to Wiebe, but he certainly could do a lot worse.

Sitting between the choir director, Byron Neufeld, and Unger, who seemed subdued still from this morning's council meeting, John forked into the *vareniki* and sliced baked ham. "That woman knows how to cook a piece of pork. How does she do that so well?" he said. He ladled some onion gravy on top.

"Unbelievable," Unger agreed. The pork gave him and the minister common ground.

Mildred appeared at the table bearing a coffeepot and pitcher of iced tea. She leaned over John's shoulder and poured with a steady hand, then eyed his plate to make sure he wasn't crowding out her dish with too many nontraditional items.

Nancy Huefflinger arrived late, as the din of conversation and rattling silverware reached a crescendo. Her face showed fatigue; she walked directly to the counter and removed little white cartons from a blue bag inscribed with the words "China Fun Best Takeout." John watched Mildred return to the counter and sensed trouble. The older woman could barely mask her contempt for the takeout, and John watched the drama unfold of women at war. Nancy wanted to put out the cartons of egg foo young and glazed snow peas as they were, spoons on the side. Mildred attempted to assist by providing serving dishes. Nancy waved off the help. "Bad move," John mumbled to himself, between bites from an Indonesian salad.

He asked Unger how business was at the print shop and listened to a treatise on rising HMO premiums. John nodded and took it all in. He learned more about his parishioners at these potlucks than at any other kind of gathering.

At the next table the graduate school crowd rambled from talk about the Patriot survivalist movement in Michigan's Upper Peninsula to the Maryknoll Order in Honduras. A young crewcut in a black turtleneck waved his arms, trying to get a word in with Wiebe, who presided with his usual blend of dictatorial charm. The crewcut said hoarsely, "Okay, so you think my position is too much like Niebuhr's"—rising cacophony of hooting, shouts—"but just let me finish!" Meanwhile, John noticed, Mildred took the strategic opportunity to remove the Andean folk music from the CD player and replace it with *500 Mennonite Men Sing*, by the Kansas Mennonite Men's Chorus.

Nancy angrily spooned Chinese food onto her plate and scrounged for leavings among the rest of the serving dishes. She came by John's table, heard the sports talk about the Bulls' shooting guard problem, and sat down by herself at the far end. After a while she looked up and made eye contact with the minister, and Unger said to Nancy, congenially, "There's room here. Come join us."

Nancy sat across from Unger and John. "Good day at the office?" Unger asked.

"So-so. What does it look like?"

"We feel your pain," John said. "Unger and I have been commiserating. Here. Try some of these." He passed the *vareniki* plate to Nancy. "Mildred has surpassed herself again."

"The best," Nancy said, trying one. "Always the best."

"Did your mother teach you how to make *vareniki*?" John asked her.

She scowled. "Don't start in with me, John. Don't mock. My generation has an impossible task living up to our elders. My mother's idea of a recipe started with the words, 'Drain a can of peas.'" Unger laughed. Neufeld, the choir director, joined in: "You're right. We don't stand a chance."

John let himself drift out of the conversation and noticed the way Nancy drank her coffee. She rested her elbow on the table in the weary manner of a Left Bank expat and balanced the porcelain rim against her lower lip, as if doing some sort of mental search, before she took a sip. Her wrist tilted and she looked at him again over the rim of the cup. He wondered if she was serious about cooking for him. He would definitely like to take her up on that. He looked back at her.

Mildred returned. "People, people! There is much food left, and no one wants to carry it home. I must insist, you have hardly touched your plates. Here, John, finish this ham. Alan, here, two more pieces, I don't want to throw it away. Please do your part, thank you, I won't take no."

"A completist," Wiebe said. John nodded.

The assault of dessert followed. The graduate students fought over a tray of lime Jell-O with grated carrots that Rachel Swartzendruber had brought as a joke. Wiebe held forth on the theological significance of kitsch and the invention of Dream Whip. The voices of 500 Kansas Mennonites echoed through the vast hall, as if to carry the sounds of gluttony to a mighty, rotund deity above.

John ached from the food. He and Unger and Neufeld carried plates to the kitchen, where Mildred presided over cleanup. She looked at the minister through a cloud of steam and held up one soapy hand to adjust her glasses.

"We would be lost without you," John said to her. She blushed and gave him a quick hug. Then she waved him off with a large yellow scouring pad and got back to work.

Chapter 19

"THE BLOOD THAT BESPATTERED the lintel and door-posts would at first be the blood of the firstborn child of the house; and when the blood of a lamb was afterwards substituted, we may suppose that it was intended not so much to appease as to cheat the ghastly visitant. Seeing the red drops in the doorway he would say to himself, 'That is the blood of their child. I need not turn in there. I have many yet to slay before the morning breaks grey in the east.'" John tore off a corner of the *Tribune*'s front page to mark his place in the hardcover volume of Frazer's *The Golden Bough*. He closed the book, removed his reading glasses, and rubbed his eyes with the heels of his hands. He once again noted that his hair needed to be cut. Mildred had commented on it while washing the dishes after the potluck. *Where would I be without my handlers?*, he wondered.

Now he sat and listened to the creaking pipes and the hum of traffic down the block on Racine. What would Milton think, he wondered, about Frazer's interpretation of the death angel? The angel as attack dog, lethal but so easily fooled. Milton's angels were lethal, too, and sometimes similarly obtuse.

John padded into his kitchen, opened his fridge, and poured himself a glass of seltzer water over ice. He returned to his study. He raised the blinds and looked down at the street, parked full on both sides, except for where the dumpster stood, now half-full, in front of the chain link construction fence.

He picked up *The Golden Bough* and read the passage again and thought about how Frazer was able to get inside the head of the death angel.

He glanced up at his top bookshelf for his Norton Critical Edition of *Paradise Lost*. He started to reach for it. And at that moment, the glass in his study window exploded.

Something warm and wet on the side of his head brought his hand into motion. There was a trickle into his eye, and then red, heavy blotches on the yellow legal pad in front of him. A gust of wind followed and the blinds rattled. He turned toward the cold and saw the glass of the window shattered into sharp spears pointing inward to an empty center. He dropped to the floor and rolled under his desk. Anxious to keep his head below the level of the windowsill, he scrambled backward toward the light switch, reached up in a quick motion, and flipped it off.

Another spray of shattering glass filled the space, and he closed his eyes and lay on the floor, fetal. A distinct thump sounded in the wall above him, and something detached from its hook and fell on his head. The hit gouged a chunk out of his scalp. He reached up and felt more blood.

In the dark now, he scrambled back to the window and peered over the top of the sill across the street at the dark empty shell of the house under construction. The empty window spaces were black. Blood dripped down his cheek in a warm, slow crawl.

He walked through his apartment, turned off all the lights, and waited some more. He stayed away from his windows. He was in a space outside of fear, in a sweaty zone of detachment. In his bedroom, he put on a pair of sneakers and a fleece and windbreaker. Then he descended the back fire escape and ran in the direction of the shots. The blood had already hardened on his cheek into a crusty mess around his eye.

John's feet carried him around the block into the alley behind the construction site. He wanted to come in from behind. There was no chain-link fence here, just a path between overgrown shrubs to the narrow backyard. He crouched beside the shrubs and waited.

A dog barked nearby. The house had a wooden fire escape painted porch gray. He looked up the stairs and tried to let his eyes adjust to the dim light. After he walked back out into the yard and picked up a two-by-two that lay in a pile of scrap, he started up the staircase.

He remembered how once on the farm his brother Andrew had rushed into a barn without fear and beaten a ten-foot-long rattlesnake into a bloody mash. Gentle Andrew. He had done the killing methodically and without any sign of fear. The problem was that during the commotion, Andrew's quarter horse Star had caught her leg in the slats between stalls. The next morning, while the crows ate the snake's bludgeoned remains out in the yard, John and Andrew had silently watched Star hold her rear leg off the floor, refusing to put any weight on it.

Andrew had said to John, "Here," and handed John the rifle. "We can't save her. And I can't do this. It's loaded. You know what to do."

Now, gripping the piece of wood in both hands, John walked up the back stairs of the house under construction.

The door off the second-floor landing stood ajar. That was wrong, John saw. He pushed the door open, stood and sniffed. There were pine wall studs, recently cut and nailed into place. The other smell carried a trace of smoke. Not cigarettes, or maybe tobacco plus something else. He let his eyes adjust to the darkness. Silence. He walked toward the openings in the wall that faced his own dark, shattered study window across the street.

He almost fell on something round and slippery. The smell in the room was distinctly gunpowder—he knew it even though he hadn't smelled gunpowder in nearly forty years. He looked down at the floor and picked up a .22 shell casing that gleamed in the sawdust. He rolled it between his fingers and then leaned down and picked up another, and another. He saw that the floor was littered with the casings, and then he walked back in the room and dropped the piece of wood on the floor. He put his hands on the frame for a new wall, vertical studs placed at eighteen-inch intervals. The two-by-four plate had been fastened to the concrete floor with spikes driven by a .22 stud gun. The heads were all recessed in the wood; he felt this with his thumb. He put the .22 casing into his pocket, confused, and wondered whether a stud gun could fire its projectile across the street. *Ridiculous. Those were bullets.*

Back in his apartment he punched the numbers on his phone for Louis Kerdigan. His finger was shaking. On the second try he got the sequence right.

"Mrs. Kerdigan?" John said. "Louis there?"

"No, I'm sorry, he's out."

"Can you call Bill?" John said.

"Is that you, John?" Mrs. Kerdigan spoke. "You don't sound so good."

"I'm fine, just in the middle of a small adventure. If you can get hold of Bill, send him over. Yes. No, no ambulance. Absolutely not. Yes, I'm fine. I'm at home. No, you should stay right where you are. Send him over as soon as you can. Thanks."

John hocked and spit into his bathroom sink. He washed his face and applied a wad of tissue to his temple. Then he walked through the dark apartment to his study.

Frazer's book lay face down on the bloody legal pad. John sat at his desk and picked pieces of glass out of both his hands and waited for the police.

Chapter 20

BILL KERDIGAN WAS EVEN bigger than his brother Louis. He loomed in John's doorway in a tailored black pinstripe suit, soiled white shirt, and red suspenders. Snowy eyebrows, with a few straggling black hairs, seemed slapped onto his angular balding head like a pair of furry animals that would not rest. He wore very scuffed oxblood tassel loafers, maybe size 15 or so, and John watched him jitter around on the front room carpet. This was a large, impatient mammal.

Bill had the knowing eyes of his younger brother, and he appraised John's condition. "You're a godawful mess. You need to take care of those cuts."

"I'm fine."

"Come here. Stand in the light a minute." He had been holding his fedora but he flipped it onto the couch. He maneuvered John beside the reading lamp and his fingers tilted the minister's head back and turned it to the side. Bill pried loose the Band-Aid at John's temple.

"Well look at this." The undertaker's brother spoke with authority. "Reverend, you're still leaking here. This isn't too big, but it's very deep. You need stitches."

"It can wait."

Bill released John's head from his grip. "Suit yourself. You interrupted my late supper, but I'm glad you called. Where is the show-and-tell?"

He shook a cigarette from a pack of 100s. His hands were enormous. He didn't light up but instead wedged the cigarette in his ear alongside his bristly skull. "Let's get down to it. Someone took shots at you?"

John was putting on sneakers. "Yes. There's glass everywhere. Be careful."

The door buzzer sounded again. Bill said, "That'd be Mark Shanahan. He said he was on his way."

John looked quizzical.

"He's with the mobile unit."

John opened the door, and the apartment suddenly filled with men, the smells and grunts of a platoon. Two stocky Hispanic officers carried leather satchels and stood in the wake of the other detective who entered and slowly chewed his gum. Shanahan looked around the room and shook John's hand. He introduced Cortez and Vito.

"You would be the priest?" Vito said.

"Call me John."

Shanahan shed his navy-blue wool coat. "Sorry about what happened. Glad you're okay." He wore a pair of black jeans and a Woolrich beige sweater. The black Nike runners gave him an appearance of speed.

The guys from the mobile unit unpacked their gear. "The front window in here, correct?" asked Vito, the shorter one. He flipped on the study's light. Shanahan and Kerdigan followed him into the room. Shanahan scratched his mustache and blew a bubble, sucking the little pink sphere back in through his teeth and popping it cleanly. Bill shifted back and forth on his big feet, hunched like a vulture over the other men.

"You haven't touched anything in here since it happened?" Shanahan said.

"Just the light switch," John said.

The wind blew through the broken window, and the air from outside smelled like cooked lamb and frying onions. Shanahan planted himself in the room like a middle linebacker and pronounced himself hungry. "Thirty-eight caliber," he said to Cortez.

The mobile unit's twins snapped some pictures. Vito surveyed the study's rear wall. He peered out the broken window then pulled some tools out of his satchel. "Two shots, am I right?"

John nodded. "That's all I heard."

Vito picked up the fallen wall plaque, looked at it, and put it on the desk. He began to use a large pick to extricate the bullet from the wall.

"That fell on my head after the second shot," John said.

"Who's the bearded guy on the plaque?" Vito said over his shoulder. He wore a short-sleeved black polo shirt and seemed oblivious to the cold.

John answered. "Menno Simons, sixteenth-century renegade priest in Holland. One of the founding fathers of the Anabaptists."

Vito worked the pick into the plaster. "Did you say anti-Baptist?"

"No, Anabaptist. Rebaptizers. Radical Reformation. We took our name after him, Mennonites."

"Maybe I should come for the catechism," Vito laughed. The other detectives joined him. John turned the plaque over in his hands. He had bought it at a World Conference in Holland and was glad it wasn't totally ruined. Menno had received a direct hit in the left eye, and the slug had not been kind. He would need an eyepatch. John ruefully fingered his own head now, noting that Menno had inflicted the pain.

Shanahan found another hole in the wall next to the light switch. "Pacifists, am I right?"

"Most of us," John said. Shanahan looked out the blasted window.

Vito went into a catcher's stance on the floor and surveyed the spears of glass. "Were you sitting in the chair?"

"Yes."

"Lucky you didn't take one of these splinters in the neck. I seen once where a man pumped like a fire hydrant from glass exploding like this. Took it right in the jugular. When we found him, we had to practically swim across the room. You anti-Baptists must be doing something right for the Man." He pointed at the ceiling and smiled, then motioned at the wall-to-wall shelves. "Maybe all the reading gets you points."

"Better install safety glass," Cortez interrupted, standing by the front window.

Vito looked at the books on top of John's desk, the spots of dry blood spattered across it. He switched on the reading lamp.

"You make anyone mad at you lately?" Shanahan asked.

"Besides a couple of people on my church council and the moderator, no one comes to mind."

"Seriously," Shanahan said, taking out a notebook. "Think about it."

"I will," John said. "But I am not thinking too well at the moment."

"We can talk more later when your nerves are settled," Shanahan said. He reached for a high-powered flashlight in a leather case on the floor.

"I think the shots came from across the street," John said, pointing. "From the street below the bullets would be in the ceiling, right?"

Vito went back to work on the wall with his tool. "John, you have it figured out. Think about a career in forensics." A chunk of metal fell out of the wall into his waiting palm. "Thirty-eight, all right. Like a little brick going through that glass. Almost went through the wall, too." He deposited the squashed bullet in a plastic baggy and handed it to Shanahan.

Cortez was working on a hole by the doorframe. "Here's the other one, it's stuck back here in the wires by the switch."

"Yeah, be careful, don't electrocute yourself," Vito said. "I know how you like hacking into wires."

"You done?" Shanahan said. "Flip that switch off for me a second, unless you screwed it up already."

Cortez extinguished the light and Shanahan aimed his flashlight beam across the street. The men looked out the broken window at the empty sockets of the gut rehab that Shanahan probed with the beam. John caught the row of new wall studs in the black interior.

"I thought I saw a light in there after the second shot."

"Yes, it could have come from there," Shanahan said. "Or from the glass in your eye." He turned toward John. "You look a little green. Wanna sit down?"

John headed for the kitchen and drank a glass of water. When he returned, Shanahan was telling Bill, "Psycho juveniles fooling around again. Goddamn kids or crackheads, doesn't matter, the little fucks all have guns now." Shanahan noticed John was back in the room. "Or somebody who just wants to send you a message." He smiled again. "That's why I asked if there's anybody who has reasons. An unpleasant question, I know, but have to do my job. In my experience everyone makes enemies. Even men of the cloth." Shanahan glanced at the one-eyed Menno on the desk. "Renegade priests, especially."

Bill looked at the second mashed slug in the plastic pouch and handed the bag back to Vito, then squinted at the empty building across the way. "If they want to kill you, this is not sniper quality. Not from that distance. Show me how you were sitting before it happened."

John sat at his swivel chair at the desk. He tipped the glass off the book and resumed his reading stance. "Just like this."

"First shot was through the middle of the lower pane," Cortez said. "That went into the wall by the light switch. On the second shot they hit the plaque higher up on the wall, which then fell on your head."

"I don't remember much. I was reaching for this book here. I think I was starting to get out of my chair like this." John pointed up above on the high shelf and pulled the paperback by Milton all the way out. He gave it to Bill. "First I felt my eye and temple stinging. Then I noticed blood on the desk."

"So you leaned forward," Bill said, "and you were starting to stand up. Actually, that might have saved you. That reach for the book. Okay, the bullets pass about a foot behind your head. Either somebody not so good missed or somebody real good got as close as possible for a grazing shot. How close together were the shots? I mean the time frame."

"I was down on the floor when the second one came. I heard that one. Maybe thirty seconds after the first shot? That's when the plaque fell on my head. I was on my hands and knees scrabbling around."

"And then?"

"I reached up and turned off the light."

"Good thinking," Shanahan said. "You switched it off after the first or the second shot?"

"I'm not sure, now that you ask."

Vito said, "That bullet so close to the switch. They might have been going for your hand. Saw the motion and fired."

"In any event," Shanahan said, "you did the right thing, turning off the light."

He exited the study to put on his overcoat. "Let's pay that construction site a visit. We'll need to cordon off the place and call the contractor tonight," he said to Cortez. "Come on, let's go." He headed for the stairs that led down to the street below.

John said, "There's something else I need to tell you. I already went over there."

Bill grasped John's arm. "When?"

"A few minutes after the shots were fired."

The rest of the men halted behind him. "Say again?" asked Bill.

"I went over there after it happened. Maybe ten minutes after. A little bit before I called for you. I went through the alley back of the construction site and took the fire escape stairs to the top floor."

"Let's go," Bill said. "Show us."

They crossed the street, turned the corner by the convenience store and the laundromat, and headed into the alley.

Bill spoke. "Let me get this straight. You went over with blood dripping out of your head, unarmed, right after someone fires two bullets into your study. Ever hear of 911?"

"Yes," John said.

"You're quite the cowboy," Bill said. "Louis has told me some things about you. What was your plan if you met the shooter in the alley?"

"Where you from, John?" Shanahan asked.

"Kansas."

Shanahan grunted. "You'll have that from Kansas." He spoke again to John: "You're damn lucky we're not zipping you into a body bag."

John bore the scolding in silence. He decided not to show them the wicked piece of wood he'd been carrying up the back stairs of the rehab.

"Next time this happens," Shanahan said, "call us first. The sooner you call, the better our chances of catching the son of a bitch."

Shanahan moved ahead to catch up with Vito and Cortez, who were already at the house's fire escape.

Bill slowed his pace and took John's elbow. They stopped in the alley. Bill said, "That stuff about pissing people off. You know, people you might have crossed . . ."

"Yes," John said. "What?"

Bill said, "Listen, you might as well know something. I know you've been asking people about the Talbot murder."

"Your brother talked to you? What could that have to do with this?"

"Yeah," Bill said. "Me and my brother talk. On a regular basis. And now I expect you to tell me what you know about Talbot. Apparently you have asked a lot of very interesting questions."

"Bill, I was scheduled to preach his funeral sermon until the alderman's office intervened."

"Well, it was his son."

"I am aware of that."

"You've been talking with his great-aunt and some girl, too."

"Bill, what do you want from me?"

"John, have you considered the possibility that this shooting is related to that? Has that crossed your mind?"

John had a sudden flash of a hulking stranger, Annie's estranged husband, sighting his head in a scope. "No, it didn't."

"Right, you wouldn't make that connection. I'm the one paid to think of these possibilities."

John was impatient. "What did Louis say?"

"We'll talk at the diner. You're going to tell me everything you know."

On the second floor of the construction site Vito and Cortez played their flashlight beams around the inside of the exposed brick walls and shook their heads.

"Somebody chews," Vito said, his light beam aimed at a clumped, glistening wad of tobacco. "And it's fresh."

"I'll bag it," Cortez said.

"Shit," Vito said, pointing the flashlight at the concrete floor to take in myriad footprints in the dust. "Don't bother. At least six different guys working this site." He looked at John. "Too many chumps walking around in the fucking crime scene."

Shanahan reached down and picked up one of the shell casings strewn about. "Well, look at this."

"They've been using a nail gun in here," John said. "It's only .22 caliber." The men listened while he explained how a nail gun works. Cortez nodded politely.

"We know how a nail gun works," Shanahan said. "Except more crews use compressed air these days."

"Yeah, they work better than you'd like to know," Vito said, sticking out his index finger. "Pow. Fine at close range. Very messy, though."

Shanahan rolled the cartridge between his fingers, and a beeper went off in his pocket. "I have to take that call in the car," he said to Bill. He turned to Cortez and Vito. "Unless we find .38 casings, I'm afraid this entire area is too cluttered to tell us anything at all. But sweep it anyway." He headed down the staircase.

Cortez said to Bill, "We got this. Thanks."

Bill pulled the cigarette away from between his ear and head and inserted it in his mouth. "It's late." He cupped his big hands around the flame and snapped the heavy lighter shut. "Vito, have somebody check around here later tonight. We want names and IDs from the foreman tomorrow morning. I'd like to know why the fire escape door downstairs was unlocked."

A crackle in the radio unit of the police van interrupted the night. Behind the van was an unmarked sedan, and Bill said to John, "Wait just a minute, okay? I need to use my radio."

When Bill got out of the car, his face was white.

"What?" John said.

The detective threw his burning cigarette into the gutter. "That was Shanahan. That call he took . . ."

"What is it?"

"Seems they got another body in Lincoln Park."

John was silent.

Bill said, "Look, now is not the time for an extended conversation. You're not telling me everything you know about Talbot. I have a bad feeling about this."

"Anything else?"

"You're going to talk. To me. A friend." Bill lit another cigarette, and the look in his eye grew darker. "We need your cooperation. You're getting into our jurisdiction. Whatever you know may help us." Bill looked up at John's study window. "You need to call a board-up service and window repairs. You may want to consider staying somewhere else for a while."

"How about breakfast at the Medinah at seven?"

"You do push it, don't you?"

"I wake up at four, five o'clock anyway."

"Lock your doors. Show that eye to a doctor."

"Goodnight, Bill."

"Yeah."

John went upstairs. He tacked up a blanket around the broken window. He'd call in the morning. He got out a broom and dustpan and began to sweep the office. He picked up the plaque and contemplated Menno's blasted eye. He tucked the plaque in on the bookshelf next to Milton, for safekeeping, he told himself.

Chapter 21

JOHN MOVED THE WESTERN omelet over on his plate to make room for ketchup. Bill ate strawberries and peaches from a bowl with milk and sugar. He eyed the fresh Band-Aid on John's brow. "You won't get it stitched, will you?"

"Nah. Little cut is all."

"You're a stubborn bastard, you know that?" Then Bill began his interrogation of John.

The minister was not unprepared. He had also phoned Annie the previous night after sweeping up the glass in the study. He had said, "Does your husband have a thirty-eight?"

Annie's voice had been clear. "I never kept track of his arsenal. I hate guns. What do you want me to say? Would he try to hurt you or scare you? Maybe. Kill you? I doubt it. Of course a lot is possible when he's been drinking."

"What you're telling me is he has a mean streak."

"Yes, he does. You're not telling the cops, are you? That would guarantee him coming after me."

John had pressed for information on finding Joey, her ex. "I need to meet Joey," he had told Annie. "I won't tell the cops. I keep my promises. But I think we need to explain some things to Joey. Could you arrange a meeting?"

"John, you're out of your fucking preacher mind."

"If you want me to find out what happened to David Talbot, a little helpfulness on your part would go a long way," John had told her.

"What do you want me to ask him?" she had said.

"Look, you want to find out who killed David. So do the cops. So does the alderman. It's only a matter of time before they interrogate everybody who has the slightest acquaintance with you, Anne Casper. Your roommate Ruth Ann, Trophy, the other waitresses at the Melrose. Sooner or later they will put a tail on Joey. Don't you think it would be better if we spoke with him before that happens?"

"How can you be so sure?"

John had ignored her question. He said to her, "This is how I see it. You don't think Joey killed David. He is a mean person, he finds enjoyment in roughing people up, he may even hate homosexuals. But he doesn't fit the spree killer type. Still, he could hurt someone who makes him angry. Excuse me, not could, but does. How is your jaw, by the way?"

"It's much better, thank you."

"Good. I think we need to talk with Joey before the cops do. We need to reassure him. I need to reassure him I'm not a threat to you or to him. We should tell Joey the truth. Once the police start to ask him about his hunting habits, he could become very angry and come knocking on your door again."

Recollections of this conversation were preventing John from staying completely focused on Bill's immediate questions.

"What do you know about this Trophy character?"

"What kind of a name is Trophy?" John asked in reply.

"Come on," said Bill. "Don't obstruct this. Food caterer in Wicker Park, overweight, apparently some acquaintance with the deceased."

"Yes," John replied. "Talbot's roommate. "He also tends bar at the Berlin."

"Okay, John, I'm impressed, you get around. What's your read: roommate, lover, buddy, what the hell was he to Talbot? I take it you spoke with him."

"Yes. I picked up David's belongings at Trophy's apartment for a friend."

"A friend? Which one?"

"Look, Bill, can we recognize there may be people who hope for privacy after all this?"

"Which friend, John? Don't make me pull my badge."

"Okay, you insist. Annie. Anne Casper. I presume you know about her. The girlfriend you mentioned last night."

Bill nodded. "Yeah, we know some things."

John continued. "Annie wanted me to pick up David's belongings at Trophy's apartment. She doesn't care for him much. The feeling is mutual. Understandable, if this was a triangle. By the way, your Area 3 buddies, whoever they were, did a messy job."

"Says who?"

"Trophy."

"Yeah, like he doesn't have an agenda. Come on, John. Can we be a little more naïve?"

John pressed again. "Did you find what you were looking for?"

Bill set his coffee cup down in the saucer. It made a sharp noise. "Hey, I'm the one asking questions."

"Okay, calm down. You want my opinion on Trophy and David Talbot. I am hardly an expert on, what do they call it, 'the gay lifestyle.'" John mopped up the last of the ketchup with the eggs. He signaled the waitress for a coffee refill. "I'm not sure. Talbot might have started out as his lover. But Trophy claims they never had a relationship."

"You mean sexual relationship."

"Yes, that is what I mean. But Trophy wished there had been."

"Did Trophy say that? In so many words?"

"More or less. He made me fill in a few blanks."

"Yeah, yeah, you seminarians are good at that. All that exegetical crap." Bill lit a cigarette and gave John a different look. "Look, not to change the subject here, but are you wise in the ways of love?"

"I was named after the apostle of love."

"Wisecrack. Listen. Let me tell you about your life. You live alone. Don't get angry at me now. Viola, your lovely wife, God bless her soul, has been in a state of oblivion in a nursing home going on what, five, six years? You are a man of considerable vitality, and"—Bill paused—"modest intelligence. As a spiritual director you consider yourself sensitive, too. If there is anything my brother Louis has made clear, it's that John Reimer connects readily with all kinds of people. You impress my brother, mostly because you understand suffering."

"Don't flatter me. Do any of us understand suffering? Louis sees my work at funerals. There is more to me than that."

Bill went on. His thick eyebrows bunched and relaxed. "No doubt. You think about people, about loneliness and disappointment. You possibly have a rich fantasy life. Like all the rest of us, you even think about sex. You maybe have an overripe imagination. Kids talk to you. You have empathy."

"Impressive speech, Bill. What are you driving at?" John wondered when Bill would start in on the subject of Annie Casper.

"I'll tell you in a moment. But there's another possibility," Bill inhaled deeply on his cigarette and ground the butt into a glass ashtray. "The obvious possibility. That Talbot and Trophy were gay, and that's why they lived together, and you are overcomplicating the issue. And Talbot was simply the next random victim of whoever is doing these crimes."

"Do you have any reason to believe it was *not* a hate crime?" John asked.

"Do you?"

"I asked you first," John said. "Do your forensics people have any doubts? What do Vito, and what's his name . . . Cortez, know? If there is a pattern, did Talbot's death not quite match in some way?"

"Preacher, you are busting my balls. Louis was right about another thing. You don't let go, do you? You don't know when to stop."

John waited him out.

"Okay, I'll give you some stuff in confidence. But quid pro quo, understand? We're checking out several scenarios. You know how it is. People sometimes talk with you in ways they don't talk to us. With, you know, men wearing the badge. Maybe you can help us with Annie Casper, which brings me back to my earlier point about your rich fantasy life."

"I don't know what you're getting at."

"Why did she get you involved? Why did she need you to get David's stuff?"

"Your people talked with Annie, too," John said. "What did she tell you?"

"She gave us nothing substantial. Absolutely riveting performance. She talked for over an hour and didn't tell us a damn thing. You know, we're usually pretty good getting people to share information. And we know when somebody is holding out on us. She seemed very upset when I mentioned David's gay network—upset, but something else. I felt at that moment she was about to say something important and then decided to hold back. I got that feeling."

"Does it surprise you she was upset, Bill?"

"You're a hard man, John."

"She told me she felt violated after you guys finished with her. Why does it have to be that way?"

"I take back what I said about you not letting go. You're a son of a bitch."

"It's my job to comfort people, Bill."

"We work different sides of the street."

"Yes, most of the time that's right. We do."

"Well," Bill said after a pause, "we are trying to figure out how many sides of the street Talbot was working, and we're not getting any answers from anybody."

"What about the alderman? Isn't he any help?"

"You know the story," Bill said. "He's not the first father to lose his kid in a divorce."

"You talked to the great-aunt."

"Yeah. She was about as helpful as the goddamn waitress. How did your interview go with her?"

"I think that Helen was more interested in hitting on me than anything else. We had tea together, a lovely time."

"The woman was pretty starchy, even for an Episcopalian," Bill said. "Where do they get off? Her father was a bloody stockyard butcher, for Chrissake. Did she know her great-nephew?"

"A little. She's unreliable, I think. She hates the alderman. Bitter old family feud and she has her own money-guilt issues."

"Well, those can develop quickly after a divorce settlement. What else is new under the sun? What I am saying here, John, is there is something I don't like. I know you're talking with people. As a professional I'm telling you to butt out for your own safety . . ."

"But you want me to share anything I learn."

"Listen to me. I know you're going to keep talking and listening because that's what you do, and I can't stop it, but you're bound to run into some different kinds of folks. I don't want you to find yourself on the wrong end of a blunderbuss."

"It's good to know you can't afford putting a tail on me," John said. "Does it ring true that the kid would move back to Chicago and never speak with his father? I mean, *never* talk with him?"

"Well, yes. Don't get me started on fathers and sons. I have a brother-in-law in Wheaton. Teaches at the college, about to retire. He has a gay son he hasn't talked to in fifteen years. I made the mistake of trying to arrange a reconciliation."

"You ever talk to the nephew?"

"Yeah. I do. It's made more complicated because he's still in the closet. A wrestling coach." Bill's face took on the drawn look of afternoon. He put the pack of cigarettes in his suit's breast pocket and his massive eyebrows drew together.

"Well, that sounds healthy," John said. "I'm sure he teaches the boys all the right moves."

"Stop," Bill said. "And, you know, it's the saddest thing. Now none of us is talking. My nephew tells me I just made things worse."

He put on his hat and picked up the scribbled bill from the waitress and said over John's protests, "I'll get this one." He held the check outside John's reach. "I was about to say. We are under a lot of pressure on this case now. Last night, the body they found, the papers are already full of it."

"What can I do?" John said. He put a dollar down next to his empty plate.

"I want you to tell me what you know when you are ready to talk. Preferably sooner rather than later. And if you hear anything more, call immediately. Repair your study window. I'll be in touch."

"Bill."

"What?"

"I didn't mean what I said about your style."

"Yeah, you did. But you know what?"

"What?"

"I forgive you," Bill said, and added, "but don't push me."

Then the condor swept out of the diner. His flaring trench coat, the belt strap flapping, created turbulence in his wake.

Chapter 22

THE SIGN WAS VINTAGE fifties "Lake Hotel: Free TV" lettered in vertical neon industrial font. Rust pocked the faded blue panels of sheet metal where the rivets puckered the surface. A curved aluminum arrow lined with little blue light bulbs pointed the way in. Underneath, smaller orange neon announced: "Private Bath Parking Available Transients $105/wk."

John pushed on a door of battered steel and glass. It didn't give, so he hit the buzzer and waited. Heads moved behind a counter inside before the buzz sounded to let him in.

The lobby of the Lake Hotel smelled of old dogs and new construction. A jackhammer distantly burped in the building's bowels, and one of the attendants behind the counter wore a fresh surgical mask. Part of the lobby ceiling hung open, shreds of chicken wire and plaster, ripped like skin, which exposed red and yellow clumps of wire, rattling duct pipe. An ancient breaker box, doorless, showed fuses like a row of broken teeth. The sunken lobby floor on John's right was chipped, inlaid black marble. This had been a good hotel once, John thought, maybe in 1927.

How can it be, John wondered, *that half a block away in Starbucks on Broadway the brokers are making calls on their new toys, those clunky cellular phones, and drinking three-dollar cups of cappuccino?* He squinted through the dust hanging in the air and walked to the counter.

"Can I help you?" A husky tenor emanated from behind the surgical mask. When the mask came off, John found himself face-to-face with Madonna hair and purple mascara. The mascara didn't do too much for her and the voice reminded John of Paladin on *Have Gun, Will Travel.* She was a big man, more than six feet tall. The top two buttons of her blouse were undone and the bulge of a faux breast pushed up under the black silk. She lit a brown cigarette and pushed smoke out of her aquiline nose.

"Yes," John said, and shook her hand. "I am looking for the building super. I think the name is Preston."

A man beside Paladin looked up from a game of solitaire. He was Latino with gentle eyes and a forehead that showcased tiny jagged mountain ranges of scar tissue. The dents in his skull had maybe healed, and they looked like the production of a ball-peen hammer.

"Priscilla Preston, honey, Priscilla on the Lake," Paladin continued. "I'm the one you seek. How may I help you?"

"I was told I could find Joey Johnson here, the electrical contractor. I want to speak with him about a job."

John leaned against the counter. Priscilla came out from behind it. Her muscular thighs were encased in skintight leopard pedal pushers. She extended a hand to John. "Pleased to meet you."

The sound of a jackhammer erupted and drowned out her voice.

"John Reimer."

"Come with me."

John followed in the acrid backwash of the super's scent, redolent of sweet perfume and tobacco. "We'll catch him before he goes on break," Priscilla said over his shoulder.

They walked down a hallway. Someone had draped a transparent plastic bag over a ficus tree that was shedding its leaves by the doorway. Someone still cared. The brown commercial carpet beneath John's feet showed stains and scars, burn marks, powdery footprints left by construction boots. There was a smell of burnt toast and something foul and meaty. John imagined old men behind the doors that lined the hall, hunched over crusty hot plates in their undershirts. SRO heaven.

The vibration of the jackhammer increased. Priscilla turned a corner. Bright light slashed out into the hallway from an open door, and the jackhammer stopped before they entered.

John had expected a redneck, but Annie hadn't prepared him for this, with her talk of Morgantown and the mountains and the rainbow bruise along her cheek.

The man turned a young, smooth face toward John, the kind of face found on surfer calendars. A portable boom box in the corner poured out the opening riff of "Street Fighting Man." Joey was hunched over a new fuse box laid across a couple of sawhorses. He twisted something with a pair of pliers and then straightened up to his full height, at least six-foot-four.

A sandy lock of hair fell across his forehead and John wondered if he were actually meeting an Eagle Scout troop leader.

"Yeah," he said simply. His eyes were flat. His partner kept busy, sweeping with a whisk broom a chipped-out trench in the floor twenty-five feet away.

"Here's somebody who wants to meet you," Priscilla said. "About a job."

Joey removed a pair of leather gloves but made no move to shake hands. "What kind of job?" He looked at John. "I'm booked through September. Give me your name and number and the secretary will call. We'll get you on the schedule."

Joey changed the subject and spoke to Priscilla. "Can you send friend at the desk out for some coffees? Large, light roast. Here." He handed Priscilla a five-dollar bill, and she sashayed down the hallway. John followed her and said, "Wait. One for me, too. Cream. Keep the change." She turned in her slippers and headed back toward the front desk.

Joey was working again on the fuse box. John said, "Sorry to bother you, it's kind of a unique job, maybe I need to explain it."

"Yeah, here." Joey reached underneath his nicked bomber jacket to his back pocket and brought out a black leather billfold at the end of a chain. "Somebody refer you to me? Have I met you somewhere?"

John read the card Joey handed to him. "Johnson Electrical Repairs. For All Your Electric Needs." Lightning bolts decorated the corners of the card. John wondered if their resemblance to an SS logo was intentional.

"Maybe you have seen me, Mr. Johnson. Let me explain my problem." John put his hands in his overcoat pockets. "I had an accident. Some bullets fired through my front window destroyed a light switch."

"That's it, a light switch?"

"Well, without light in my study I can't do my job. And I think there's also a short in the wiring inside the wall now."

"Turning on your lights could be hazardous to your health." Joey turned the pliers. "You could burn down your house."

"That's right," John said. "Everything could fry. I heard you're a good electrician and you have reasonable rates."

Joey looked at his assistant rolling up a loop of extension cord. "Turn off that compressor. Go ahead and load up. You can get started over on the Damen job."

John and Joey were left alone in the room. Bad light from between brick buildings filtered through frosted glass panes. Joey gave John his full attention now. "Yeah, I'm reasonably competent. And I'm pretty cheap. Now who would want to shoot at you?"

"I thought you could maybe give me some clues after you look at the wiring damage."

Joey picked up a pair of wire cutters and began to clip at a nasty-looking hangnail beside his thumb. "Oh, I'm good for clues, if the money is right. Tell me, is your electrical system totally out? Did you turn off the main box? These freaking knob-and-tube circuits can go poof just like that." He spread his fingers to illustrate.

"I turned off the circuit to the study. It's an inconvenience. Late nights, I do a lot of work in that study."

"Look," Joey said, "you don't have to bullshit me. I know all about you. You think Annie doesn't talk? Come over here. I want to tell you something."

Joey's voice was little for his frame, slightly squeaky. He clipped more skin beside his gnawed thumb and winced.

"Here. You need the proper tool." John held out a nail clipper across the sawhorse table.

"Thanks," Joey said. "You're a kind, sensitive man. I appreciate that." The squeak in his voice carried a hurt sound. He sauntered around the table until he stood beside John.

"You think I did him, don't you?"

"What?"

"You're not here about an electrical job. Don't fuck with me." Joey's thumb was bleeding thoroughly now. He took a hankie out of his back pocket and wrapped his hand. "I'm not an idiot. Annie's told you about her faggot lover boy and you think I have a motive." When he said the words "you think," he pressed his index finger into John's breastbone until it hurt.

John deliberated. "Mr. Johnson, I'd have to say this. Don't take this the wrong way, it's for your own protection. The way you hit your wife is going to make the police *think* you have a motive."

Joey removed his index finger from John's chest. "Annie can be a sweet little bitch, can't she. She told you that?"

"She told me nothing of the kind. She said she walked into a door. Next time you hit her, try for a light touch. You have big hands that leave marks."

Joey looked at his wrapped thumb. He put an arm around John's shoulders and gave the minister an affectionate squeeze. "Reverend, you and I need to have a serious talk."

"Take your hands off me and we'll talk," John said. "Calm yourself down."

"Okay," Joey said. "Talk. Or else."

John sat down on one of the sawhorses. "First thing," John said, "tell me if it was you who shot out my window last night. Second, I am curious what you know about David Talbot's death. I'm wondering if you're on the fringe. You look and talk like a redneck but do you quack like one? Is this just working-class affectation? Third, what can you tell me about something called 'faggot-bashing'?"

"Jesus Christ, reverend, Annie says you're a preacher, but you sure as hell don't talk like one. No, about your window, absolutely not. I don't even know where you fucking live. Why would I shoot out your window?"

"I don't know, maybe silence me the way you've silenced Annie? Maybe you think I know something about Talbot that could get you into trouble? Any number of possibilities." John wanted that cup of coffee now. He could feel his legs tremble. "But they haven't hauled you in because they don't know about you yet. I want to assure you of something, okay? For Annie's sake, I'm not talking about you with anyone.

"But how much did you hate David Talbot, Mr. Johnson? Enough to kill him? I just need some clarity in my own mind."

He thought Joey might hurt him with the wire cutters then, perhaps take off a pinkie, but Joey said with quiet menace: "Okay, that's enough. You don't want to insult me." He dropped the wire cutters on the table and adjusted the hankie wrapped around his thumb. A red patch was soaking through the cotton.

"Listen to me," John said. "I want to give you some reassurance. I have said nothing to the authorities about you or Annie. It's not for your sake, believe me—though I am compelled by my faith to feel compassion for you, at the moment I am finding that to be very, very hard. It's for Annie's sake. But in exchange for that confidence, you owe me just a little bit."

"I don't owe you jack shit, preacher."

"Calm down and hear me out. I can understand why you'd feel paranoid right now. I understand. I'm thinking out loud here, that's all, so don't get jumpy when you hear what I say. You hated Talbot because he was sleeping with your wife. Then he was killed. It's just a matter of time before the cops look you up as a suspect. They're going to run files on Annie and learn she's married. They've probably already figured that out. It's tough to keep marriage a secret, you know."

The misery showed in Joey's eyes. "So I get carried away a little bit sometimes, Annie isn't above slapping me around either, but I'm not a serial killer, all right? The cops talk to me, and I'll tell you this much: Annie and you both will have some accounting. You hear?"

"Mr. Johnson, try to make sense. Think about your own interests. I know you beat her up, and that makes me sad and Annie afraid, and both of you insist I keep quiet about it. I've seen strange things, but I tend to respect a couple's wishes. Professional confidentiality is the word. But the more you beat her up, the guiltier you will look. Do you see what I mean?"

"What are you, man? My goddamn therapist or legal counsel?"

"Do yourself a favor," John said. "Lay off a little. They're going to track you through legal records. Anyone connected to the victim once, twice removed. Now would you rather talk to a couple of tactical officers who kick you around a metal room for sixteen hours or would you rather talk with me? I'm a reasonable man. Annie asked me to look into this murder. She claims he wasn't gay, he wasn't cruising."

"Yeah, right."

"You must have considered him competition. So you must agree with her."

"Tell me more about Annie's theories. You've obviously done a lot of thinking about all of this."

"You still haven't answered my question. Did you do it, Joey?"

"You have a lot of balls."

"Did you do it?"

"No. I told Annie she was crazy to go out with this bisexual freak, okay? That if she wanted to risk her life with somebody who takes it up the ass, that was her problem."

"Did you know he was the alderman's son?"

"No. Not until the news story after his death. I was totally surprised."

"She doesn't think David was cruising the park. And she doesn't believe the newspapers or the cops' version of what happened, or the alderman's story either, for that matter."

"Yeah, that's my Annie all right." Joey walked toward John. "Finds it hard to believe anyone, but her head crawling with some fucking conspiracy theory all the goddamn time. You better watch out, mister—"

"Reimer. You can call me John."

"Watch out, she loves getting men to listen to this shit, okay? And in you she has found a great listener."

"That's part of my job," John said. "I listen."

"Just know after a while that she's jerking your chain. She gets you to go through interesting little motions on her account. You don't know her—or her family—like I do."

"I do know something about your personal family values, however, and I would suggest you stop beating her up. Talbot is dead. He's no threat to you anymore. Let it go."

"So who are you? A friend trying to help her out? Come on. If there's anything I hate more than a preacher, it's a Bible-toting lech. I know what Annie can do to a guy. You can tell me all about it. I will understand."

"Joey, you're not making sense. Let me explain to you one more time how I see this. You're mean and vicious, though probably not a murderer. If you are lying to me now, then you are very convincing. Maybe you don't know where I live. I can't read you. But if you know anything about this Talbot kid, or any of his connections, I'd like to know what you know."

"Annie and the pretty boy didn't talk to me, understand? There was no talking whatsoever. Zip. I was cut out. I didn't see her for a year. I got back in touch only when she phoned and told me he wanted to keep living in Wicker Park. He wasn't interested in moving in with her."

"What did she say about that?"

Joey folded his arms. "She said she was disappointed."

"Why did she call you?"

"Maybe I'm a big strong shoulder to cry on. I don't know. I was fucking confused. I asked her the same thing. I didn't think she wanted to talk with me anymore. I figured she was starting to understand the little fairy."

"She called you. It gave you hope."

Joey looked down. He scratched at something under his eye. "Yeah, that's right. She gave me hope." He looked straight at John. "You know, I'm not just an electrician, okay, not just some lug. Like, Annie and me, we met at a poetry slam."

A movement in the doorway interrupted them. The brown man with the dented skull delivered a paper bag with tall cups of coffee inside. He put the bag down carefully on the sawhorse table, took the coffees out, and obsequiously set out napkins, sugar packets, and stirrers.

"Thanks, Gino," Joey said. The man put all the change on the table and Joey handed him back a single.

"Third world," Joey said, after Gino left. "I think we should keep that term, don't you? They're just fabulous when it comes to errands."

John looked at Joey Johnson and tried to gauge the man's command of irony. "You design your business card yourself?" he asked.

"Yeah," Joey said. "Annie told me I should go to design school. She has an eye for that shit, told me I have talent. I like to think about architecture."

"Poetry and architecture," John said. "Then it all fell apart for you two."

John got Joey to talk about architecture and a half hour later the electrician agreed to come over and rewire John's study. John gave him his address.

"If you ever hit Annie again, the cops will know about it, do you understand?" John said. "Otherwise you have my word that I'll stay quiet."

Joey flashed a wide surfer-boy grin. "You're threatening me now, aren't you?"

"No. You've told me your limits. And I'm telling you mine."

John left with a strong urge to see the interior of Joey's apartment. That's what this kind of work does to you, he thought. It makes you want to see the inside of people's houses. He wondered if Annie might still have a key.

On his way out he asked Priscilla Preston whether Joey had been hired at the Lake Hotel on account of his strong references.

"Oh, he's the best," the Queen of the Lake said. She raised her eyebrows above the clotted lashes. "If you know what I mean."

The brown man behind the counter bowed his head over a newspaper. John gazed at the battleground of that shiny skull and buttoned up his coat to face the wind. He went outside and stood under the awning.

Poetry and architecture, he thought.

Chapter 23

MILDRED UNRUH VOLUNTEERED TWICE a week in the church office to keep
track of phone messages and organize John's life, which without her help
would slide into irreversible disarray. She occupied herself now at his desk,
regally ensconced in his padded chair. A letter opener like a stiletto lay
on the glass writing surface beside the day's mail, which she sorted into
three stacks: the junk, glossy magazines, supply catalogs bearing computer-
generated labels; letters directed to the church address; and, finally, mail
addressed specifically to John that she decided qualified as personal.

To the first two piles she applied the blade. She straightened up when
John entered. A paper clip jiggled between her lips, and she removed it to
say, "There's a fresh crumb cake in the kitchen, if you want some."

"Fresh?" John said. He walked away two steps and came back to poke
his head through the office door. He noticed she was making adjustments
between piles two and three. "Did you put enough brown sugar on this
time?"

"I am in no joking mood, this morning, pastor." She put the paper clip
back between her lips and continued grimly at her work.

John saw she would occupy his chair a while longer, and so with no
other recourse he sauntered through the darkened sanctuary up the middle
aisle toward the side door that led out to the church fellowship hall. He
paused in the doorway and fingered the sensitive flesh above his eye. It was
still tender, but he had removed the Band-Aid. No need for alarm.

He found the pan of cake. Mildred had already cut him a slice, a middle
piece, the kind he liked. He moseyed back toward the office, balancing the
cake on a napkin, and wolfed it all down before he returned.

The office was his again and he occupied the big chair while Mildred sat primly in the easy chair, crossing her legs. Her blue dress had little daisy patterns that jumped out and announced springtime.

"Did the window repair people come yet?" John asked.

"Yes, here and gone already." Mildred opened and closed her mouth, and began, "I went ahead and vacuumed your study afterward. There was still a lot of glass."

"Thank you. I need to get back to work today. I work better in my study."

"What about that light switch?" Mildred said. "I saw the tape over it. It's not safe, is it?"

"I arranged for a repair. They'll do it tomorrow. In the meantime, I'll use a lamp and an extension cord."

"I'm worried sick about you, pastor. How is your eye? Here, let me see." She came around the side of his desk and with authority took his head between her hands. "I need more light," she said. "Lean this way. Close that eye so I can see the lid." She pushed his head back and examined the laceration that ran into his eyebrow.

"So many people taking liberties with my head," John said.

"Not as bad as I thought," Mildred said, and returned to the easy chair. "I don't think you need stitches."

"Thank you. I heal fast."

"Yes, perhaps you do, but Mrs. Maasser does not, and her daughter called to ask if you can visit. She is in Columbus Hospital."

"Did they X-ray?"

"Yes, it's what they thought. Broken hip."

"That's bad. Any other calls?"

"Here, I wrote a list." She held a yellow legal pad covered in cursive. John reached for it, but Mildred pulled it back, pretending not to notice his reach. She read: "A call from Unger about the new member class. And a call from Miss Casper, you are to call back. One other person, who just called herself Helen." Mildred's eyes inspected John for clues. "She seemed very impatient."

"Did she say what about?"

"No. She said you would know."

"Anything else?"

John at times resented the way Mildred could drag out this ritual, but he tolerated it in return for certain useful information about his parishioners. Mildred was a reliable barometer. "Any word from the AA group? Did they get my letter?"

"What letter?"

"Council agreed they can use the social hall for their meetings. I sent them a letter of invitation. I also left a phone message."

She looked at the yellow pad. "Oh, yes," she smiled, "it's all written down here. Yes, they called, too." She gave up the pad to John. "Oh, there are two other things. I didn't have time to write them down."

John looked up from the mail.

"Nancy stopped by and asked where you were."

"I'll call her."

"She said not to call her at work."

"Okay. What else?"

Mildred gave him a strange look. "That young man Chris. You know, the one they call Crazy Chris? He came by. He banged on the door and was very anxious. He wanted to talk with you."

"Talk about what?"

"Here." Mildred handed John a sealed envelope. "He told me to give it only to you."

"He has schizophrenia, Mildred. He's unpredictable. Be careful with him when I'm not around. Were you here that Sunday he walked in during the service? When he doesn't stay on his medication there's no telling what he can do."

"He seems to be a sincere young man. And he always has a good Bible thought for the day."

"It must be his good Moody Bible Institute training. Mildred, how have you survived in Chicago this long?" John shook his head slowly and ripped the envelope open. He took out the note.

Dear Pastor Reimer,

Now I've done it. Yes, I've committed the unpardonable sin. I know we disagree on a lot, but where do you stand on this question. Or have you gone liberal on this one too? I hope not . . . Broad is the path that leads to destruction.

I need to know,

Chris (1 John 5:16)

Mildred watched John read. "He kept mentioning the unpardonable sin. I wasn't quite clear what he meant," Mildred said.

John smoothed the note on top of the desk. "Do you think there is one, Mildred?

"One what?"

"Unpardonable sin."

"Our minister in South Dakota used to think so."

"I heard sermons about it at least twice a year when I was growing up in Meade," John reflected. "We always felt terribly afraid. But disappointed, too, that the elders couldn't be more specific. Maybe that's what made it terrifying."

Mildred seemed uncomfortable with this particular theological turn. She asked John if he wanted another piece of crumb cake.

John shook his head. "What else did Chris say?"

"Not much. He brought his bike into the foyer and sat on it most of the time that we talked."

John stopped her. "A bicycle?"

"Yes, why?"

"I didn't know Chris had a bike. When I see him he's always walking."

Mildred took a Kleenex out of a mysterious place at the front of her dress and blew her nose. "He said he was getting lots of exercise and that you would like that. He said he has been riding on the lakefront between four and five o'clock. He was specific about that. It seemed odd."

"A bike," John repeated. "What kind of bike?"

"How would I know? I don't pay attention to such things. Why are you so interested in this? This is a young man worried about the unpardonable sin and you . . ."

John stood up and looked for Trophy's phone number in his address book. "Thanks, Mildred. I need to make some calls. Why don't you go home early?"

She knew when she was being dismissed, but she took the cue, lips pursed tragically, as if surveying the damage done by Cossack riders to a Mennonite wheat farm in the Ukraine. She sighed and stood up.

"You are a mystery to me sometimes, pastor." She watched him take the phone receiver off the hook and begin to punch numbers. He studiously ignored her.

"And by the way," she said, on her way out of the office, "that's not just my opinion of late."

"Really?" John said, the phone pressed to his ear. "Someone else thinks the same way?"

"Yes," Mildred said. "Nancy. She is very concerned."

"Please, Mildred," John said, as he heard the ringtone on the other end of the line. "Not now."

She left him finally to his thoughts. Trophy was not home. John debated what to do. He could call Annie. He could try to catch Trophy at Berlin again. Or he could go running at four o'clock and hope Chris rode by the rocks at Belmont Harbor.

He wanted a look at that bike. He tried to remember how Trophy had described it. As he dialed Annie, he found a Bible and flipped it to the passage in John's first epistle.

"If any man see his brother sin a sin which is not unto death, he shall ask, and he shall give him life for them that sin not unto death. There is a sin unto death; I do not say that he shall pray for it."

A bicycle. He felt a pain above his eye and looked in his desk drawer for two Tylenol. Crazy Chris on a bicycle. Something about that image hurt his head. He thought about calling Detective Kerdigan and then decided not to.

Chapter 24

JOHN CHANGED HIS SHIRT. While still knotting his tie, he called Nancy. He talked his way through a receptionist and personal secretary. When Nancy finally picked up the phone, her voice was steel.

"I had said don't call me at work . . . News on your investigation? I guess I shouldn't have made that slam about you getting hurt. How is your head?"

John imagined her unsmiling face, her shellacked red fingernails smoothing her hair behind her ears and then the clicking of her nails against a can of Diet Coke.

"This has become quite involved, Nancy. I think I need to talk with you about it."

"I expect you'll install bulletproof glass in your study. Please do."

"Okay, you can stop."

"And another thing. Investigators need to carry higher insurance premiums than clergy. I can look into that for you. You are definitely moving into a riskier line of work."

"Well, only in certain respects."

"The bodily harm part is what I refer to," Nancy said.

"Look, I think this was totally random."

"But you are not one hundred percent sure."

"Nancy, let's get coffee. I have to tell you in full what's happening."

"Why all of a sudden? First you push me out, now you want my undivided attention. Is there a big break in the case?"

"Actually, there just might be. I may know more by supper tonight."

"Terrific. Let's have Mildred prepare you a press kit."

"Nancy, stop it, please."

She didn't say anything. Then came her voice, which John realized he was hanging on to, waiting for it. "I'm worried sick about you. There are people who want to hurt you and you seem oblivious. The slug in your wall was intended for your head."

"What are you doing for dinner tonight? I'll tell you everything. I promise."

"Let me cook for you."

"Not now. You don't cook on week nights, remember? We can meet at Ann Sather's. I like their mashed potatoes, and I'll be at my usual table."

"In the back?"

"Yes. Seven o'clock."

He combed his hair and put on a pair of oxfords. He would drive over to Columbus Hospital to visit Mrs. Maasser, and afterward he would return and write for an hour or so before his run on the lakefront.

He was thinking about Nancy and the worry in her voice when he got to his car. All four tires had been slashed and the vehicle sat heavily on its rims. John stepped off the curb and walked around to the driver's side.

The swastika and neat block letters etched in soap covered the window above the door handle: faggotlover. Whoever it was, John decided, they wanted him off the case, and off the case right away.

He walked to his apartment and wearily climbed the stairs. Changing back into sweats, he set the alarm for 3:30. There were no phone calls he wanted to make now. He checked all his doors and double-bolted them. He turned off the answering machine, climbed under his covers, and went to sleep.

Chapter 25

SOMETHING LIKE RAIN BUT nastier slanted out of the sky. Without the wind, the driving needles would have been a pleasing mist. But this was no Oregon cove. The wind coming off the lake rebuked all the premature celebrants of spring.

Only hard-core runners persisted in these elements to prove themselves. A blonde woman and a boxer dog at the end of a chain leash came swiftly toward John. The woman fiddled with her Walkman volume at her waist and shook the chain to slow the dog's speed. The dog's young face was wet as a contented seal's. Canine and woman passed, trailing a double whiff of dog and Chanel.

John pulled the stocking cap around his ears, then retied the hood of his windbreaker around the cap. Five degrees lower and it would be unbearable. He put on a pair of ski gloves. He looked north and then south toward the Gold Coast, wondering what the chances were that Chris would be riding in this storm. The waves on the rocks covered the sidewalk with intermittent foaming sheets of water. John hoped the bicycle had good tires.

He set off at a slow jog south, running by the North Pond again. He had memorized the details of this path, every tree, the muddy slope toward the water, the chain-link fence, the façade of Columbus Hospital above the trees inland. He had often stood at the window of the eighth-floor cafeteria in the hospital during his visits to the sick and looked down on this very scene. *Mrs. Maasser is waiting for my visit*, he reminded himself.

He needed to do something about the car. Let Nancy know? She would call the cops herself. Perhaps he could spare her the trouble and go straight to Kerdigan on his own. The swastika reminded him of Joey's calling card with its lightning bolts in the corners. But then again, pinning the swastika on Joey seemed premature. How many slashed tires did the Chicago police investigate per week? How many swastikas?

He remembered Joey's remarks after Gino brought the coffee. A supremacist group wasn't out of the question. Joey could fit that nicely. The young man's use of wire cutters on his own ragged cuticle now came back to John as sign of a deeper unrest. At what point would Annie end up strangled or beaten? And at what point, John asked himself, would he begin to act?

Calling Kerdigan seemed imperative. He couldn't put it off any longer. He thought more about Joey and Annie, a deranged couple from southern Ohio who insisted he share in their dirty little secret and help keep it. They reminded him of something, and then he realized what it was. Picking up his pace a little now, his mind turned to books. They were Nancy and Bill Sikes in *Oliver Twist*, but unfortunately not very many people would understand the allusion if he tried to explain. Nobody read Dickens anymore. John thought of giving Annie the book, his worn Penguin paperback. He could circle the Nancy and Sikes chapters, assign the homework, then ask if it provided insight into her own condition. He would perhaps read to her that passage about Sikes's club lying in a pool of morning sunlight the morning after, sticky with drying blood and hair. How about that for pastoral counseling?

He knew the other Nancy—Nancy the attorney, Nancy his church moderator—had begun to question his judgment, and perhaps even his ability to reason. Maybe he was losing it. Nancy no doubt could see that. He ran harder. He thought about turning sixty. He had always thought that after Vi went into the nursing home he would have to stay young to compensate, to stave off mortality, as if there were some kind of scales of justice balancing out in God's infinite mercy. He knew he was a fool. Any Mennonite with a thimble full of historical memory knew better.

But now, to the immediate situation: his tires had just been slashed, threats against him, a sniper had fired two shots. And here he was running like some idiot in near-tempest conditions on the edge of Lake Michigan.

If someone chose to follow him now this would be a perfect place to terminate all further inquiries from the clergyman. Of course, they could carve up his chest, too. He wondered what Mildred would say to the tabloids.

He wiped water out of his eyes and kept going. He thought of all the people he hadn't spoken with yet about David Talbot. He had made a silly promise to a young and unbalanced, albeit very attractive, woman to keep the professionals out of it. Why? For all he knew, she was dealing drugs out of her apartment, a front for the man threatening to kill her. He tried to refocus, attempted to bring back to memory the face of the dead man in the Cook County morgue.

He wondered about speaking with the alderman himself. But what was he supposed to say? Maybe present him with Helen's hypothesis: "You're a man capable of killing your own son, did you know that? By the way, where were you the night of the murder?" John saw himself accompanied out of the man's office between large male security goons and receiving a libel suit via registered mail several days later.

He had become too involved with a dead man's lover and that was why he felt paralysis. It was basic. She had charmed him. The flesh is weak. Annie Casper had been mediating far too much of his reality, and that was why he had ignored the alderman father. He thought of the alderman on TV: the tears, the dignity, the indignation, and yet the manufactured sense of it all. But then all political stuff seemed manufactured to him, it always had, so he didn't know how to read it or he just didn't pay much attention. He wished he could bring the alderman's ex-wife back from the dead.

His cheeks felt numb in the cold. He looked for some sign of Chris.

Maybe Chris did it, he thought, *and wants to confess*. Chris of the unpardonable sin. Chris riding a bike, a special bike, a bike that was maybe witness to the crime.

Still, in spite of John's warnings to Mildred, it didn't seem likely that Chris would kill anybody. John couldn't see it. If Chris had done it, how would the tabloids report the deed? "He was a quiet and moody boy, sometimes given to spells of guilt and anguish over his own sins. He admitted to not following medical advice and experienced periodic fits of rage leading up to his encounter with the alderman's son by the North Pond."

No way. Dodging the waves washing up on the concrete walk, John lost his rhythm and his wind. He slowed to a fast walk. Ahead, the John Hancock Tower loomed, its top caught in a thick ruff of dark clouds. The rain had stopped; now it was simply cold, but the wind drove harder, with bitterness, to the bone.

John needed warmth and light. His thoughts turned to survival, to life, to sitting across from a beautiful attorney in the comfort of Ann Sather's. He visualized Nancy's hands and her face as he recounted his adventure to her.

Thinking about her eyes made him run harder, again.

Chapter 26

CHRIS WAS WAITING FOR John at Fullerton Beach.

At least that's how it appeared. Chris was kicking sand around in front of the boathouse, watching the sky. Approaching him, John looked for the bicycle.

Chris's lips were going blue from the cold. He wore black straight-legged dress pants with a rip in one knee and a stained green parka with the hood pulled back from his head. He had a green backpack. His high-top tennis shoes were caked in wet sand. From a distance, Chris could pass for merely eccentric, maybe an undergraduate environmental studies major who was jamming poetic thoughts by the lakefront.

Up close, he spoke in a high voice that sounded as if he hadn't properly negotiated puberty. "I tried to see you," he told John. His face looked scuffed, his nose raw. He didn't look at John when he spoke; his tendency was to look away when speaking with people.

"Where have you been, Chris?"

"I have been walking to and fro upon the earth, Pastor Reimer."

"Mildred said you stopped by. I read your note. Do you want to talk?" A squadron of five seagulls wheeled overhead and for a moment hovered motionlessly against the wind blowing inland. Two of them swooped down to the sand to fight over half a hot dog rolling out of its shredded wrapper.

"Let's get out of this cold," John went on. "Are you hungry?"

"No."

"Do you know what day it is today, Chris?"

"No."

"Can you tell me when you last took your meds?"

"Maybe. Two days ago, was it? I think."

"Let's go to a diner. Mildred said you had a bike. Where is it?"

"I don't have it any more. They took it from me. I got a nice lock for it but they broke it."

"When did they take it?"

"The gears weren't working anyway. They can have it. God will punish them all right, like he punished me."

"How did you get the bike, Chris?"

Chris started to sniffle. He pulled the hood over his head. His thatch of hair stuck forward underneath the edge of the hood and came to a point that dripped rain directly onto the tip of his nose.

"I said how did you get the bike, Chris?"

John walked swiftly. This forced Chris to keep up. "What are you afraid of, Chris?"

"The angel. They weren't as big as the angel though."

"What did the angel look like?"

"He's big and his head is on fire. He has a shiny tool, a sharp and shiny tool. He moves it fast. Yes, he is very, very fast."

"How big?" John stopped Chris and held his hand flat about six inches above Chris's head. "This tall?"

Chris pushed John's hand away. "I couldn't tell. His head was on fire."

"You saw the fire, Chris?"

"Yes. Shooting flames."

"What did he say?"

"He didn't speak. He just moved really quick. Too fast for this world, pastor."

"He took your bike?"

"No, he didn't take it." Chris's gaze went back over his shoulder toward the lake.

"You sound a little confused, Chris. I wish I could have seen that bike."

"Yeah, they took it. They took it away."

"What can you tell me, Chris?" John began to feel desperate.

Chris began his familiar litany. "I'm on the highway to hell, Pastor Reimer. Oh, you know that, don't you? It's too late for me, man, you can't save me. I know you want to try. But I can help warn others. I just want to help people, you know?"

The young man fumbled with the zipper of his backpack. "Man, I have a mailing list I wish you could help me with."

John spoke: "'There is a sin unto death; I do not say that you should pray for it.' You wrote me that note because you want to talk with me about something specific, Chris. Tell me what you saw, Chris, tell me exactly."

John steered them into the Lincoln Park Zoo. Chris needed a distraction from his own interior mental landscape. They stopped in front of the tigers. John began to speak.

"You saw this angel with a knife in his hand, is that it? Did you see him use it? What did he look like? Tell me about his face. Did you take a bicycle nearby? Somebody died by the pond very close by here, Chris, and you could do a lot of good if you tell me what you saw."

"They stole the bike from me because I stole it from him." Chris started to cry. "I deserved it."

The crying turned to sobs. "I deserve everything I get in the next life. Maybe if I didn't steal his bike, he wouldn't be dead."

Inside the cage a Bengal tiger got up from its nap and stretched. It opened its black lips in a gigantic yawn, then swung its head down to lick the bottom of its paw. Chris paid attention, distracted momentarily from his own personal psychotic vision.

"The angel used his shiny tool to kill him. Then he wrote something. He wrote very fast."

"He wrote on the boy's chest," John said. "How did he look when he wrote?"

But Chris quoted poetry now, removed again at least one dimension from the world John wished him to live in for just these few moments. "'What the hammer? What the chain, in what furnace was thy brain?'" Chris chanted.

"Under the fire around his head, Chris, what did he look like?"

Chris moved on now toward another cage, where a black jaguar lay on its side, back pressed against the bars. Its side rose and fell regularly with its breathing.

"Like that," he said simply, pointing to the big cat, and then looked directly at John for the first time this afternoon. "I was scared. He ran fast when he was finished."

"Did you look at the boy he killed?"

"No. I didn't want to get close."

"Did you hear the man and the boy say anything?"

"I was running, I found a bike. I tried to forget. I rode as fast as I could."

John took him to Peter's Diner and made him get his medication bottles out of the backpack. After reading the labels, John bought Chris a tuna salad sandwich and a cup of coffee. He put some of the pills in Chris's open palm and made him swallow them with a glass of ice water.

He listened to Chris talk about Paul's thorn in the flesh for fifteen minutes and then decided he had had enough. When he returned from paying the cashier at the front desk, Chris was waving his arms at an imaginary person sitting where John had been. John grabbed one of Chris's wrists and sat back down.

"How did you know it was the boy's bike you took?"

"I saw him riding before it happened."

"Which direction was he riding. From the north, or from downtown?" John took Chris's wrist again and repeated his question.

Chris's eyes glazed. "For he should ride from the north. I think the north."

"Is there anything else you can tell me?"

"Goodbye, Pastor." Chris pronounced the words with a decidedly new expression. The yellow plaque on his incisors shone in the light. "You do not pay enough attention to the word of God, do you hear me? You read books about the Bible but you do not read the Bible itself. The road is wide to destruction, pastor. Nobody is safe, not even you. Do you understand? There is a sin unto death; I do not say I will pray for it. Nobody is safe!"

Chris knocked over his glass of water. "Now let me go."

People at the surrounding tables looked at them. John noticed he had Chris's wrist in his grip. He also knew the hair on the back of his neck was standing up.

The young man named Chris rushed out of the diner uttering a string of expletives. John sat frozen in the booth. The waitress came by and asked him if he was okay. "I'm fine, thanks," John said. She mopped up the mess on the table.

John's hand was trembling as he swilled the last of his coffee and made his own ungraceful exit.

Chapter 27

BECAUSE HE WAS IN the vicinity, and because he needed to settle his nerves, John stopped by Columbus Hospital to say hello to Mrs. Maasser. The nurse at the visitors' desk winked and said, "A little informal today, aren't we, Reverend?" He requested Mrs. Maasser's room number, signed in, and then walked the corridor toward his destination. He greeted doctors and staff as they passed. People knew him here.

She lay in the bed with the covers tucked tight under her arms. A portable cassette player on the bedstand played schmaltzy piano music. John recognized it: Rudy Atwood. His older sister in Kansas liked this music, too, and he had once thought of telling her it suggested an interesting fusion of Liberace and the Blackwood Brothers instrumental section, except that she wouldn't have had the foggiest notion what he was talking about. He imagined her asking, "Liber*who*?"

Mrs. Maasser turned rheumy eyes in his direction. She took his hand in both of hers. "We are safe, thank you, Jesus, in the *heilige Hande*." As she talked, the German language steadily overtook the English. John's own German was rusty, but he tried out some Plattdeutsch anyway. A nurse poked her head into the room. John asked, "Is she getting enough pain medication? German is her language of anxiety."

"Reverend Reimer, I expect she is as high as a kite." The nurse flashed John a huge conspiratorial smile. "But she will mend. Feisty, this girl. Almost nothing, just a hairline fracture. She'll be up and about with a walker very soon."

"How can a hip fracture be nothing?" John asked.

The hoarse voice from the bed spoke. "It is nothing. Now go, pastor. This room is starting to smell. You need to take a bath, I think. Go."

The nurse grinned. "You heard the lady."

John considered his outfit, self-conscious. "You see, I was out for a run . . ."

"Yes, yes," Mrs. Maasser said, as she strained her neck against the pillow. "You run and you must always talk about it. Too much maybe about the running, and not enough about your walk with the Lord. Now you are a sweet man, I know, in the *heilige Hande,* and I am glad for your visit. A dear man. Come here and give me a kiss."

John took his dismissal in stride. He touched his lips to the withered cheek and Mrs. Maasser settled back with her eyes closed and began to snore. After gently turning down the volume of the music, he tiptoed out.

He went home and showered, then turned on the TV. A segment of the alderman's news conference was replayed. The story segued to a press conference at City Hall with the police chief, who seemed less comfortable in the glare of the lights. "We are following every lead," he intoned like a mantra.

"Is it true the department is internally divided on whether to treat these as hate crimes?" a reporter asked.

"There are too many rumors for me to respond to here. We are calling these events hate crimes for lack of a better term at the moment. What is important is that we find the perpetrator or the people doing these things. Now if you will excuse me, ladies and gentlemen, I have work to do." More garbled questions and shouting, and the chief waved off the press. "That is all I'm at liberty to say."

John dried out the inside of his ear with a corner of the towel. He pointed the remote at the set and switched it off. He phoned Joey Johnson's answering service and canceled the repair. He decided to have Mildred find someone else to do it.

He played back his messages. Annie Casper and Helen. Both wanted to be talked to, did not want to be forgotten. John noticed that neither sounded as if she were in tears, so he decided to let them wait. They couldn't solve his problems now, and it was time to consult with people who could.

After he got dressed, he felt better about himself, though the image of Chris's twisted face still bothered him. He knotted his tie and put on a black sweater under the tweed jacket and trench coat. He wanted to be presentable when fielding Nancy's questions. Anything to give him an edge during her cross-examination.

He went to his study and absentmindedly flicked the ruined light switch. In the gloom, he found his briefcase. He turned it upside down over his desk, emptying it of loose papers and several shards of glass. He got the

Dustbuster from the kitchen utility closet and came back to vacuum the interior of the briefcase. Then he packed a couple of books, a volume of Frazer and also Moltmann's *Crucified God*, several magazines from his unread pile, and a manila folder with some articles on Girard. He threw in a lined yellow legal pad. He decided to walk over to Ann Sather's early because the storm had subsided and the booths there afforded comfortable reading space.

Outside on the landing he furled his compact umbrella and tucked it into the briefcase's side pocket, just in case.

He walked past his car again to make sure the tires were still slashed—to make sure he hadn't hallucinated.

The car horn sounded immediately behind him, almost upon him. He hurled himself out of its way and landed, half-crouching, against another parked car on Racine.

Nancy leaned over and spoke through the open passenger window of her black Chevy Blazer. "Get in, if you want to live."

She gave him one of her incandescent smiles, looked at John in his defensive crouch and seemed to enjoy the moment of his terror.

Once he was situated in the front seat, she pulled away, rolling up her window. He waited for an explanation. She drove several blocks and then glanced over at him. "I'd say you're pretty tense. I have a surprise for you." Her black hair was pulled back with a rubber band and showed her high, smooth forehead to good effect above her sculpted eyebrows. She wore a Levi's jean jacket over a tight white button-down blouse.

John gripped his briefcase. His heart was still pounding. "I'm in no condition for this, whatever it is. You don't know what I've been through today."

"Oh, but I think I have an idea." She slowed to a partial stop at the stop sign, turned the corner, and put the vehicle smoothly into second, her fist closing competently over the knob of the stick. "I thought you were developing a taste, a liking even, for this crime thing."

"Yes, you nearly just ran me over and ended a budding career."

"Matters of church polity may be getting too bland for you." She turned to drill him with a quick glance. Her fist on the knob of the stick shift tightened. A couple of rings twinkled. "We're going to my place. I believe you are a man who needs some anonymity at the moment."

"What are you doing? A kidnapping seems extreme."

"No, I don't think so."

"What do you mean, you don't think so?"

"I received a call from your detective friend, what's his name, Bill? I will call him Wild Bill from Area 3. You didn't tell me what happened to your car. How come?"

"Bill Kerdigan called you?"

"Yeah, Kerdigan, that's his name. Is this a buddy thing?"

"I didn't tell Kerdigan about the car." John tossed his briefcase to the back seat. "How did he find out?"

"Ever hear of license plates? Did you know you were illegally parked? The parking violations people found the markings of sufficient interest to report it up the chain to violent crimes. One thing led to another. Kerdigan was suddenly hot on your trail."

"Okay, yes, somebody slashed my tires."

"The writing on the windows is what intrigued them, I think," Nancy said. She gave John another look that could draw blood. "Kerdigan says you're in danger, and he wants you to stay away from your apartment for a few days. He ordered it."

"You're not serious."

"I may jerk you around a little, but I don't lie. We're taking care of you now. Relax, enjoy yourself, and stop being a damned Boy Scout. I've had enough. The shooting, the slashed tires—what next? Are there any threatening phone calls you've deleted? You know, more stuff you should be telling me?"

"No." John wondered if his conversation with Joey Johnson at the Lake Hotel would qualify as threatening.

"Now we're going to my apartment for dinner and then we will decide what to do, or better, what not to do. Kerdigan wants you to call him."

"Do you have any other orders?"

"No. Now try to show some enthusiasm for my cooking."

"I thought maybe Mildred sent home the chow mein with you after the potluck."

Nancy gave his arm a light slap with the back of her hand. "You're a bad man, John Reimer." Then she smiled again. Her warmth scared John just a little bit on this late afternoon. "It's a surprise." She turned up the volume on the music. The complex layers of dubbed and redubbed horns on Miles Davis's "So What?" knifed easily through the padded leather interior of the vehicle. Nancy rumbled smoothly through the heavy traffic, seeking the open lane and finding it. John admired her driving. But he wasn't so sure about being taken care of. This was not what he had in mind.

After a while Nancy said, "John, I think you have an authority problem."

"That makes two of us, doesn't it?" John said. He flipped the sun shield down in front of him and inspected his eye in the little mirror on its back.

Nancy told him she thought he was healing beautifully, but he didn't say thank you. He could tell she was more interested now in negotiating traffic, imposing her will at the wheel of the car, the immediate task of bringing him home. He looked again at the mysterious smile on her face and found himself curious about the destination.

Chapter 28

TEN STORIES UP IN her loft, he occupied an airplane chair by one of her floor-to-ceiling windows that looked down on the tar roofs of the South Loop. In her kitchen she uncorked a bottle of Chardonnay and poured herself a glass. She asked John if he wanted one. He didn't.

John remembered when the area had been a dismal void of abandoned buildings. The change had come suddenly. Now he wondered how bagel shops and bookstores and a new Kinko's could have signaled the renaissance of an entire neighborhood. Of course, all these empty warehouses had cried out for loft makeovers. There had even been a red brick Victorian train station full of interior oak waiting to be stripped down to its original splendor, ripe for rediscovery.

He gripped the flared armrests of the chair and looked at Nancy's ceiling. Eighteen feet above, it was printed metal, painted forest green and held warm globes of frosted light at fifteen-foot intervals. The space was big enough to hold a double-decker bus. He pulled an ottoman under his feet. He noticed that Nancy's wool rug was a Bokhara. Making partner had been good to Nancy.

"Do you have any coffee?" he asked. He heard her move around by the front entrance, hanging up his coat. He felt restless and got up to inspect an Amish quilt hanging beside one of her oak barrister bookcases. Upon closer inspection he realized it was no quilt at all. Carefully arranged industrial warning labels in orange and yellow, almost fluorescently bright triangles and squares, were arranged in the geometric rectitude of a familiar Lancaster County pattern. The labels bore unmistakable text, alternating two perfectly distinct phrases: *toxic* and *keep back.*

"I love that piece," Nancy said. She reached up to take the rubber band off her ponytail and let her hair hang free. "The artist told me they refused to auction it at the MCC sale in Goshen. I got it so cheap I felt bad, but I think she is going to go very far. She lives in Baltimore now. Her dad worked in the shipping department at GE."

"I take it this is a critique of the quilt ethic?" John said.

"God help us," Nancy said. "Our people's quilt fetish could use some criticism."

John looked at Nancy's wine glass. "Do you have any coffee?"

"That's part of your problem, one of the reasons you're so jumpy and tense. Too much coffee. Drink the wine, just a glass, it will relax you. I promise espresso after dinner." She returned to the kitchen, poured him a glass of wine, and brought it back. "Here, come toast my new kitchen. Your cabinets inspired me." He took the glass.

She sat him down at a barstool next to a zinc counter that looked as if it were taken out of an old hotel. He watched Nancy on the other side of a cooking island put on a red apron and beam at him over the top of her six-burner Viking stove. John admired the cabinets and the butcher-block countertop that segued to a marble surface.

"Why the marble?" John asked.

"That's for pastry. Marble is good for pastry because it stays cold."

"Oh."

"This feels like a date," John said. "I haven't been on one of those in a while."

She pretended a demure innocence, then batted her eyelashes at him. "I know."

"You know this feels like a date, or I haven't been on a date in a while?"

"Both."

She measured a couple of tablespoons of olive oil into a saucepan and quickly minced a clove of garlic into the mixture. She threw in bay leaves and let it cook. After a while she added white basmati rice and then water. She stirred. She diced vegetables on the butcher block. She rinsed shrimp in a colander, cubed some ham. He drank some wine and went to the fridge.

"Pour me some more, too."

He said he liked her kitchen.

She looked up once and blushed. "No Martha Stewart jokes, okay?"

"I'm just admiring the food," he said.

She quartered an onion, sliced a shallot. She threw these ingredients and some other vegetables into a hot wok where they sizzled in oil. She sliced in a cup of okra, which made sticky tendrils when it cooked. The wine slipped cold and smooth down John's throat and he felt hunger. Nancy replenished his glass. He didn't fight her. He struggled to remember why he was here.

"I want you to start at the beginning," Nancy said. She spooned rice and the sautéed ham into a casserole dish. She opened a can of Ro-Tel tomatoes. John noticed that her lilting Southern accent, usually suppressed, became more prominent under the influence of the wine.

"How about I call Kerdigan, let the professionals handle it, and let it go as you have been asking me to. Then we can eat and discuss the impending split on church council."

"I *am* a professional, John." She measured a couple of teaspoons of deep red powder into the vegetables. "We'll get around to the church council. What I want to know about now is the alderman's son. The recent victim of this homophobic killer stalking our fair city. How did you get mixed up in all this?" John watched her powerful wrists as she ground black pepper over the wok.

"I thought I told you."

"You only started to. Something about a waitress at the Montrose."

"Yes. She told me she was David Talbot's lover, that he wasn't gay, and that she didn't trust the media. She was very upset. Plus, I discovered shortly after that she has her own problems with an estranged husband. He periodically beats her up. One thing led to another. She wanted me to ask a few questions."

"Go on. You think the husband killed Talbot?"

"I asked a few questions. Here and there."

"You had no business getting involved this way. You should have reported it immediately to the police."

"I thought of it as a counseling situation. And she entreated me to confidentiality. I'm breaking it now by talking with you. And the cops did speak with her," John continued. "Whether about her husband or not, I don't know."

Nancy tried pouring John some more wine, but he put his hand over his glass. "Look, you know as well as I do that domestic cases are dicey. She was afraid for her own life if the cops talked to her husband. I didn't see how breaking the confidentiality would necessarily benefit her."

"You could also be criminally accountable, you know, for not reporting a case of spouse abuse." Nancy hefted the wok by the handle and with a spatula spooned its contents into the casserole dish with the shrimp and rice.

"I know that," John said. "I also heard her tell me this guy would come over and kill her if the cops ever called him in for an interview. Then after I met him, I decided that was a distinct possibility. In fact, he might come after me, too."

"A little intimidation, a little extortion. John, maybe your courage doesn't go as far as I thought."

"I didn't see how a restraining order would necessarily prevent him from shooting either Annie or me."

"What's this guy's name?"

"I don't know if I should say."

"These are special circumstances, John." She adjusted the temperature of the oven and pushed the casserole dish in. She began shredding leaves for a salad from some kind of greens John had not seen before. "And someone wants you out of the way. I'll bet you've never been hunted like this. What's the guy's name? Sounds to me like he would be capable of killing Talbot if he knew he was bedding his wife."

"That's a rough way to talk for a Mennonite church moderator."

"I'm not your average Mennonite church moderator."

"I see that."

"What's his name, John?"

"Joey. Joey Johnson. He's an electrician. But I don't think he did it."

"Why not?"

"I just don't think he did."

"White male in his thirties."

"Well, yes."

"Fits a serial profile. Or what do they call the variant now . . . spree killer?"

"Oh, come on, he's a hardworking electrician with a lot of resentment, some of it justified. Another interesting side of him: he told me he met his wife at a poetry slam."

"Oh, yeah, right."

John continued. "Besides, if it were a revenge killing, I don't think he would have carved the word *fag* into his chest."

"How do you know that?"

"Like I said, I've asked a few questions."

"But he might do it as camouflage. You know, a copycat, make it look like a genuine faggot bashing."

"Interesting, but he didn't strike me as that smart."

"John, you appall me. Here you meet this man, he beats up the girl, what's her name . . . ?"

"Annie."

"Beats up Annie, and you defend the bastard as if he's some kind of choirboy. Like he couldn't possibly be a suspect."

"But you know what interests me the most about all this?" John said. "Pardon me for changing the subject. I keep losing sight of Talbot. He gets lost in all these other questions."

"Here, set the table, you big, strong man." Nancy directed John to the plates and glasses and silverware. She continued: "Correct me if I'm wrong. The question that bothers Annie the most, next to Talbot being dead of course, is why the media insists he was gay."

"Everyone presumes he was. He was found by the North Pond, a cruising area. He was a little bit of a pretty boy, judging by his pictures. It was hard to tell, looking at him at the morgue. Then there's this other complication. He was rooming with a gay fellow over in Wicker Park, a bartender who works at Berlin, on Belmont. Annie and this guy, named Trophy, hate each other's guts. It all adds up. There is no reason to believe David Talbot wasn't gay or bisexual."

"But the cops interrogated Annie. Didn't they believe he was her lover?"

"I think they concluded that she was mixed up about him. Easier to write it all off as youthful confusion. They called her a fag hag, she said. It made her livid."

"That is such an ugly term. But maybe she is."

"But what if she is right and the cops are wrong?"

"Wrong about what?"

"Wrong about representing the murder as part of a series. Maybe that's just untrue. Maybe something else happened that can't be explained," John said. "I don't know."

"You notice you've said very little about the alderman," Nancy said.

"What else is there to say? You and I have both heard what he had to say. Excuse me, but wasn't I supposed to call Kerdigan?"

"Why don't we eat first. Then you can call."

"I thought you were in a hurry to turn this over to the police."

"I was. But I like listening to you like this." Some bangles on her wrist moved as she checked the oven. When she straightened up, she unconsciously moved her hands down to smooth the blouse around her waist. John watched the motion of her hands on her hips.

"Thank you."

"Egos, all of you. Men. Have you talked with the alderman directly about his son? Did you know he has surged in the polls since his press conference? It's good timing if you ask me, so close to the election."

"Now you sound like the conspiracy nut. One can understand the sympathy factor."

"Then why did I feel so little sympathy, and mainly disgust?"

"Come on, the man was crying," John said.

"Never trust a man's tears, especially when he stands on a podium in front of microphones in the 44th Ward."

"You're cold, Nancy. Cold as your marble countertop. The man's son was murdered."

"You're innocent. The man didn't know his son. You don't cry for a son you've never talked to."

"You know nothing about fathers and sons, Nancy. That's precisely a reason for crying."

He looked out the window and realized he had cut Nancy off. Her face flushed.

"I'm sorry," he said. "Explain to me what you're trying to say about the alderman." Helen's words about the family came back to him. Recalling the miscellaneous, absent quality of David's personal possessions stashed in those liquor boxes, John went to the sink and filled his empty wine glass with water. He drank it quickly.

"I know there's a lot about fathers and sons I can't understand," Nancy continued, gently. "I'm an only child, and my father loved me unconditionally. But hear me out. I'm saying it bothers me that the alderman could turn the death of his son into a campaign rally. Not that he planned it that way."

"I think he wanted to make the announcement before the papers did it for him," John said.

"You keep defending unsavory men, John. Didn't the alderman's talk of such total estrangement tell you anything? Didn't you think it was bizarre?"

"It does. Very much. And I was surprised when the body was whisked out of Kerdigan's for the funeral at Our Lady of Mount Carmel. It seemed abrupt to me. But if it was a case of father reconciling with son, better late than never at all."

"But that is what bugs me. The timing was so convenient."

"Look, Talbot's parents separated when he was an infant. His mother died a few years ago, but her aunt, this woman Helen, told me a long, tortured story about money and abandonment. Seems she is operating out of a lot of guilt for not helping Talbot's mother more after her separation from Fitzsimmons—who, at the time, was a callow law student."

"So you're saying originally Fitzsimmons deserted them."

"I didn't say deserted. That's how Helen made it sound. In fact, the mother moved out on Fitzsimmons. People do separate and divorce. It is never simple. There are many versions of the same story. A little like the synoptic Gospels. Personally, I believe Helen has demonized the alderman on account of her own guilt. He didn't take good care of his family, but when she could have stepped in and helped, she didn't either."

"Really?"

"Yes. That came out when we talked. She's nursing her own bad conscience. She lives in decaying splendor on Orchard Street in Lincoln Park. A grand house. A daffy old woman. By the way, she hates lawyers, even more than most people. She came along with me to the funeral. You'd love to meet her."

Nancy ignored the last remark. "Why do you think Fitzsimmons left his wife?"

"I don't know. Helen said he wanted access to the family fortune. But it is more complicated than that. Tell me, though, it's interesting to speculate on the alderman's past, but what exactly does it have to do with his son's murder now?"

"I don't know that it does. It probably doesn't. It's the way he's worked the boy into his political campaign gives me the creeps. Just a feeling I have. What I want to know is why he left his wife and son."

"Well, when he makes a bid for mayor, I'm sure someone will do a deep background check," John said.

They sat at one end of an antique jury table by the main loft window. Nancy put seven black candles in an iron stand and lit them. She opened a second bottle of wine. The jambalaya smoked on John's plate. He kept talking, voluble now, forgetting that somebody in Chicago wanted him out of the way.

He was surprised by the way Nancy took his hand and asked him to say grace. Her hand made him momentarily lose his words.

"And keep us from harm," she added after he said amen. He had always known that in spite of her jaded exterior, deep down she had a pious streak. Who knew that she could cook like this? It made his eyes water, but he bravely partook. She apologized that the food tasted a little "bland."

He smiled to himself. She was a rough kind of Mennonite girl, he thought, but put the Mennonite women in the kitchen, and the similarities grow. She would never forgive him if he articulated that thought, so he smiled again and decided to have seconds.

Chapter 29

NEARLY ALL THE LIGHT had bled from the sky when John stopped eating. He said, "I'd better call Kerdigan." In the distance the Amoco Building shimmered, fading from ivory to yellow to salmon, then that, too, transformed as the grid of lights in its rectangular bulk began to flicker on.

"Kerdigan can wait," Nancy said. "Can I hear it from you first, exactly what you plan to say? All I need in my life is another four days of wondering where you are. That you're locked in somebody's trunk in Gary or something. Can you finish talking to me?"

"You run me on too short a leash." John waited for her pained expression, got it, and raised his eyebrows for emphasis as he continued. "You want honesty, I'll give it to you. I mean that."

"John, don't be a fool. Kerdigan meant what he said. You're in danger. Please tell me who you talked to. You don't think I cooked all this for nothing, did you?"

"You want me to name everyone I've spoken to in the last four days?"

"Yes." She tended to the espresso machine and returned with a yellow pad and a pen. "Remember that I am a highly paid professional. Now please begin."

"Okay. Annie first. Well, no, not exactly first. Her friend Alex at the Melrose, one of the older waitresses, said Annie needed someone to listen to her story.

"I spoke with Talbot's roommate, this young man, Trophy, Trophy Gallante. A bartender at the Berlin club. He lives in Bucktown. I have talked with Joey Johnson, Annie's estranged ex-husband . . ."

"Estranged, that's pretty understated, isn't it?" Nancy continued, "Am I correct about him being redneck? You know, bigot, homophobe, the works?"

John saw Nancy's pen writing the words on her yellow pad next to Joey's name.

"Whatever," John said. "Yes, all of the above. Maybe not a skinhead. I spoke also with Talbot's great-aunt Helen, actually met her at Cook County morgue on Saturday and visited her again. I have spoken with Louis Kerdigan, the undertaker on Lincoln Avenue."

"Did you speak personally with the coroner?"

"No."

Nancy put a check mark by the word *coroner*. She continued, "And you spoke with Kerdigan's brother, the detective, right?"

"Yes, with Bill. They both grew up in Lakeview. Old-timers. What are you planning to do with your notes?" John waved at her pad. She left the table to bring the coffee and a bowl of unrefined brown sugar cubes. The smell of the strong espresso filled the room.

"I just need to know who to talk to if anything happens to you, okay?" She smiled and came around to his side of the table to pour his coffee. He could smell her perfume and a faint trace of sweat. It felt like the most intimate act of the evening.

He tried to recover his train of thought.

"I talked with an attendant at the morgue, by the name of Julius. I talked with three other detectives besides Kerdigan from Area 3. Another detective, name of Shanahan, and two forensics specialists, Hispanic guys by the names of, let me see, Cortez, I think the other one was Vic, maybe Vito—that's it, Vito. They came over the night my study window was shot out. Then this afternoon I talked with Chris. Crazy Chris."

"The schizophrenic?"

"Yes."

"What about Mildred?"

"I haven't told her a whole lot. Of course she screens all my phone messages in the office so who knows what story she has cooked up by now."

"You keep us in the dark, so we have to form some theories," Nancy said. "Where does Crazy Chris fit in all this?"

John hesitated. "Well, that's really what I have to call Kerdigan about. Chris could have been an eyewitness."

Nancy stopped writing in her pad. "Eyewitness to the murder? And you're jawing away with me here and haven't called Kerdigan? What's wrong with you, get on the phone!"

John sipped more of the espresso, faking calm. "Chris takes about fourteen kinds of medications, Nancy. When he stops the meds, which frequently happens, his visions multiply. I don't think we will find out anything from him. He's obsessed with someone's head being on fire."

"You mean like red hair?"

"No. You don't understand. When Chris sees a man's head on fire, he sees the fire. Literally."

"John, just make the call now, please."

"Have you heard enough? You sure?"

"Go to the phone."

John paused as he picked up the phone. He said, not sure if Nancy was within earshot, "Maybe when you kidnapped me, you threw off my timing."

Bill Kerdigan added his reprimand to Nancy's. John held the receiver with weary patience and listened.

"You must by all means stay away from your apartment, do you hear me? Whoever wants you out has upped the ante. I would hate to find you with your telephone cord wrapped around your neck. They did bad things to your car. You still there? John?"

"Yes. How did you contact Nancy?"

"Church secretary. She was very cooperative. Nancy said you could stay at her place. That is wise, I think. Do it."

"A lot of people are suddenly making decisions for me," John said.

"I don't want to hear your resentment," Kerdigan said. John heard the cigarette lighter click. "We towed your car. We need to look at it some more. Don't worry, you'll get it back."

"Where did you tow it?"

"Look, just thank the God you pray to that you didn't get in."

John's stomach did a half turn and a shimmy. The okra wasn't sitting well. "So—you mean—why would they warn me away with graffiti and slashed tires if . . . ?"

"It's illogical, you're right. Whoever is after you may be breaking down. But if you'd gotten into the car, you would have blown yourself all the way to Navy Pier. This guy is going to show himself sooner or later."

"You presume it's a man."

"This is not a lady's style. Trust me. Look, if you need a couple of things at your apartment, make a quick run, pack a suitcase. Call for your messages. I'm even afraid you're being tapped, though. And one more thing, the most important thing. Let's hear what you know. I've been quite patient to this point."

"I wanted to call earlier, Bill, but a determined woman at this end who controls my salary insisted I speak with her first. Do you understand?"

"I understand. Keep the stuff about the car under your hat. Nobody knows that. I have about five minutes here before I have to run. Now talk to me."

"I ran into one of my marginal counseling cases, guy by the name of Chris, this morning at Montrose Beach. He might be an eyewitness."

"To Talbot's murder?"

"That's what I think. But I'm not sure. He has a severe case of schizophrenia. He takes a lot of drugs, has more visions than Emanuel Swedenborg."

"This happened this morning, and you get around to telling me now?" Bill's voice rose.

John resumed. "He is highly suggestible. He claims to have taken a bicycle, he kept talking about a bicycle."

"Wait a minute, what does a bike have to do with any of this?"

"Talbot had a couple of bikes, and the one he was riding the night of his murder disappeared."

"It did?"

"Yes. You didn't know that? I thought you people were thorough."

"Dammit, John, we're going to have a nice, long talk, you understand?"

"Calm down. Listen. It gets more complicated. Chris says he took a bike in the park, I think after he saw the murder. Mind you, I'm speculating here. I filled in quite a few blanks for Chris. Then, he says somebody stole the bike from him later on. So I never saw the bike, you understand? I'd like to confirm it was Talbot's, but I can't. My church secretary saw it, but she didn't have any reason to think it mattered.

"She can't even describe the bike. Chris was probably hypnotizing her with his talk of the apocalypse. He told me someone's head was on fire. He mentioned a shiny tool and pointed at the tigers in Lincoln Park Zoo. This is not much to go on."

"We have gone on much less," Kerdigan said. "You let us determine what's useful. Now where can I find Chris?"

John admitted he had no address but described Chris's appearance.

"If he's not in Lakeview, where do we look?"

"There's a corner diner in Uptown. He's sometimes there," John said. "That's about all I can do."

"Can you be a little more goddamn specific?"

"I'm trying to remember. Couple of blocks east of Truman College. You don't need to swear at me."

"Name of the place?"

"Inside it has both a bar and a lunch counter in the same room. If anybody would know where Chris lives now, someone there might."

John listened to the detective talk a little longer. Then he said, "I'm tired, Bill. I'll see you tomorrow." He hung up and looked at Nancy. "I'm through for this evening. Please don't ask any more questions."

She didn't. Instead, she led him to a leather sofa and handed him the remote. She swung the wooden doors open on a cabinet holding a TV. "Here, veg for a while. It will do you good."

CNN put him effectively to sleep.

Nancy loaded the dishes in the washer and came out from behind the lacquered Japanese screen to watch the man on her sofa. He was a loud snorer. He snored with conviction.

She sat at the end of the sofa and undid the laces on his oxfords. She held his ankles and pulled the shoes off his feet. The remote lay on his chest, loose in his thick paw. She carefully straightened his fingers to remove it and switched off the TV.

She returned from her bedroom with a blanket. He stirred when she covered him up. She stood with her arms crossed and deliberated. Then she switched off all the lights in the loft except for the glowing lamp on an escritoire by the window. She looked down the list of names on her yellow pad and considered the lake from one of her big windows. The bow light on a lake cruiser winked in the distance. Patiently she appraised it, until certain it was out of range of her naked human eyes.

Chapter 30

A PRICKLING CLAMMINESS, THE throb in the neck brought on by an unfamiliar pillow. The flood of light in Nancy's loft came like a red swirl through his closed eyelids. He squinted. His left leg was doubled up against a sofa's leather back. He remembered where he was, though he didn't recall taking off his shoes. There had been some wine, to which he was unaccustomed. His head felt clogged.

A clock ticked somewhere in Nancy's kitchen. He heard the crash of metal doors and whine of a cargo elevator further away in the building. He consulted his watch. Seven-thirty. He'd put on his coat and shoes and quietly slip out before Nancy awoke. He needed to get back to Lakeview.

He had no car. Pieces of yesterday came back now like flotsam. He would take the L. He found his way to the bathroom and urinated. He washed his hands and took a look at himself. The tangled growth on his head, still a little bit of salt and pepper but mostly salt, resembled the vertical thrust of Van Gogh's cypresses. One of Nancy's brushes lay beside the sink and he picked it up. He looked at the black lustrous hairs caught in its bristles. He picked up the brush and caught her good, clean scent that traced strong lines in his head. He rammed the brush through his hair, attempting to create some order.

Only on his way out, while congratulating himself on how quiet he could be, did he find her note:

> John,
> I'm off to the office for an early meeting and I didn't want to disturb your slumber. There's cereal in the cabinet by the sink, bagels and OJ in the fridge. The thermos of coffee is fresh.

I think it best you call Kerdigan and get advice on what to do today. I thought of waking you up to go running but you looked like a man enjoying his sleep.

You were fun to watch.

Three miles tomorrow morning, maybe? Can you handle it?

Love, Nancy

P.S. An observation. Look at your list again. I left it on the writing table. You were right about Talbot getting lost in all the other details. Details such as women. With Annie, eros has clouded your reason. I mean no disrespect here. I can tell by the way you talk about her. Talbot's roommate almost certainly knows more. You might talk with the alderman, too. That's a no-brainer. What does Fitzsimmons really think and know when he's not in front of a TV camera?

Gotta go, N.

John folded up the note and put it in the breast pocket of his jacket. He stood at Nancy's zinc breakfast bar, poured himself a coffee, and felt like a commuter in a train depot.

First, she had told him to leave matters alone; now she was providing supervisory advice like chief of the station. Her very note had preempted Kerdigan's advisory. In a manner of speaking, John thought, turning dick herself.

What did this woman want?

She was right about Annie, he had to admit. His face grew warm at the thought. Funny, then, that he felt the need to see Annie once more. He dialed her. He was lucky; she picked up.

"I need to come over immediately. Do you still have David's things in those boxes?"

"Oh, it's you." Annie's voice came like a low sleepy purr over the line. "I'm glad you called. I was about to heave the whole works. I'm trying to clean up around here. You got me started, you know . . . ?" Then, accusingly, "You didn't return my call."

"I'm returning it now. I'll explain when I come over. Can you give me an hour to get to your place?"

"Sure. I don't start work till three."

John rode the elevator down to the street. There was something about not having a car that felt freeing. At the corner, he turned and walked by the Pacific Garden Mission. He remembered when it had anchored the neighborhood. Now it survived as a strange fossil from a different era. A couple of winos, a black guy and a white guy sporting matching Chicago Bulls warm-up jackets, grinned in unison. The sign above them said "Jesus Saves" and in the window of the rescue mission John noticed the announcement that visitors were welcome to each Saturday's taping of the radio show, *Unshackled*.

"Hey, bro," the white wino said. "Spare five dollars?"

John said sorry and made a palms-out gesture. At the next corner, trying to get a *Tribune*, he wasted two quarters in a malfunctioning vending machine. He slammed the metal side of the machine in frustration. He got on the L and rode northbound. He read and reread Nancy's note. That and the clatter of the steel wheels soothed his nerves.

"You're lucky. I was about to heave all this stuff." Annie toed the Bacardi box at her feet. She wore black combat boots and overalls over a torn T-shirt. Other boxes stood stacked in her kitchen.

She had propped open the door to the back porch fire escape with a broom handle. More cartons balanced precariously next to her garbage can. "I have to get rid of it, you know? His stuff?"

"I know."

"I can't bear to look at it anymore."

"It's the right thing to do," John said. "Your business is with the living." Annie had on a baseball cap turned backward, gangbanger style. An open bottle of Lysol stood on the counter beside a pair of yellow rubber gloves. The ammonia and lemon aroma pierced the room. Annie squashed out a cigarette and adjusted her cap. She smiled quickly at John. The plastic strip at the back of the cap left a neat horizontal crease on her forehead.

"You look like hell," Annie said. "You sleeping okay?"

"It's been a tough week. May I take a look?"

"Be my guest. You know, I get enthused about a cleaning project like this, I like to go all the way. I'm even doing cabinets, new shelf paper. When I do cabinets, I don't know, I just feel . . . *cleansed*." Annie cleared half the kitchen table. John opened a box and hoisted it to the surface.

The bulk was back issues of *Cycling* magazine and a few comic zines. A Quimby's promotional flier. John found several articles stapled together, torn from somewhere. Eclectic clippings. Stuff on right-wing deep ecology. Flakier material on New Age alternative medicines, including aroma therapies. These clippings were yellowed. They seemed older. John wondered whether they were Talbot's or his mother's. A treatise on mind-body unity. Science and postmodernism after the Sokal hoax. Tantric yoga and Christian Buddhism, written by a Jesuit priest from Jersey City. There were a couple of brochures for skateboard shops with Venice Beach addresses. *California was still very much with him*, John mused.

Lots of receipts. David had been something of a packrat. Caribou coffee, White Hen Pantry, Subway coupon books. A written invoice for $91 from a bike shop, for a carrier pouch.

Working through the strata of paper, John realized the older stuff was on top. More Chicago, less California came to light as he worked his way down. A flier for a zoning dispute at a drive-through bank in West Lakeview made him pause. A pencil mark circled the meeting time, and the brochure was folded up and appeared slightly concave. On the back of it was a schedule penciled in with a neat hand: "9:30 zoning board. Lunch: Ann Sather's. Afternoon: ward council." The word *zoo* was followed by a question mark. John realized he was reading David's notes.

More fliers. John separated these out and looked for more handwriting. A meeting with the Lakeview neighborhood association. A party at the Jane Addams House, to welcome the food pantry's new board of directors. A Friends of Halsted neighborhood meeting on proposed zoning board alterations. Commercial versus residential interests, the usual conflict. No surprises here.

Interspersed with these came clippings on the alderman himself, from both mainstream and alternative sources: the *Tribune*, the *Reader*, and *Windy City Times*, as well as more marginal venues including those for which John's friend Modeski liked to write.

Was David Talbot really this civic-minded? Unlikely. Trophy had implied he was more of an anarchist, like many of the bike messenger crowd. These were meetings for property owners by property owners. What was this stuff about, then? The fliers lay in a pile on the table. Most of them were folded into quarters and bore the same wrinkled concave shape. John looked at them again.

That was it. They'd been carried around in someone's back pocket. He looked at the writing again on the back of the invoice.

Surely not David's schedule. No. His father's.

It dawned on him. The son had been following his father around, watching him. He'd been going to meetings, watching, observing. But for what? John tried to remember Fitzsimmons's words at the press conference. Hadn't he specifically said that he and his son hadn't spoken for years? John went through the remainder of the boxes' contents, hoping to find a "Dear Dad" note.

Maybe Fitzsimmons didn't recognize his son at all those meetings. But surely the son recognized his father. Why go to all those meetings if not to approach him?

"Have you read all his letters?" John asked Annie. She was scrubbing in the cabinet underneath the sink. She poked her head out from the space and said, "That's what I read first. It's all outgrown skateboard buddies in California. If you're looking for correspondence with his dad, forget about it."

"Nothing?"

"His mom never said a word about Fitzsimmons either. That's what you're looking for, right?"

"I want to look at all the papers, if you have any more."

"Yeah, one more box." She stood up. "Over here." She toed the box and returned to her scrubbing.

"The problem with your generation," John said, "is that you've never learned how to read closely. What they say is true. Your attention span is nonexistent."

"I know," Annie said, from the depths. "We've turned into mindless consumers with no sense of history. Like, am I a total fluff chick, or what?"

"Will you allow me to take any of this?"

"Anything you want. I'm dumping it today. Be my guest."

John finished his work quickly and gathered a pile of papers together and put them in a zippered side pocket of his briefcase. He debated asking Annie if she knew David had followed his father around. But she was engrossed in her own tasks now and let him out of the apartment quickly, with a crisp and impersonal, though friendly, peck on the cheek.

He walked the ten blocks to his apartment. When he turned the dead bolt, he felt like an intruder in his own habitation, and when he got to the top of the stairs by the landing door, he heard his message machine start to play inside.

It was Bill Kerdigan. "John, if you're there, please pick up. This is very important. John, please pick up the phone."

Inside his door, John lunged for the receiver.

"Reimer here." John heard the sound of crackling car radios in the background.

"Is that you, John? I want you over here immediately."

"Where are you?"

"You were right about the diner in Uptown. Listen, I'm going to radio a unit to pick you up outside your front door, okay?" More noise crackled in the background, and John heard a voice say, "We want a positive ID *before* we morgue him, you got that?"

John said, "What happened?"

Bill spoke tersely. "Just move. We'll talk when you get here. I think we found Chris."

Inside the police cruiser two minutes later, John watched the driver pick up the mic and say, "Yeah, Unit 7-0, we've got the preacher and we're on our way." He started up the siren and did not slow down until Uptown.

Chapter 31

THEY DROVE NORTH TO Uptown by the upscale secondhand shops and funky cafés; then the convenience stores and gas stations and taquerias flashed past until John stopped looking and began to wonder what he was about to see at the end of the trip. The driver chewed his gum and tromped the gas. Under the dashboard, a little evergreen air freshener dangled from the cigarette lighter knob.

Leaning forward in the back seat, John glimpsed the clutter of wrappers and soiled napkins at the feet of the cop on the passenger side. Ho Hos, burritos, doughnuts, the works. John thought about the cops' caste system and the seemingly iron laws of body types. Detectives and tactical officers tended toward lean. Fewer flabby endomorphs among them. These guys, by contrast, were pooching out like there was no tomorrow.

"Did Kerdigan tell you I'm clergy?"

"Yeah," said the driver. "You're practically famous already in the district. Your troubles are well known. You staying safe? Being a good citizen, sticking to your regular duties?"

"I try."

"What's that accent, Reverend? You're not from Chicago, are you?"

"No. Kansas. Western Kansas." After all these years, John was beginning to realize that for nonnatives the regional niceties meant nothing. He still said "western" anyway.

"That's funny for Kansas, even. Is English your second language? Pardon me for asking. Daughter teaches in a community college and I pick up on this stuff." The cop daintily sipped his coffee and wiped his lips with a napkin. John wondered if he were being insulted.

"Low German is my first language. You have a good ear. I learned English when I was seven."

The cop ignored the compliment. "Okay, listen, Reverend, I presume you see a lot of caskets, right? You ever see a body on the street?"

"No."

"I'm telling you just to let you know in advance, okay? It can be a little rough the first time."

John looked at the driver's soft under chin that drooped a little over his collar. "Not on the street," John said. "I've seen some in apartments."

They drove through an arched entrance cut into the middle of a building that housed a pizzeria and a Muslim religious articles store labeled "Islamic Books and Things," and then several empty, burnt-out spaces. Once through the entrance they emerged into a back parking lot with a new fence that was topped by razor wire. Reconstruction had begun where a fire had toasted a section of the long building's guts. A yellow Bobcat front-end loader stood parked against the building's flank next to a pile of white sand.

Four men stood under the unused L platform on the far side of the lot. John saw tufts of grass waving atop the concrete pylons. He recognized Kerdigan stooping over something in the distance.

Shanahan was there, too, going into a crouch and listening to what Kerdigan had to say. Four other tactical officers sporting sidearms and white running shoes stood with their hands in their pockets, waiting.

Kerdigan broke away from the cluster and approached. John tried to take in as much visual information as he could in the parking lot. He noticed a black man sitting in the back of one of the cruisers.

"I'm glad I caught you at home. Still alive. Good to see." Kerdigan grabbed John's shoulder and gave it a quick squeeze. "What time did you see Chris yesterday?"

"Probably around eleven. At the beach, near Fullerton. I took him to Peter's Diner for lunch. Who's that in the car?" John pointed to the black man.

"Man who made the call. He may know more than he's telling. We picked him up at the diner around the corner and plan to ask him more questions. Lives in the same flophouse as Chris. By the way, what'd Chris have for lunch yesterday with you?"

John thought for a moment. "Tuna sandwich? A piece of blueberry pie, I think. Why?"

"Stomach contents, just to be sure. We're having a hard time making out the face."

It took John several moments to comprehend what he was looking at. He knew from the clothes it was Chris. Several bottles of pills lay uncapped beside him, their contents strewn out in the rank weeds. Sunlight dappled through the spaces in the vacant L platform above.

"Was there a backpack around?" John asked. "He carried his pills in a backpack or briefcase. Also a Bible most of the time."

"No," Kerdigan said. "This is what you see."

But John did not wish to see. What had had been the face was peeled down from the hairline and hung from the chin now in what was an inside-out and upside-down bloody scrum. The exposed skull's mouth was open, as if forced, and something pink and visceral had been stuffed inside, glistening between the teeth. Not the tongue.

"What?" John said weakly.

Kerdigan's eyes followed John's and the taller man pointed at the crotch of the victim, where the blood had flowed in considerable quantities. The pants were askew.

John walked a few yards away and held onto the steel mesh fence with his hands while he threw up. When he finished and came back, two more men had joined the cluster. John recognized Vito, who carried a camera. He walked around the corpse and snapped pictures. Without looking up he said, "Sorry to meet you in these circumstances, pastor."

The other men considered the corpse. Shanahan stood beside John and waited a decent interval. He put a hand on his shoulder. "Can you tell us who this is? Is this the man you had lunch with yesterday? If it is Chris, we need to be sure."

"Yes, that's Chris," John said.

"We have to ask you a few more questions," Bill Kerdigan said. "Over at my office. There's nothing more to do here."

"How did he find the body?" John said, pointing again to the black man in the back of the cruiser.

"That's what we'd like to know." Kerdigan nodded slowly. "More to the point, I'm afraid that someone out there right now thinks Chris told you something very important. Especially if he was an eyewitness, as you said. Are you sure he was just babbling? Sometimes babble has its own sense, its own logic. Did he give you no description of any kind?"

"Bill, are you positive this has to do with me?"

"Yes, I am afraid so. Which is why it's high time we have that good long conversation. Do you understand me?"

"I'm not sure."

"John. Don't be such a dumb fuck. Do I have to spell it out? If that someone thinks you heard something important, he's coming for you next."

"You know it's a he."

"You asked me that once already. Girls don't do this shit. To pull the skin off someone's face takes upper-body strength, okay? That's what you just saw. Somebody strong and efficient. A sick, ruthless bastard."

John paused before getting into Kerdigan's green unmarked Dodge. The voices of the men under the L platform drifted across the lot.

"I haven't seen this since 'Nam," one of them said. "It's what the VC did to informers."

"It's not a gang marker thing, is it?"

"Latin Kings?"

"Cut the speculation, guys. Let's get on with it."

"Jesus fucking Christ," said Vito. "I thought I seen it all. Look at that face. I'm going to lose my religion here."

"Not to mention your breakfast if you keep talking," Cortez said. "Just shut up and finish the pictures already."

Vito's camera shutter whirred on its motor drive. John looked at the men beside the corpse and Kerdigan, growing impatient, told him to get into the car.

He obeyed the man and thought maybe the Ho Ho doughboy in the uniform a half hour ago was right: he should leave this stuff to the hardened professionals. The bile burned in his throat. Kerdigan offered him a breath mint.

Chapter 32

AT AREA 3 HEADQUARTERS John sat in a plain gray metal chair by a plain gray metal desk while he waited in Bill Kerdigan's office. He drank a Coke to settle his stomach. The detective stood by a table in the larger work space outside and talked into a phone. More men in plainclothes sat at their computer terminals and sighed over scribbled notes. John considered their dilemma: crime fighters chained to electronic screens, unhappy with this part of the process.

The office smelled of Windex, and on the spare desktop a clean ashtray squatted next to a black phone. There was no clutter and the office had a monastic feel.

John sat and wondered how much confidentiality he still owed Annie Casper. He knew well enough that time erodes promises and changing circumstances often require revised plans. Of course it was situational. He had been accused of that kind of thinking before, not only by his brother Andrew but also in more recent years by his Mennonite colleagues across the land. If faith is communal, then the community to some extent fashions the faith. If theology requires the work of the imagination, then imagination must be given its due. He had said that once at a western district meeting, and not everyone had been pleased.

Who could possibly want to kill Chris? And if it was connected to what he told John, who had known about that? And if Chris had been an eyewitness, what did he know?

John had told Bill Kerdigan about Chris. The only other person he'd told this to was Nancy. Less than twenty-four hours later Chris was a dead man.

Who else had Chris regaled with his hallucinatory visions of cats and angels and fiery auras? And, John wondered, what had he told them before his balls were cut off and stuffed into his skinned face in Uptown?

John finished the soda and crumpled the can in his hand.

I talked to the cops and Chris is dead. Was such a sentence a case of bad reasoning?

Annie didn't trust cops either, but she was mountain people. He was Plains people. He thought there were common elements between them: the distrust of office, of authority demanding respect. Deep down, a lot of resistance. Not a foreign idea to him. He'd lived that, too, finding the inner resources to reject the Kleine Gemeinde community in Meade when he was still an adolescent. It was the rejection that he would still have to call the defining moment of his life: telling his brother Andrew that no, he could not remain within his church.

You have forsaken the one true community of faith. We give you up now to the world and works of the devil. Yours is the pride of rebellion and so we give you up to the father of pride and rebellion.

John looked around at his ascetic surroundings. On the wall behind the desk hung a black-and-white framed photo of two boys, Bill and Louis. Louis, in shorts and basketball jersey, stood next to his brother, who wore street clothes. The boys had curly black hair and sported immigrant smiles and their arms were around each other's shoulders. Louis was giving a thumbs-up sign in the photo. John considered the Kerdigan boys, one a future undertaker, the other a detective in the Chicago PD, forty years earlier, about the time when John himself was leaving home and his older brother's reach. Giving himself up to the works of the world and the devil, about to attend college and seminary.

Now Kerdigan and Shanahan stood outside in the main work area conferring with one another. John tossed the crumpled soda can in the trash. Nothing was right, and he wasn't getting anywhere trying to make it right, and he would be expected to trust these two men who turned his way and entered the office. They closed the door. John looked at them and trusted in neither God nor men.

Shanahan started. "What did Chris tell you yesterday? Try to be as specific as possible, verbatim if you can."

"Very little that made sense. We walked through the zoo after we met at the beach. Chris pointed at a tiger and talked about a head on fire. He spoke of a shiny tool. That's what he said: 'shiny tool.' He didn't say knife."

"What was Chris's mental condition at the time you saw him? I understand he was diagnosed with schizophrenia."

"He is psychotic and delusional if he doesn't maintain a strict regime of medication. I mean, he was. The problem was he often lost track of his prescriptions. I think he went between overdosing and then ignoring the meds altogether. This has happened with many of the mentally ill, ever since we decided to turn them into outpatients. Mix up his theology and his mental illness and you have a recipe for serious confusion. He did say something specific though: 'If I hadn't taken his bike, maybe he wouldn't have been hurt.'"

"It ever cross your mind that Chris could have done it?"

"It crossed my mind, yes. But that's very doubtful. I think Chris lacked the focus to kill someone."

"This bike you say Chris rode, the bike stolen from him later on, this bike that places Chris at the scene of the crime," Shanahan said, scratching his head. "I don't get it. We saw a bike at the roommate's place, what's his name?"

John thought of finishing the sentence for him but held back.

"Anyway," Shanahan said, looking directly at John and then through a manila file. "Here, Gallante. Trophy he's called. He said nothing about Talbot owning another bike."

"How much time did your men spend when they questioned Trophy?" John said.

"That sounds a little hostile, Reverend Reimer," Shanahan said, "but I'll pretend I didn't hear it. We're doing our very best. May I presume you talked with him? With Trophy?"

"I've met him," John said.

"You met him," repeated Shanahan. "Kerdigan tells me you've met a lot of people lately. We're trying to figure out what's in it for you. Why you would keep risking yourself when you have apparently become so unpopular in Lakeview?"

Shanahan sat at the edge of Kerdigan's desk and crossed his arms. He looked at John and didn't blink.

"Make that unpopular with some," John said.

"You know what he means," Kerdigan said, speaking for the first time since he had sat down behind his desk. "There have been two attempts on your life now. You are some kind of lucky." He doodled on a pad that was resting on one knee. "Shanahan is absolutely right. We are wondering what's in it for you. You are taking terrible risks. You might want to think about taking an interim pastoral assignment downstate. Get away for a while."

John waited. Kerdigan continued: "And each time I try to talk with you I get vague answers, as if you know a lot more than you're letting on. I'm a little bit tired, too."

Shanahan spoke. "So now you have a strange encounter with someone you call Crazy Chris, and you think he was an eyewitness but you replay nothing but zoo talk and something about a shiny tool. Half a day later somebody whacks him."

"Yes," John said, looking straight at Kerdigan. "I thought about that. And I thought about the fact that I told only two people about Chris and one of them was you. And yes, half a day later Chris is dead. Of course, Chris could have babbled to other people. And other people obviously saw us together. What did the other guy you arrested in Uptown have to say?"

"We're asking the questions here," Shanahan said.

"You ever discover who it was that shot out my window?" John asked.

"We're working on it," Kerdigan said.

"I imagine that forensic evidence is tied up," John said. "I hear it can take a long time." John took a deep breath and thought, *Okay, calm down. A little civility.*

Shanahan's face had gone from sober to displeased. He started to speak but John cut in.

"And my car. I'd like the car returned, let's see, what do you think is reasonable? Within a week?"

"Why would an obscure Mennonite minister become interested in a faggot bashing? Why are you asking questions about Talbot's murder? What's in it for you?"

Shanahan got off the desk. He pulled a wooden chair out of the corner of the office and scooted it up beside Kerdigan's desk, closer to John. He settled into it and drummed his fingertips together. "You haven't answered this question yet and it is fundamental."

"We're stumped," Kerdigan said.

"Are you investigating me or the murder?" John asked. "And what makes everyone so sure David Talbot's murder was a faggot bashing?"

"Come on, Reverend, let's not waste time. That's never been in doubt."

"Why not?"

"The evidence was clear from the get-go."

"It was?"

"Yes."

John realized Shanahan was answering his questions now. He pressed on. "Evidence such as what?"

"Okay, that's enough," Kerdigan said, leaning forward behind his desk. "You seem to forget. We're here to ask you the questions."

Shanahan resumed. "We've checked you out a little bit. Your congregation, while priding itself as progressive, is not exactly a hotbed for gay activists. Am I right?"

"You've been interviewing my parishioners?" John raised his voice slightly. "What does that have to do with your investigation?"

"Hey, not so loud." Kerdigan stopped his doodling.

"I don't need this," John said. He got to his feet and looked at the cops. "I've told you what I know about Chris. Your job is to find a murderer, and my sense is you're straying from that. I don't see the point of these other inquiries."

"We need to know who you talked to, Reimer." Shanahan gently nudged him back into the chair. He attempted to inject a note of kindly patience. "Let me remind you that we have no idea what Chris said last night before he died. If he mentioned you to whoever it was who did him, you could be in considerable danger. And we're worried you're not telling us everything you know. Did anyone you talked to threaten you in any way? Is there any reason you're hiding what you know?"

"Funny that the same thought crossed my mind," John said. "Anything you guys should tell me?" John knew it was a mistake once it was out of his mouth.

"You're out of line, John. I like you, but you're out of line." Kerdigan showed no anger. He put the doodle pad on the desk. It teemed with life, covered with miniature sketches of Disney characters, rocket ships, finely drawn human faces. "Do you know anything more about the bike?"

"I never saw it, and Chris was unable to describe it."

"This is bullshit and a waste of time," Shanahan said, getting to his feet.

"Exactly my feeling," John said. "I really must be on my way." He put his hand on the doorknob.

Shanahan spoke. "There is someone out there who doesn't like you and we are here to keep you safe as a citizen of Chicago and of this precinct. Okay? Do you understand that? And we can't help you if you fail to cooperate."

"Everybody in this room is suffering from frayed nerves," Kerdigan said.

John wondered if the interrogation was about to turn into group therapy. "Maybe we should join hands and sing a verse of 'Kumbaya.'"

"Look, stay out of trouble, okay?" Shanahan smiled. "For your sake and ours. Stick to the word of God. Leave law enforcement to us. Please?"

"Yes, sir," John said.

"You want a ride?" Kerdigan asked.

"No, thanks. I'll walk."

It was almost noon. John was hungry and not happy with the confrontational tone he had taken. It had emerged out of a raw part of himself he hadn't heard in years. But the walking cleared his head, and he felt the return of equilibrium. He stopped at a taqueria, where he sat down in a booth and had the burrito plate with a side of rice and beans. He read the *Trib* and ordered coffee.

They had not done a very thorough job of investigation. They hadn't gone through David's papers at Trophy's apartment, the papers stored securely inside his briefcase now beside him in this greasy little Naugahyde booth.

They had either been sloppy or else intentionally ignored things. *Why?*

He went home and let himself into the apartment. The kitchen smelled damp. He looked in the fridge and noticed there were Tupperware meals that needed to be tossed. He opened a carton of milk and sniffed. Gone sour.

In the bedroom he folded slacks and a couple of shirts as well as a heavy sweater into an oversized sports duffel bag. He found his overnight kit in the bathroom, packed his toothbrush and razor. He checked his messages before he left. "Reimer? I need to see you right away. At the usual. Afternoon is good. Later."

John replayed the message to make sure he recognized the voice.

"I can't talk now, okay?" Trophy was stacking longnecks into the cooler compartment beneath the bar. Three women in black leather jackets sat at the back end of the bar drinking martinis. One of them motioned Trophy her way and called for another round.

Trophy nodded, "Be right there." He looked back at John.

"You called. You said you wanted to talk. I figured this was the usual."

"Let me very precise about this. I can't talk right now, you understand. Meet me tonight, ten o'clock, at the Lucky Horseshoe on Halsted."

John looked at him. "The Lucky what?"

"The Lucky Horseshoe. You'll think I'm perverse, but there's a reason." Trophy looked as if he had lost weight. He wasn't wearing mascara.

"Use the back entrance off the side street, not the Halsted entrance. And one more thing. If you think you're being tailed, please don't come in."

John nodded. All of a sudden the duffel bag felt heavy on his shoulder. He adjusted the strap.

"You traveling somewhere?" Trophy said, looking at the bag.

"In a manner of speaking. Who would want to tail me?"

"Cops are pretty obvious at the Lucky, though they're working on that. Know what I mean?"

"Yes, I think so."

John took the L downtown to the South Loop and walked the three blocks to Nancy's loft. He found the key under the mat and let himself in. He took a long, hot shower and put on running shorts and a T-shirt and curled up under the blanket on Nancy's sofa.

There was too much light flooding in from the expansive multiple-paned windows. It was gorgeous light but bad for sleep. He dreamt he was running on top of unused L tracks. Clumps of tall waving grass that grew in the cracks kept tripping him up.

Someone chased him, someone he couldn't quite see. But he could hear his mother's voice in Low German saying, "Shut your smart mouth, young man."

When he tried to reply to her in English, he didn't sound smart at all. All the eloquence of his pride and rebellion were gone.

Chapter 33

JOHN HAD ONLY INDIRECT knowledge of the Lucky Horseshoe. A couple of years earlier Wiebe had told him it was the favorite spot for one of America's leading church historians, who, after writing two definitive works on nineteenth-century pietism and social reform, had strangely disappeared from his seminary teaching post in the suburbs.

How did Alan know this, John had inquired. "I saw him there," Alan said. "Very adept at putting dollar bills into a G-string." And what was Alan doing in such a place? "Part of urban pastoral education," he had replied, "for the consortium. Urban anthropology course. You should do the tour some time, I could set you up with an orientation leader."

John hadn't asked any more questions, nor had he found time to take the tour. However, he read the evangelical historian's writing with a new eye. It felt, as Wiebe might say, thoroughly "defamiliarized." John recalled a similar sense of vertigo thirty-five years earlier when a liberal Baptist professor shocked a seminary class with tales of Paul Tillich's pleasure chest full of sadomasochist fetish toys.

John had gained a small portion of fame by inquiring, in his still rather thick German accent, whether Tillich was merely investigating the Pauline meaning of bondage to sin. The professor had replied over the laughter, "Perhaps, following Paul, each generation experiences its own thorn in the flesh. Who among us really knows what the apostle was struggling with?"

Afterward, John had entertained second thoughts about Tillich's talk of the "ground of being" and "ultimate concern." And in the ensuing years he had become a neo-orthodox follower of Karl Barth. But why, he wondered now, should he have ever presumed that theological liberals cornered the market on sexual kinks?

Especially considering what he knew about the home community in Kansas, where the most extreme instances of shunning and excommunication had involved crimes so grave that John had never coaxed a complete explanation out of his older brother. Andrew would simply shake his head in pained dismay. These were sins so lurid they were unmentionable, if not unpardonable. John was eight years old when he heard dark murmurings about the elder *Krimhofer* in the next county, something unseemly about his use of bucket calves.

In fact, John recalled now, he had first heard that conversation among the old Mennonite men pitching horseshoes at the Friesen place.

Which brought him back to the present, walking north from the Wellington L stop on his way to the Lucky Horseshoe. His head felt full of fog. The long walk afforded him the opportunity to pause a couple of times and look over his shoulder. It was good Nancy was working late; she would have offered to drive him over and asked far too many questions.

He looked over his shoulder again, trying not to be obvious. Ridiculous. He didn't know how to spot a tail, or if he had, he wouldn't know how to shake it. He considered the word *tail* and thought Trophy would enjoy the pun. Seriously, though, maybe the occasion called for a gray fedora. Stopping at Borders, he picked up copies of the *Reader* and *Windy City Times* in the front foyer and then, putting them in his briefcase, continued on.

He searched the sidewalks for low foreheads and jutting brows that were perhaps after him. Normally on Friday nights he put the final touches on his sermon draft.

He was about to spend time in a male strip bar with a homosexual bartender given to making paranoid pronouncements about the Chicago PD. He remembered the advice Andrew had given him once when they were young, about to go into Dodge City together on a Saturday night: "Don't act surprised. Even if you are."

John believed that certain aspects of the male code of the West still worked.

Chapter 34

HE WONDERED WHETHER TO wade through the throngs of men crowded around the Lucky Horseshoe's multiple bars, watching the dancers dance. Maybe Trophy would shout his name above the tumult and beckon him over to some strange grotto.

His eyes and lungs adjusted to the scant light and thick smoke. Pausing just inside the rear entrance, he felt overdressed. There were at least three rooms, maybe more, laid out in an L-shaped grid, awash in sweaty testosterone and the chatter of conga rhythms. The bar nearest the back entrance, to his right, looked staid, with no live entertainment, just a horseshoe-shaped counter with yuppie executive types in polo shirts lounging over their beers. *Nothing exotic here*, John thought.

The conga beat subtly transitioned to techno thrash, picked up in volume, and pulsed in and out, spilling against the walls of the bar. To his left, a film played on a widescreen set mounted on the wall. He could glimpse the movie through an antechamber that featured a live dancer in a Napoleon haircut. The dancer, who gyrated on top of a modified pool table, sported a purple G-string and high-top laced Doc Martens. He was busy busting out a repertoire of leg-crossing moves with all the enthusiasm of a young Richard Simmons.

But it was the film that caught John's eye. Two young cowboys gave each other some direct pleasure. The words "Get Out of Dodge," in frontier calligraphy, filled the screen, after which the action cut to the bunkhouse. One of the boys stood bent over in nothing but his boots and a ten-gallon hat, his hands and ankles bound with rawhide. A stern trail boss prepared to administer discipline in the form of a braided leather whip handle. The boy's mouth made a moaning shape.

John gripped his briefcase handle and walked through the antechamber. The dancer in purple writhed like a cobra rising from the piper's basket. He lip-synched naughty words while tweaking his nipples. He glanced down from his platform at John, and John looked away.

Another young man with a pitted complexion walked past John and spoke with an Aussie accent. "Welcome to the Lucky, mate. Care for a drink?"

"Thank you," John said. "Seltzer, with a lemon twist." He found the only available booth not too far from the dance platform and hoped the information Trophy promised to bring would make this visit worthwhile. A graybeard walked to the edge of the pool table and fondled the dancer's bare buttocks. The dancer squatted athletically in a catcher's stance and when he stood up from the embrace there was money in his string.

John read his papers and waited. He put his trench coat on the back of the chair opposite and was startled when a man took that seat. His shirt was starched and white and the tie spoke of Savile Row elegance in slanted blue stripes. The man's curly hair was black and cropped short, his jawline was clean, and the horn-rimmed glasses suggested a young associate professor.

John looked again. "Is that you?" He tipped the glass and drank the bubbly water. It was relief on his parched throat; the air was thick and hurt his lungs. "You leave anonymous messages. You come in disguise. What does this mean?"

"This is partly a new career phase," Trophy said. His ears were free of metal accoutrement. He glanced at the dancer who nodded and smiled back, and then said to John: "You came here. I didn't know if you would."

"You're testing my patience. Why?"

"Look, Reimer, understand this is more than a private mindfuck, okay? They're on to me. I thought if we were going to talk, this would be a good place. I'll spot them if they're in here. He's watching out for me." Trophy pointed a thumb back over his shoulder toward the dancer. "I'm pretty sure someone's tapping your phone, by the way. Have you received any odd messages?"

"No, not besides your own. What do you mean, they're on to you?"

"I got a hate call today."

John thought of Chris and wondered if he needed to tell Trophy about the risks people took lately when they spoke to the Mennonite minister from Lakeview.

"Let's try that room," John said, pointing to the bar surrounded by young brokers. "More my type. It's quieter, too, and at my age, the hearing starts to go." He stood up and took his coat and briefcase. They pushed their way through the crowd to the other side of the horseshoe.

This room was an addition-in-progress. Recently installed Sheetrock panels, still unplastered, contrasted the backlit panes of art nouveau leaded glass. The glass ran around the top edge of the wall, just above oak molding that carried indirect lighting.

Trophy burrowed his way toward two unoccupied bar stools and pounced. He ordered a martini straight up.

John began. "Are we okay here?"

Trophy nodded and lifted his glass.

"You didn't tell me Talbot was watching his father. I went through those boxes of stuff again at Annie's place. Fliers on zoning board meetings, ward meetings, public hearings, fundraiser. And the funny thing is all these notices were folded up and looked like someone had carried them in his sweaty back pocket. A biker, I think. David Talbot might have been a Boy Scout, but I don't think he attended these meetings out of a deep sense of civic responsibility."

"Go on," Trophy said, and lit a cigarette. "You're doing good."

"I read those clippings on Fitzsimmons, too. Clippings his son apparently found important enough to keep."

"And what did you learn?"

"Insightful stories in the marginal press, stuff the *Trib* and *Sun-Times* didn't run. The far-out anarchist and libertarian publications. Presumably rumor. About the hard line he was taking against police brutality in the precinct. Not just brutality, but reports of torture. Illegal use of stun belts and cattle prods. The water and wire treatment, as one writer put it."

"Apparently Fitzsimmons had said, off the record of course, that he would investigate these reported abuses no matter where they led. Virtuous Democratic Party stuff. Nobody's rights to be violated in the 44th. Et cetera. Including the people who can't defend themselves in court. The Democratic Party standing up for the little guy. You know."

Trophy snorted. "Yeah, the usual. Yadda yadda."

"Angry words had been exchanged with the police commissioner over these accusations by the good alderman . . . inside sources claimed."

Trophy sipped from his martini and chewed on an olive. "You read anything about zoning?"

"Yes. Lots of zoning board meetings. It seems a few lonely voices in our town asked questions about construction companies and campaign financing. Were the big donations a mere coincidence, coming at the same time that petitions rolled in to change the zoning? Why the big donations at the same time that petitions were filed for high-rise condominiums in parts of the West Side?"

Trophy spoke. "Everybody is happy if enough interested parties get a piece of the action. Distribute the wealth: isn't that what progressives want? When real estate is hot, no one wants a spoilsport. If it's good for developers, it's good for Chicago." He smiled like a broker after a solid day on the floor of the futures market. "Bigger tax base, better city services, everybody scores. Might be able to pay the debt on the cops' pension fund and massage the angry egos in the teachers' union. Actually, if I live long enough, I have my eye on a great building in Bucktown. Excuse me, Wicker Park."

John reached for his briefcase. "One other thing of interest. A piece of notebook paper with writing on it. This fell out of a magazine. Lined paper, nothing on it, with just two words.

"I expected to find this. And I did. It's the start of a letter. Like you sometimes start if you're writing in a restaurant. Two words: 'Dear Dad.' And then nothing. You want to see it?"

Trophy looked into his glass. He did not look surprised. "No, I believe you."

"You knew he was obsessed with his father."

Trophy nodded.

"He was sketching out his father's schedule in places. He was practically stalking him," John said. "Yet he told you he hadn't talked to his father or that his father even knew he existed in Chicago. How do you square this?"

"I couldn't," Trophy said. "It took me months to figure out what he was doing. All straight boys think they're more than prodigal sons—maybe he wanted Daddy to be proud of him. Even though he must have come to realize his father was a piece of shit."

"Did Annie know about this?"

"I don't think so."

"You knew about it, but you lied first to the police and then to me. Why?"

Trophy said, "Give me a little time here."

"Okay," John said, and looked at his watch. Loud whooping noises erupted from around the billiards table in the next room, and a purple jockstrap flew through the air. "I keep a late bedtime on Friday nights. Stop me at any point here as I ramble. It is helpful to have you listen.

"What bothers me most is how the Chicago Police Department, in their infinite pains to be professional, should have overlooked all this stuff at your apartment. How is that possible?"

"Maybe more interesting is that Fitzsimmons never asked for any of David's personal effects," Trophy said. "What do you think about that?"

"When there is alienation, you don't necessarily take a personal interest."

"Reimer, you're smarter than I thought. I underestimated you."

"I'm a slow starter," John said. "Did you get the names of the detectives who interviewed you?"

"You'll get me into trouble, preacher man."

"Who were they?"

"A Spanish guy, a joker, cracking bad jokes, annoying as all hell. The other guy bigger, black hair combed straight back at the temples, going a little gray. Snappy dresser."

"You can do better than that. Names?"

"Look, I didn't call to ask. I'm petrified. You have to understand something about my work," Trophy said. "In my job, you hear things. And there are those things you'd rather not know for your personal safety."

John answered: "In my job we leave certain things to faith but we still try to know as much as we can. I need your help. Can you give me any better descriptions than that?"

"I wasn't entirely sober the evening they came, okay?"

"Either of them named Kerdigan or Shanahan? Does the name Vito come to mind? Cortez, maybe?"

"Sorry," Trophy said. "I was out of it. Really."

"Mr. Gallante, Trophy, you were mincingly, touchingly drunk. And tonight you say you're petrified, and yet you take the risk to meet me here in this public place and you think I might be tailed. And you still haven't told me why."

"*Petrified*, not *patrified*."

"You are the second person today to mock my foreign speech. You still haven't explained this business about the tail."

"It's like this," Trophy said, and took a small spiral-bound notebook from his coat pocket and laid it on the counter. "If you're looking for the rest of your 'Dear Dad epistle.'" He looked across the room in the mirror above the bar and said, "Just put it away."

John flipped the cover open and saw on the flyleaf the name David Talbot. "Why didn't you give this to me earlier?"

"Just put it away, all right? Fold it up in your newspaper."

John did what he was told. "You held it back from both the cops and from me."

Trophy nodded. "If they find that on you, you are going to be in very deep shit."

"So, what, now you want me to carry this around?" John patted his briefcase.

"Look, I didn't know where else to go with this. I couldn't sit on it anymore."

"Frightened into silence by bullies."

"Yes."

"But the still small voice within began to speak. Okay, I'll keep it. But my eyes aren't what they used to be, and the smoke hurts them here. Can you give me a quick summary?"

"I'll try."

"Why don't you take a break from the gin? Two coffees, please," John said to the man across the counter.

The bartender was new and had just started his eleven o'clock shift. He looked at the geezer in white hair and the young man in glasses next to him. He thought the younger man looked familiar, and the bartender wondered if he was into bizarre partner playing with Mormon types. But they looked like they were enjoying each other's company, and the bartender knew the Lucky was about nothing, if not friendship, so he kept his observation to himself.

Chapter 35

IT IS A SHORT walk down Halsted to Belmont, where John turned in the direction of Ann Sather's Swedish restaurant. This was his most frequent stop for comfort food, not only the cinnamon rolls but also the mashed potatoes, or if too late for supper, then the boysenberry tart with vanilla ice cream. Now he was going to ask a few questions. He'd had too much coffee already. The briefcase weighed heavily in his hand, and he reeked of tobacco. His lungs had been abused. He had seen things he didn't want to dwell on.

He tried to comprehend Trophy's story.

The night was clear and cold, and it was good to walk. He passed a new restaurant whose manager stood outside the door, dressed in a soft chocolate flannel suit and a wide tie. John imagined that he spoke Russian. Everyone inside, bathed in the gentle glow of little lamps set on starched white tablecloths, looked successful, beautiful, and twenty-seven years of age. To John, their faces seemed unaware of life's terrors and pain.

John imagined traveling with Nancy, maybe to Moscow and then the Ukraine. Perhaps a stop in the Molotschna colony. They could look at their ancestors' graves, and Viola's, those lost butchered relatives who hadn't made it out, some scythed down in their fields by Cossacks, some shot by the Bolsheviks, some executed for the crime of speaking German or making considerable sums of money, or angering the kulaks and serfs alike, or growing red winter wheat and resisting collectivized farming, or practicing a strange religion. The authorities had found plenty of reasons to kill them.

He felt the heft of the briefcase. He wanted to read the notebook, but he wasn't sure of a safe place to do that. Sitting down and reading. To think that in this country you could get shot for such audacity.

His eyes burned with exhaustion. He wanted to sleep in his own bed tonight, not somebody's sofa, even if it were Nancy's. How much sense did it make to involve Nancy in all this? At some point they'd be tailing her too, or worse.

He entered Ann Sather's and did something he'd never done before. He sat at the little bar by the front cash register. Lately he had become adept sitting at bars.

A blonde maître d' in a black dress with a white apron held the phone receiver against her ear and looked at him. A slightly chipped front tooth made her smile more winsome.

She put a hand over the receiver. "Don't tell me you're drinking. I don't believe it."

"Coffee, please," John said. "Decaf." He looked at boxes marked Robert Mondavi to his left, stacked up on the bar. "Lots of parties tonight?" He glanced up the polished staircase to his left that led to the second floor's atrium and Scandinavian meeting rooms. Laughter emanated from upstairs and the foot traffic up and down was heavy.

A waitress climbed the steps. Her muscular arm supported a tray full of cocktail shrimp and scampi, sauce, mounded heaps of fresh lemon slices. She spoke to the maître d' on the way up. "Terri, Fredo wants these wine boxes upstairs right away. Can you get Carlos and Pedro to help?"

Terri picked up the intercom phone and said something in Spanish.

"Strong girl," John said to the maître d'.

"Yes," Terri said, "that's the kind Fredo hires." She put the phone down.

John stirred half-and-half into his coffee. "You do lots of parties on the weekends here, don't you?"

"Too many," Terri said. John noticed the sheen on her fine blonde hair, as if it were moussed. She had it tied back with a black velvet scrunchie, and she wore double silver earrings that bobbed in her lobes, picking up light from the restaurant's dusky red interior. She, too, he realized, looked successful and twenty-seven years old.

"You work here on Thursdays?" he asked her.

"Yeah, why. What's with all the questions tonight? You're starting to sound like the rabbi and that wacko journalist you hang out with."

"Please speak kindly of my friends," John said. "Actually, Terri—it's Terri, isn't it?"

"Yes."

"You would do me an enormous favor if you answered these questions I have tonight."

Terri poured him fresh coffee. "For the preacher, anything. If you're sitting at this bar it must be something important. Ask." She pronounced the last word with the high northern Great Lakes diphthong, the long *e* sliding into the vowel.

Two Polish women who looked like twins appeared from the kitchen, muscled the wine boxes off the counter, and headed up the staircase to the party rooms. "Thanks," Terri said to their backs. "Tell Carlos and Pedro their ass is grass." She turned back to John. "Now what can I do for you?"

"Last Thursday night, a little over a week ago, there was a meeting here with the alderman, I believe? A citizens' meeting upstairs?"

Terri looked blank.

John continued. "Fitzsimmons. 44th Ward. He has his office a few blocks from here, I think he's a regular."

"Wait a minute, everybody's a regular here, if you know what I mean."

"Fitzsimmons, the alderman whose son was killed."

"Oh."

"Yes, that one."

"Why do you want to know?"

"I'm doing someone a favor. Somebody who needs to know. Can you trust me?"

"Is that rhetorical?" Terri looked at the stubble on Reimer's cheek and wondered what kind of man of God he was. His hands seemed younger and stronger than his face.

"No, I just need you to know you can trust me. This is important."

"Okay."

"You were working the night of the meeting, right? Are there any details you remember? I'm especially interested when the alderman left that night, if you saw him. Anything that stands out."

"Okay. I remember. I was waiting tables that night, too, because we were running shorthanded. There was the crowd upstairs, a couple of different parties. They were demanding, know what I mean? Emotionally needy. The alderman's group, the citizens' group, ran up a pretty big bar tab. I mean, respectable tab, okay? Real noisy if I remember correctly."

"Noisier than now?" John asked, pointing upstairs.

"Yeah."

"Did you go upstairs?"

"Yes, some of them thought the cash bar upstairs was inconvenient so Fredo had me carry drinks. He'll go that extra mile for the big spenders."

"You said they got loud. Do you remember what about?"

"Geez, you want some details here, don't you?"

"Some."

"Yeah, well, a couple of days ago a big guy asked me some of these same questions. Tall, hunched over. Reminded me of what, a giant pelican, kind of fatigued like. Hair wasn't quite as white as yours."

"Thank you very much."

"I thought you'd be interested to know."

"I am, but I'm more curious about what happened Thursday night."

"Wait a minute," Terri said, "that was Thursday evening. The alderman . . ."

"The body of the alderman's son wasn't found until early Friday morning, and it got reported in the Saturday papers," John finished for her. "But you don't read the papers. That's okay. Let's focus now for a moment on that evening. Were you there when the party broke up upstairs?"

"Yeah, they finished up with espresso and had a couple bottles of Sambuca and ouzo circling the table. They were arguing. But the political people argue as a matter of course. I think it was mostly friendly."

"Zoning talk or the police? Do you remember the topic?"

Terri stopped and looked at John with a new expression of fear and respect. "Say, where are you coming from on this, anyway? You're ahead of me here. They talked about zoning. I've never waited a ward party or alderman gathering where there wasn't talk of zoning. Lemme tell you, that talk bores the hell out of me."

"Yes, that's the way they like it," John said. "It's so boring that nobody pays attention. Your concern is how well these guys will tip you, not who owns the town."

"Are you making fun of me?"

"No, I'm talking about most of us. Including myself."

"Okay, well, the alderman got into a pretty intense exchange during the main course. But it wasn't about zoning, it was about something to do with the 23rd Precinct."

"Were there any cops at this gathering?"

"How should I know? What do you want from me, a seating diagram? A flow chart? Full bios?"

Terri flagged one of the Polish twins who swept down from upstairs. "Take the desk here, could you, for five minutes? I have to talk with this man. He's from the mayor's office." The Polish girl took up her station behind the bar.

At a table in the back of the restaurant, John resumed his questions. "They argued about the 23rd Precinct, but what about? Do you remember?"

"The only phrase I kept hearing one of them say was, 'Call off the investigation. Cease the investigation.'"

"What investigation? Do you have any idea?"

Terri shook her head. "No. One guy was more sober than the rest of them. He said something I remember. I came in with the dessert cart. He said, 'You want to investigate the people trying to solve the case, what the hell is wrong with you? You're going to piss them off? Something to that effect."

"What did the alderman say?"

"He mumbled. It wasn't clear. Something about a no-win situation."

John paused and smiled at Terri. "You certainly remember a lot for someone who didn't recognize the alderman's name ten minutes ago."

"And who doesn't read the papers," Terri added. "I'll let that insult pass."

"What time did the party break up?"

"Around midnight."

"Did you see who left with whom?"

"Why would I pay attention to those details? I was down here at the bar, trying to total up tabs."

"Did you notice anybody different hanging around here about that time? Say, a young man who could have ridden in the Tour de France?" John took out one of the old pictures from his briefcase. He showed it to Terri. She got a frightened look in her eye.

"I'm afraid to say much more. What kind of divination are you into?"

"My grandfather was a water witch in the old country, in the Ukraine. Before he found Jesus. I got some of it from him maybe."

"No, I mean it." Terri smoothed a napkin beneath her well-manicured fingers. "He sat at the bar where you sat tonight when you came in. Exactly the same place. He had a bike helmet under his arm, blue windbreaker. Long spandex racing pants. He didn't look like a bike geek, it seemed natural on him. He drank one beer. He had a nice face, just like that picture."

John looked hard at Terri.

She went on. "He talked with me about apartments in Edgewater. He went upstairs once to use the telephone in the hallway."

"The one just outside the meeting room."

"Yeah, that one."

"Did it strike you as odd that he was drinking beer at this ornamental bar that almost nobody uses?"

"I was too charmed to notice. Let me tell you, I look at a person's shoes and his butt and I can tell you the world about him. This kid was, like, seriously toned."

"Straight or gay?"

"The way he talked I'd certainly want to put him on my list." Terri bit her lip.

"When did he leave the bar? Before or after the party upstairs broke up?"

"Almost immediately after. In fact, I didn't see him actually leave because I was cashing out such a long line of customers at the front desk. A
real late-night rush. It was about midnight. When I looked up he was gone.
He left cash on the bar counter. That was after the party upstairs left."

"And how did the alderman leave? With a group or by himself?"

"He was pretty wasted, if you ask me. About half the table left earlier
in the evening around ten-thirty, then the alderman and four or five others
stayed longer. I took it to be more of the inner circle. The alderman was
ordering doubles. Bourbon."

"This was after Sambuca and espresso."

"Yes."

"A serious drinker."

"Very serious. He was unsteady on his feet when he left. At the front
door he told his staff to go home, there was a little protest, but he said he
needed the air."

"Do you remember anyone else who might have left shortly after the
alderman did? Say, somebody on the big side?"

"You're asking me to remember too much. Like I said, there was a rush
here about that time. A lot of people cashed out. I admit I was disappointed
the biker disappeared without saying a proper goodbye."

"A lot of us are disappointed."

"What are you saying? What do you . . . ?" A shadow passed over the
young woman's face. John waited for her to figure it out; he wondered how
long it would take. "Oh, shit, no," she said.

"Maybe you see a lot of bikers. That one happened to be the alderman's
son."

"How could I have known?"

"Try the papers, maybe. Didn't the big hunched guy who asked you
questions tell you?"

"He didn't get that far," Terri said.

"I'm curious," John said. "Would you vote for this alderman?"

She gave John a look that suggested the friendly vibes were gone. "I
don't talk about my voting, okay?"

John was tired now of the nightlife. Terri's smile didn't look winsome
anymore, just wan, and if she were twenty-seven, much of the vitality had
evaporated. This was no glamor job. She suddenly looked down at the place
mat between her strong hands and said curse words again, under her breath
to herself, as if John were no longer there.

He told her thank you, but it didn't sound right, and he pushed his
chair away from the table.

"Wait," she said, as he stood up. He looked at her and she was crying, crying maybe about the dead young man or about her lousy job. John couldn't tell.

"I want to help you, Reimer, and I don't mind answering your questions. But don't be such a judgmental prick, okay?"

He hesitated. "I'll have to apologize now and explain later," he said. "I'm sorry I can't do any better than that."

"Yeah, that's just the kind of shitty thing a man would say." She dabbed at her mascara with the corner of a Kleenex.

John knew he was not going to win this round. On his way out he heard the Polish girl at the front desk tell him, "Good night, Reverend," but he was already through the door.

Chapter 36

THE THIRD NIGHT IN Nancy's apartment was no good.

A brief note on the kitchen counter told him she had flown to New York on business. "Please be careful. Don't do anything stupid."

He was relieved to have solitude, yet felt a twinge of disappointment; he thought of her greeting him at the door, just out of the shower, with her splendid short wave of black hair dripping wet, and smelling of bath soap and wrapped in a terrycloth robe. Again he thought of traveling with her on a train across the Western Steppe of Russia.

He put these thoughts out of mind. He dead-bolted the door and had a tall glass of milk. After he showered and dressed, he opened the briefcase and spent an hour studying, in the pool of light on Nancy's escritoire, the spiral notebook that Trophy had given him. The chair made his back hurt. He wanted his own study and his own office chair.

He called his home phone for messages but after a while realized that it wasn't working. What had Trophy said about phone taps? He wondered how far his paranoia could go. Something was about to snap.

It took a very short time on Saturday to find out how soon. At the church office his secretary gave him a withering look. He still had the duffel bag slung over his shoulder, and this and the briefcase strap made him feel like a water carrier. He needed to go running to get some kinks out.

He said lamely: "Aren't you here a little early? The mailman doesn't arrive till noon."

"I don't think you've spent more than ten minutes in the office this week."

"I am a minister, Mildred, not a copyeditor. Some of my work happens outside the office."

"Look, pastor, I know there is something—there is something going on, and it's not right, I just know . . ."

"And you feel like I am not communicating so well, is that it?"

Mildred nodded.

"I have reasons for my silence. Did Mrs. Maasser call?"

"She was very glad you visited her, yes."

"You see, I have not been a total derelict."

Mildred eyed the duffel bag. "Somebody called and asked if you were taking his advice, not to sleep at home for a while. I asked him to identify himself."

"Was it Kerdigan?"

"Yes." Mildred hesitated again. "That is Louis's brother, right?"

"That's the one."

"Well, you should maybe know that when he came by here earlier this week, Alan Wiebe and I talked to him. A lot of people are getting worried about you. Alan said he thought you needed a long vacation, out of town." She paused and the vertical lines between her brows deepened. "Is all of this connected to the shooting?"

John rearranged a stack of manila folders on top of the file cabinet. "Some of it may be."

She looked again at the duffel bag.

He sighed. "Okay, you want to know where I've been sleeping. I'll tell you, I'm awfully tired of not sleeping in my own bed."

"Where have you been?"

John felt like a schoolboy caught by the Sunday school teacher. He debated not telling her; there would be older parishioners who wouldn't approve. "Nancy's," he said. "Don't worry. She is away in New York."

He tried to gauge the mixture of confusion, judgment, and sympathy in Mildred's face and gave her his full attention. "You must listen to me, Mildred. Look at me." He sat her down in the chair across from his church office desk. He kicked the duffel bag and briefcase aside with his foot. Mildred clutched a stack of bulletins.

"What I tell you now I tell you in absolute confidence," he started. "I have been shot at, my tires have been slashed, and threats have been made. Kerdigan advised that I get away from the apartment for my own safety. I have been staying at Nancy's. It is possible that someone who is after me might also go after Nancy if he knew.

"Mildred, look at me. Stop folding bulletins."

"I'm listening," she said.

"It is imperative that you don't communicate to anyone what you just heard me say or where I am staying. Do you understand?"

"Yes."

"Good. Now I hope this will all blow over in a few days. You have to trust me."

"I think I do," she said. "Please let me finish these," she said, pointing to the bulletins on the desk. "I'll leave them in the front foyer, then I'm going home. I want to call Alan. I think we should talk about this if you're in so much danger."

"The more people you talk to the more danger I will be in," he said.

"You haven't told me everything."

"I can't. Not right now."

Before he left the office for his apartment, she interrupted his thoughts once more. "The nursery and social hall are reeking of tobacco smoke."

"I'm sure we'll discuss the problem at the next council meeting."

"Good," Mildred said. "If you don't bring it up, I will mention it to Unger."

In the apartment, his phone rang. Like a fool, John picked up the receiver and spoke.

The voice did not sound like a normal human voice. After the first few words, John realized it was filtered through some kind of electronic distortion.

"You don't give up, do you? If you want information about Talbot, come to Waveland Golf Course clubhouse, two a.m., Sunday. That's after midnight. Dark clothes. There are occasional police patrols. Avoid them. Don't try to bring a vehicle. And sure as hell don't bring anyone else. Good-bye now."

He hung up the phone and held out his hand to see if it was shaking. Just a little.

He needed to make one more social call before taking a daytime run past the Waveland clubhouse. He dialed the number to make sure there was room on the appointment schedule.

This visit would call for power dressing. He found his charcoal pin-stripe suit reserved for special occasions. He stripped. In the bathroom he shaved and ran a hot washcloth over his face. He put mousse in his mane of unruly hair to keep it down, and washed his face again.

He decided to wear cuff links, and dug out a white shirt in the back of the closet to accommodate them. The cuff links, a twenty-fifth-anniversary gift from his wife, were silver with polished shell interiors. He hadn't worn them in years, but now they seemed right. He knotted a Brooks Brothers tie that his daughter Sarah had given him.

When he finished, he got to his knees by the bed and prayed. The last time he had done that was also a lifetime ago, the day after Vi was diagnosed in Minneapolis at the neurology clinic. He remembered that day now. And now he felt an identical hollowness in his heart.

In his private moments, John Reimer did not often engage in prayer. But it was not often that he paid a visit to the alderman, either, and certain old habits were hard to break.

Chapter 37

Shortly after eleven John walked into the 44th Ward Office. He read the neat handbill in the glass front before pushing open the door:

> The Following are Against the Law in the Lakeview
> District: Panhandling, Open Liquor, Peddling, Use
> And Sale of Illegal Drugs, Posting of Flyers.

He looked around a well-lit work area formed by a short counter and a couple of desks behind it, no cubicles but empty space, minimum clutter. It was the very embodiment of the corporate good citizenship and decency conveyed in the handbill. *Talking the talk, walking the walk*, John mused.

A young man with wire rims and red hair cropped in the bowl-cut style of an Amazon Indian tribe looked up. His zipped backpack and bike helmet at the end of the counter suggested the day's work was done.

"Appointment with Alderman Fitzsimmons?" he asked. He spoke crisply, like an overachieving graduate student in a seminar. He was both authoritative and eager to please his superiors. John nodded. The young man unfolded his lanky frame from the chair and walked to the back of the office where he knocked on a closed door. "Yeah," came a muted voice from within.

"Name?" the assistant asked, looking back at John.

"Reimer, John Reimer, I'm the minister at Lakeview Mennonite and have an appointment."

"Yes, the minister," said the assistant, cracking the alderman's door a bit now, then returning to the counter. "He's expecting you."

The alderman came out of the office looking rumpled but successful. Even the khakis looked tailored. He wore Asics runners and had a fountain pen behind one ear.

He extended a hand to John and began. "You're the Amishman, I gather. Pardon me, Mennonite. Didn't we meet some years ago? I hear wonderful things about your congregation and have been meaning to come to one of the ministerial alliance breakfasts."

"Third Monday of each month," John smiled. "It's a nice gathering."

The alderman bubbled on. "I have to tell you, your people are known for their spirit of building community, I'm sure I'm not the first to tell you that. Mennonite Disaster Service? No one does it better. We need more like you. Come on in back here, what can I do for you? As you can imagine, this last week has been very hard in the neighborhood."

The assistant shouldered his backpack and fastened the chin strap under his helmet. "I'll lock on my way out," he told the alderman. "He's your last appointment this morning."

"Thanks," the alderman said. "See you Monday." He turned his attention completely to John. "Coffee?" He carried a mug with a Cubs logo to the Mr. Coffee machine beside his door. He poured it full and handed it to the minister. "Let's sit in the office."

There were no windows, but four tall barrister bookcases, full, and a few framed prints on the walls under little brass shaded lights. The photos of the skyline at midcentury seemed familiar, but there were others that seemed strange, including one that looked like a newspaper photo of a car crash but was indeed some kind of painting. It seemed to John unnecessarily morbid for a man in Fitzsimmons's state of affairs. A small crucifix hung beside a spacious generic calendar.

Diplomas and other framed certificates announcing various awards for community service clustered on the wall directly behind the alderman's desk, which bore a phone, a hefty Rolodex, and ringed loose-leaf binders in various states of assembly.

The condolence cards and a glass cylinder full of wilting roses stood on the oak surface of a shorter bookcase.

"I've received some very kind ministerial calls," Fitzsimmons said, putting on a pair of gold-rimmed bifocals. He let them ride down on his nose.

John nodded at the flowers. "It must have come as a tremendous shock."

"Have you ever lost someone close, Reverend?" the alderman asked, and then answered his own question, "Of course you have. This was a terrible thing. I hadn't seen my boy since he was eleven. One gets estranged by family circumstance, but never forgets. It's like I lost him, what, lost him twice."

"I think I understand." John thought he might share some thoughts about Vi, whose loss was stretching out now over a couple of decades, but he wasn't here on a mission of empathy. "But I guess I'm a little confused about several things, Mr. Fitzsimmons. Starting with the funeral service that the boy's great-aunt Helen asked me to do last Saturday."

The alderman removed his glasses and looked at John. "Okay," he said. "I'm pretty good at getting trash picked up in the ward. I'm a simple, direct man who can deal with those kinds of things. It's much less complicated than family affairs." He gave a pained smile. "How is Helen? Tell her if you see her that we need to get reacquainted. Now how can I help you this morning, Reverend?"

"I don't think you are that simple a man."

"Come again?" The pained smile on the alderman's face began to erode.

"I said you're not that simple. No, actually you are quite complex, and very smart."

"Reverend, can we cut to the chase here? Now what is it that you want?"

"Be patient, I'm coming to my point. Let me start with this."

John pulled a folded piece of white paper from his suit pocket, unfolded it on the desk surface, smoothed it out deliberately, and pushed it gently toward the alderman. He watched the man's face get pasty.

"Please tell me in your own words what it says, Mr. Fitzsimmons," John said. "A paraphrase. Could you be so kind?"

The alderman took a gulp of coffee and looked at John. "What is it that you want?"

"Feel free to keep that. It's a copy. You can put it in your dead boy's funeral album."

"You may be a man of the cloth, Reimer, but you're starting to act like a son of a bitch, you know that? I have better things to do."

"No, you don't. Not right now. Let me read this document for you. It says, 'Dear Dad.' You will notice the letter is not finished. He wrote a lot of other things, too, things you don't seem so interested in. I should let you know they do not corroborate the story you're floating around."

"Where did you get this?"

"There were many people who loved David and mourned his death. Which is a lot more than I can say about his father."

"You've got some fucking nerve." The alderman's face was going through transformations now, from fear to fury. "Okay, Helen got to you, that's what this is all about. That crusty old bitch. I should have known."

"Yes, I partly agree with you. *Crusty* pretty well sums her up. But she is only part of this story. Tell me, how estranged can a father and son get? Not even there to claim your own son's body. When did you decide it was politically feasible, and who told you?"

The alderman leaned forward with his mouth open.

"Let me finish. I'm still not clear on how the connection was finally made that you were his father. Is that something you let the inner circle in on?"

The alderman consulted his watch. "I don't have time for this shit."

"Yes, you do. You want to know what I know. Now hold your tongue and listen to me."

The alderman reached for his phone. John stood up and loomed over the desk, and his large hand closed over Fitzsimmons's, forcing the receiver back into the cradle. There was a brief struggle. It was the hand of a farmer crushing the hand of a lawyer, and for one moment John felt a great inner surge of justice. But rage stirred him, too—vicious unregenerate rage. He wanted to make this little man pay.

"You call whoever you want to after I leave," John said. "And only then."

The alderman pulled his shaking hand out from under John's vise-like grip and collapsed back into his chair.

"Thank you," John said. He removed the phone from the desk, receiver in its cradle, and then, for emphasis, ripped the cord out of the wall.

"Now. Let's start again. From the beginning. Your son was not gay. Your son was a young man you rejected and never talked to. And he was killed.

"I can't believe you would exploit your own son's murder for political gain, but that is precisely what you did. I have seen people get hurt in this life. I have seen bad things. But I have never seen anything this cold and this evil.

"Where I grew up in Kansas, when I was a boy, there was a lot of speculation about the unpardonable sin. You have perhaps shown me what it is."

Fitzsimmons tried to speak. "Hold on just one second."

John cut him off. "Shut up and hear me out. I don't think you killed your son, although for a while I did. And, yes, crusty Helen thought you were quite capable of doing such a thing. For a while, the extent of her anger is what made me mistrust her.

"But to my point. You were in the park that night, too, weren't you? Some late-night cruising, Alderman? Out to look at the stars? Or out for what they call a happy blow job? You tell me."

The alderman started at John's language.

"You didn't think I could talk that way, did you? You have nothing to say for yourself, pleading the Fifth, are you? No, you didn't kill your son. But what you did was more evil. You destroyed his identity and covered up your own. Your son wanted to talk with you, but you never let it happen.

"He just wanted to talk, do you hear me?" John's voice shook with rage. He waved the sheet of paper above the alderman's desk.

"He knew who you were, but you lied about him. You lied in order to win this coming election, a cheap, lousy, political campaign, and you made your son's sacrifice literally part of your platform. I have seen some things, Mr. Fitzsimmons, but never like this."

"Reimer, you're mistaken. This is outrageous."

John came around the side of the alderman's desk and leaned down to peer directly in the politician's face. He planted his hands on the chair's armrests and spoke. "Don't lie to me anymore, do you hear me? No more lies! To me or to anyone else."

"But . . ."

"Don't. Don't say it. Enough." John relaxed his grip on the armrests and walked back to his own chair. He sat down and spoke quietly. "It gets more interesting. Your son was not gay. Calling him that suited your purposes.

"And, Mr. Fitzsimmons, how about you? People are born different ways, with different orientations. Ten years ago I wouldn't have said any of this. What's wrong is not that you're homosexual, or that you found you couldn't live with your wife, or even that you abandoned your son—though that's pretty rotten in my book.

"It's that you lied. It's the lie that matters. And the idea that you would hide an identity of your own and create a false one for your son—if there is an unpardonable sin, and I don't know if there is, then that's it, you've done it."

Fitzsimmons said, "Are you finished, motherfucker?"

"Who killed your son?"

"I don't know."

"Your son followed you into the park that night. I think he was following you because he was afraid for you. You had been drinking, pretty steadily, for a couple of hours. You know he followed you, don't you? Did you recognize him? He went to meetings, he saw you on the job, you know. He knew a lot about you. There were a couple of things he was curious about, though."

"Like what?"

"Like how a man so principled about police procedure in his ward could be corrupted by the zoning board and the developers. Perhaps your own personal accounting system to balance your virtue with your vice? My own theory is this: simple greed gets a lot of us, and most of us learn to ethically posture at the proper moment. Look, neither of us is a virgin. For crying out loud, this is Chicago. You shun the media spotlight so that when you're in it you can bask in your humble virtue. You pathetic fake. Did you ever hear the line about whited sepulchers?" John pointed at the crucifix behind Fitzsimmons's head. "He was describing people like you."

"I don't know what you're talking about. You're mad."

"I'm angry, I'm not mad. And I know for a certainty that your dead son was afraid you would get blackmailed for cruising."

Fitzsimmons shouted. "That is a bald-faced lie! How do you know this?"

John quietly continued. "Was there someone in the police department? Is there someone in the police who knows now and who you're paying off? Or does someone out there want to whack you because you've stepped on toes in the precinct office? That is one of the virtuous planks in your platform, Mr. Alderman. And if the police are torturing people, you end up looking pretty good, don't you, if your investigation of them hits pay dirt?

"Tell me, though, I'm not so clear on this. David suspected there was a cop who had it in for you. Someone in particular."

"Are you threatening me, Mr. Reimer? Because if you are . . ."

"I am not threatening you. I am asking the questions David would ask were he alive now. That's what I'm doing."

"You crazy fucking Mennonite. I should have you locked up."

John said, "I can give you the rest of the copies of David's papers if you're interested."

"You can't blackmail me."

"This isn't blackmail. I'm trying to explain a few things. You lack a cooperative spirit, Mr. Fitzsimmons."

"Enough," Fitzsimmons said, finding the will to rise to his feet. "Nobody is going to believe your cockamamie bullshit, you hear me? Nobody."

"Who said I would talk with anyone but you?"

The alderman was all business now. "My citizens' hours on Saturday run nine to twelve and it's twelve now. I have a ward to serve and a campaign to run. Time for you to run along. And you should know I'll be keeping an eye on you."

"No," John said, on his way to the door. "I think it's the other way around."

"I'll be sending you the bill for the phone repair."

"No, you won't."

John's rage had left him. He looked at the alderman who let him out the front door of the office to the street. Physically they stood very close, so close that John could see, and smell, the alderman sweat. For one pulsing moment John wished he could drop the pacifist mantle and smash this lawyer's face into the pavement outside, once, twice, grind the man's nose in his own blood and make him pay.

His brother Andrew had always told him violence accomplished nothing. John felt empty. He wanted to tell Andrew that words weren't any better.

Fitzsimmons turned away behind the handbill on the glass door that forbade liquor, panhandling, drugs, and peddling. The key turned in the lock.

Liberal leadership, John thought, *has its privileges.*

Chapter 38

THE BLANKET OF FOG coasted in, swirling, and dropped down on the land mass. It bejeweled the lights on Lake Shore Drive, enveloped the cars which moved in little isolated pockets of speed toward their unknown destinations. It quieted their sound and subdued them in the larger frame of nature. The fog worked like a palette knife, smearing all detail into a uniform smudge.

John watched the traffic and wondered what kinds of people drove after midnight. What kinds of transactions awaited them? Who would they encounter when they stopped? All at once he grew afraid. At the Irving Park Road intersection, he nearly turned back, and then forced himself to press on. He ran in a slow jog toward the lake in black sweats and a black stocking cap, to all appearances a silly aging ninja. He zipped up the front of his windbreaker and pulled the nylon hood over his cap.

He gazed at the Kwanusila thunderbird above on the totem pole, and the human immediately below gripping the harpoon. Leviathan, immutable and inscrutable, bore them all on his back. Fog settled at the base, causing it all to appear as if floating in a strange sea.

He slowed to a walk and continued toward the green of the park, except that the green was now black and the birds in the sanctuary did not sing. The archery range lay silent.

Though I walk through the valley of the shadow.

He thought of David Talbot and he thought of the other David, the warrior David, walking alone onto the field, looking a little absurd himself, the unassuming farm boy who would slaughter Philistines like grouse, screaming through the blood and battle-ax the name of Yahweh. Slashing off foreskins and carrying them back in triumph to Jerusalem.

At the core of the warrior king, John thought, stirred the solitude and isolation of the prairie.

He knew that solitude. *Though I walk through the valley of . . . Thy rod and thy . . .* The problem was, courage provided no guarantees. Talbot hadn't lacked for courage when somebody smashed his skull and carved him up.

On the farm, John had carried a .22 or a carbine when he went out at night to find coyotes. They were elusive, but he was patient. Sometimes they remained invisible for hours, but he had learned the virtue of waiting. Now he carried nothing. He wondered what kind of coyote, what kind of animal, he would find tonight at the Waveland Golf clubhouse.

To the south, the Loop skyscrapers appeared as a vague, glowing mass that periodically achieved the definition of orderly dots of light but then melted back into the inchoate glow of the mist. Across the expanse of the softball fields, the fog drifted like torn patches of bedding carried in from the black water, affording a surreal and shredded light of a minimal kind available only to fully adjusted night vision. The globe lamps, eight of them between the bird sanctuary and the tennis courts, emerged as feeble beacons. John used the available light and pondered the layout of these grounds that he had memorized earlier in the afternoon.

Ahead, the clock face in the clubhouse tower glowed yellow like the unpupiled eye of a night predator, its numerals undecipherable. As far back as John could recall, it had never kept good time, but its face was always lit up.

The clubhouse buildings on the Waveland—which had been renamed the Marovitz, but no one ever called it that—had been constructed for the World's Fair of 1933. All the structures—the starter shack and concession stand, even the bathroom facility with its peaked row of leaded windows—showed the uniform faux Gothic design, and the comprehensiveness of the architects' plan made it easy to forget that this little world was part of Chicago at all.

The notched battlement profiles fronting the slate roofs could only barely be made out in the dark. John walked slowly, straining to see, then headed toward the water, with the clubhouse off to his left fifty yards away, and the maintenance buildings to his right shrouded in a large cluster of old-growth hickories and oaks.

He could hear the water lap on the stonework of the lakefront. The fog, patchier now, broke up and reconstituted itself like a primordial living thing.

John looked at his watch dial: still not quite one. He wondered if he had already been spotted and where his contact would appear. If the fog broke up any more, he could possibly spot the person arrive.

The obvious question now was who was stalking whom. John swung a leg over the low stone wall and sat down on the rock escarpment leading to the water itself. Then, listening to the waves, he turned back to watch the clubhouse.

He knew its layout by heart. On this side, a series of stone arched porticoes hid a recessed, urine-soaked stone floor. Peaked windows inside the portico enclosure revealed the Waveland Pro Shop, not yet open for the new season.

Around the corner of the portico, on the north end, a concrete ramp ran down to the clubhouse basement for storage of maintenance equipment and tractor mowers. Partly obscured by trimmed shrubs, the ramp managed to achieve near-perfect invisibility even in the daytime until you stumbled onto it, a concrete slope slanted down to the padlocked wooden doors twelve feet below ground level. It made John think of a cattle chute, and he didn't like it.

The coyote might be there, but other possibilities intruded. He could be out here on the lake walkway, just around the bend. He could be a hundred yards away crouched down against the stonework, or he could be passing time in the restroom. The Depression-era designers had determined that even taking a piss ought to attain a certain dignity; thirteen solid marble stalls with archways over each toilet door ran the length of the mosaic tile floor. Opposite the stalls, a row of urinals as big as sarcophagi beckoned. Was it possible to turn the activity of relieving oneself into high church ritual? John had wondered earlier in the afternoon, standing there, feeling as if he were inside an Anglican church choirboys' loft.

Now he thought one of those stalls would be a good place to wait, or to kill somebody. John began to shiver. He blew into his gloves and flexed his hands, and moved around restlessly behind the wall.

He couldn't see the patrol car ease slowly down the road beyond the clubhouse, its lights off, and disappear south into the fog. John drifted into reverie. He felt his concentration lapse. He thought of Nancy, and he imagined she would be very warm.

When he saw the ember of a cigarette glow under the clubhouse porticoes he ducked down beneath the wall and cautiously looked again. The direction of the wind, blowing in from the lake, did not allow him to pick up any scent.

There it was again, that glow. He dropped down two steps on the walkway so his head would not show above the wall and he moved quickly two hundred yards south before peering over it again. Now the clubhouse was invisible, out of range. He picked up two golf-ball-size chunks of concrete from crumbling masonry at the wall's base and put them in his pockets. Then, with both hands on the wall, he swung easily over onto the other side. He walked inland, circling back toward the clubhouse, glad for the fog now.

He didn't want to approach the porticoes frontally from the water's edge, but from around the corner of the main building. At the northeast corner of the building, he waited another fifteen minutes. The bushes and concrete maintenance ramp were behind him. He waited to smell the smoke from the cigarette and wished for a break in the cloud cover, for just a little moonlight.

He was torn between the need to keep a good distance and his desire to see a face. He debated what to do if the coyote decided to take a stroll around the building. He realized he didn't have a clear plan.

At exactly two o'clock in the morning, John removed both his gloves and took one of the concrete chunks out of his pocket. He hefted the rock in his right hand, stood a little bit away from the building's corner, and took careful aim. It was a good throw; the rock arced through the fog and struck the slate roof of the starter shack. It made the sound of a flat wooden ruler slapping a desktop but there was a crunch, too, and John figured he had broken a shingle. He waited twenty seconds and then threw the other rock. Once more he drilled the roof of the starter shack, this time with more conviction.

And this flushed the coyote. A figure stepped away from the porticoes and walked slowly toward the starter shack, stopped midway on the cropped lawn, and turned around.

He took a slow drag on his cigarette, making the glowing ember tip flare. He tossed the butt away on the green. Looking in the direction where John stood, he said, "Old man, you're good, but you're not that good. Hell of an arm, though. Now step away from the building so I can see you. I know you're not in the starter shack."

John could not make out a face, but the voice he knew.

The fog turned ragged and John looked up where the moon now traced a circle in the churning gray thickness of cloud, tight whorls like the surface of a brain. The figure on the green took something out of his jacket pocket and spoke again.

"Okay, you can come out on your own, or I can walk over there and stick the barrel of this gun up your ass. Which do you prefer?"

He waited a moment and resumed speaking. "Glad you got my message. I was hoping we could meet like this. And don't even think about running. I know you're in shape, old man, but I'm a lot faster than you are. I would like to make this as painless as possible."

John stepped out from the protective corner of the building. "Shanahan," he said. "I expected it would be you."

"Let me tell you something," the detective said, flipping the object he held from one hand to the other. "You impress me with your mental quickness. But you're also something of a bungler. Like showing up here tonight, you dumb fuck. You haven't learned the difference between bravery and smarts, but then you never had combat training. I can understand. You don't know when or how to stop yourself. I had you pegged for it."

Forty yards of inconsistent fog separated them. Nearly half a football field. John debated how to conduct the interview, and decided which direction would be best to run, if he had to. He thought of stepping back behind the corner of the building and making a full-out sprint for Lake Shore Drive. But the odds were not good. Then again, getting off a clear shot in these conditions wasn't a sure thing, either.

John found his voice. "You think I'm alone. Think again. I may be a farmer to you, but I'm not completely stupid."

"Yeah, I've heard all that cowboy lore you've fed Kerdigan." Shanahan lit up another cigarette. The glow of the lighter briefly illuminated his shadowed face and the blue metal of a pistol in his hand. The steel top of the lighter snapped shut. "Speak up a little bit when you talk. I want to hear you. I've staked out this place since midnight so you have nowhere else to go and no one else to talk to."

"You would like to be sure of that, wouldn't you?"

Shanahan laughed but he didn't come any closer. John's heart beat a tattoo under his sweatshirt. He found his voice again, the preacher's voice.

"You killed Talbot. You killed a kid on a bike. At the time, you didn't know he was the alderman's son. What did he say to you that made you so angry?"

Shanahan was silent and John continued. "It's interesting, because you went into the park that night to nail the father, to blackmail him. You followed him out of Ann Sather's. You didn't know the bike messenger kid sitting at the bar was his son, did you? Well, don't feel bad, very few people did know.

"You wanted to take down the father." John paused for effect. "Instead, you got the son. How am I doing so far?"

The figure was silent.

John resumed. "Fitzsimmons knew about the water and wire torture going on at headquarters. Were you a part of that, Shanahan? I'm betting you were. So Fitzsimmons started to ask questions because these practices did not reflect well on his leadership in the 44th Ward. His enlightened liberal constituency would not tolerate it, no, not in their ward.

"Fitzsimmons actually wanted to clean up the Chicago police department. Pardon my barnyard language here, but he either was incredibly naïve or had a bigger set of balls than anyone gives him credit for. He wanted to be known as a decent man, a reformer, a man of judicious but principled action."

Shanahan laughed again. "Preach on, Reverend. I'm listening."

"It was dumb and idealistic, and you have to wonder if the alderman understood the weight of Chicago history. Still, it was also a product of incredible ambition. Had he pulled it off, he'd have a clear path to becoming the next mayor."

Shanahan tossed his pistol back and forth between his hands, bored. "Yeah, I'm still listening. But wrap it up in the next thirty minutes, okay? This isn't your pulpit on Sunday morning."

John said, "It was of course much more complicated than this. You were on to him about the zoning board dealings. Even better—ideal, in fact, for your purposes—you knew he was a closet homosexual. A man proud to flaunt his liberal tolerance but terrified of coming out. Something of an anachronism, I know, for this community. A kind of flipped version of Roy Cohn. The world provides us with many strange examples of human behavior, does it not?

"But to continue with how you fit into all of this, Mr. Shanahan. You worked vice years ago, didn't you? Where did you first run into the alderman? Over here in these marble bathroom stalls? You had him where you wanted him. One thing I wonder about. Did you proposition him or was it the other way around? How did that first encounter go?"

"Don't get cute, Reimer. You're starting to annoy me."

John watched Shanahan play with the pistol as he continued to speak. He wondered if he could dive behind the corner of the building before Shanahan tried to pot him. He was grateful to keep the distance.

"So you killed the boy in the park, who had somehow come between you and the father. You wanted the father, but you got the son, and after you killed him in a fit of rage you thought fast enough to make it look like a hate crime. You would know how to do it, wouldn't you? Nothing like being on the inside of the investigation. Did anyone in Area 3 see through the, what do you call it . . ."

"The copycat?"

"Yes, the copycat. Thank you. I'm guessing they didn't all believe it." John waited for a response but heard only a grunt. He continued. "You must have been livid after the alderman used the boy's death to his own advantage. You hadn't anticipated that one. How could you? The alderman's cleverness and audacity were breathtaking, even for you, and you've seen it all, I mean . . ."

"Your time is about to expire, Reverend. Wrap it up."

"I knew it was you when you interrogated me after Chris's death. You got carried away there, the passion started to outstrip the reasoned planning. You went a little bit too far.

"I figured it had to be someone on the inside. I began to understand why so many of my friends think of the police as the Gestapo. I had talked with Kerdigan about Chris, and next morning, just hours later, Chris is found under the L tracks in Uptown. Almost obvious. Coincidence? I don't think so.

"I'm curious. What did Chris tell you he saw the night of David's murder, just before he discovered the boy's bicycle and rode off with it? Did he tell you anything before you killed him? Did he mention me?"

"I was coming for you before that talk, Reverend. I knew from the start you'd be a problem."

"You knew I had to be silenced, but why? These were extreme measures, don't you think? The bullets in the window, the slashed tires, even a car bomb. Was I such a threat? You threw some very heavy stuff at a humble preacher."

"Reverend, shutting you down was essential. It was a matter of finding the right time. Actually, I still have no idea about those window shots, if you really want to know. But it's time now for us to get on with our business."

John imagined he could see Shanahan smile and then figured out he was actually seeing the curl of the man's lip. The fog had cleared and the man standing forty yards away had a loaded weapon and no doubt would prove a very good shot, and the only reason John was still alive was because this psychopath had lived the preceding minutes in some unpredictable bubble of patience and grace.

That bubble was about to pop. "Step away from the building where I can see you." Shanahan motioned with the pistol, waving it like a school traffic cop waves a wand. He took something out of his pocket now and screwed it onto the barrel, extending the length of the weapon by another eight inches.

Shanahan's voice rang out now, hard and unyielding. "Take off your clothes, starting with your shoes. Put them in a nice, neat pile. I would like to make your body a public example. Sorry I have to do this."

John froze, like a rabbit caught in the searchlight atop the cab of a pickup truck, waiting in a stubble field to be blasted by the hunter's lead bullet. Time slowed down. He had killed rabbits this way once in winter, when he was twelve and on the farm. As he stooped to unlace his shoes, moving now in uncoordinated panic, he recalled borrowing his neighbor's .30–06 rifle once for the novelty. Andrew had shaken his head when John brought the eviscerated frozen carcasses into the barn where Andrew milked the cows, and his older brother had said, "Don't do it again. It's not right." And John had said, "I won't."

Shanahan's voice returned him to the present moment. "Good. You're doing nicely. Now I am going to march you over to one of those pretty bathroom stalls to shoot you in the head. I need to make you quiet and then I will write some messages on you. We will give the people the word. Surely as a minister you understand. Have I made myself clear?"

John stood in his boxers under the moonlight and Shanahan was in motion and could not have been more than thirty yards away when John said in low tones to himself, "Okay, it better be now, come on, man."

Then he heard the tread of someone big behind him, and the shambling figure of Bill Kerdigan stepped into the clearing directly to his left, and his voice rang out. "No, you don't."

Kerdigan's big coat flapped as he ran up beside John, and then John felt a heavy hand on his shoulder rudely shove him to the ground.

Shanahan ran toward them now, pistol raised, and Kerdigan stepped in front of John and swung up in one easy motion from under his coat the sawed-off twin barrel of a twelve-gauge shotgun and crouched and fired from the hip once, twice. The roar of successive blasts next to John's ear made the world go suddenly silent, but he could see through the curl of smoke from the gun barrels the figure of Shanahan tumble on the dark grass, cartwheel almost, then miraculously land on its feet. And resume motion toward them, in a kind of broken but relentless lope.

"My, my," Shanahan said. "How on earth could you miss with that thing, Bill? Gentlemen, I'm afraid you're toast." He raised the pistol and fired once as he walked, the flash from the muzzle sharp yellow against the night, but the aim was high. He chuckled. "That was on purpose," he said. "Just a practice round. The next shots are for real." He continued his walk toward them, but the shots didn't come, rather a repeated clicking from the weapon, and the limp grew more pronounced.

"Fuck!" Kerdigan said under his breath, and John could see he was fumbling badly as he ejected the spent shells and tried to reload, then he gave up and dropped the shotgun and went into a two-hand stance with his standard-issue Glock aimed at Shanahan's advancing figure, firing three, four times, but the cloud cover once again killed the light of the moon and Shanahan was zigzagging. Kerdigan pulled shells out of his coat pocket and shoved them in John's chest. "Dammit, John, give me a little backup here. Do you know how to reload?"

John tasted fear, then Shanahan was gone, evaporated as if by magic, raptured from the field of battle.

"His gun must have jammed," Kerdigan said. "Miracles happen. But where the fuck did he go?"

"What did you say?" John was holding his ears, still ringing, then he witnessed his hands move like foreign objects, scrabbling in the wet grass to pick up the shotgun, and moving with muscle memory to eject the spent shells.

"Where is he?" Kerdigan repeated. "This is not good." The men stood back to back, straining to see. "Dammit, if we don't get cover we're dead."

Scrambling after Kerdigan in a low crouch to the north corner of the clubhouse, John leaned against the building and pushed two shells into the shotgun chambers, all muscle memory. "Here," he said, handing the weapon to Bill. Bill peered around the corner of the building and motioned for John to follow. John thought, *We're making far too much noise, not smart*, and he was right, but he didn't figure out Shanahan's angle of attack or the timing of it until the big lieutenant was on them and it was too late.

It was the blind spot by the sloped concrete runway that led up beside the clipped shrubbery, from the bowels of the clubhouse. At that exact moment, when they arrived there, John thought, *Yes, of course, this would be the place.* Shanahan came out of the ramp like a bull out of a chute, a projectile on afterburner, and Kerdigan took the hit on his side in the split second after he sensed the direction of the assault. He had no time to react, much less turn or swivel the shotgun into the face of his assailant.

Nevertheless he tried. Shanahan smashed into him with a full body tackle, and then they were grappling in the grass, like furious beasts, for their lives. Kerdigan was lucky to hold onto the shotgun. Shanahan grabbed its short barrel and pointed it away from himself, and even though Bill exerted tremendous torque on the stock and the lower part of the twin barrel, his effort to twist it toward his target was in vain. Shanahan was too strong. The barrels pointed skyward just as Kerdigan's finger hit the trigger and emptied the first chamber. The blast staggered all three men. Then the clouds parted around the moon and John could see Shanahan's bloody face, one side looking as if it had been scraped across a dirty sidewalk. The shotgun had done damage already, but judging by Shanahan's ferocious energy, not enough.

Kerdigan was bigger, but also unfortunately two decades older than his assailant, and now Shanahan's right hand closed over the end of the shotgun as he and Kerdigan fought. The younger man struggled to get Kerdigan in a neck lock, and Kerdigan saw the enemy's hand close on the end of the barrel, and just before the lieutenant could get it off the scorching hot metal that toasted his fingers, Kerdigan managed to thumb the second trigger.

The blast tore off a chunk of Shanahan's hand. There was a brief moment of silence and then a shrill scream erupted from his throat.

But Shanahan wasn't finished yet. Kerdigan went for his pistol at the same time the lieutenant brought out a serrated knife. With his other hand, now just a partially functioning stump of gristle and spouting blood, Shanahan managed to neutralize the motion of the pistol. With his remaining good hand he brought the knife up above his head, ready to plunge down into Kerdigan's chest. The older man rolled sideways and missed the point of the knife, and then he was shouting at John, "Pick up the shotgun, for God's sake! Use it!"

Time slowed once more. John saw Shanahan's arm raised again, bearing down with the knife, and then he gripped the barrel end of the shotgun and swung the heavy stock like a baseball bat at the kneeling figure of the lieutenant. All John could think in that moment was that he wanted to smash the man's head like a melon, but Shanahan was too fast; he instinctively ducked when he heard Kerdigan shouting directions, and the stock of the shotgun only grazed the crown of his head.

It was John and Bill's good fortune that the continuing arc of that desperate swing carried through and sent the knife spinning away out of Shanahan's grip and into the darkness. Line drive.

"Pacifist, my ass," Shanahan snarled.

Still gripping the shotgun, John launched himself at the killer. The dimension of time disappeared entirely. John thought, *I knocked the knife loose. Maybe all the blood made the handle slippery.* There was a slick of blood everywhere. Maybe it was the element of surprise. Shanahan to that point had been fighting one, not two men. Now it was a melee of a deadly and confused threesome, nothing but darkness and wet grass and grunting, mortally angry men. The Glock was firing, again, uncontrollably, impossibly, in every direction, as Shanahan and Bill fought to control it. It, too, was slippery with blood.

The dimension of time disappeared entirely, all that was left was bloody, primal space, moves, countermoves, futility. The Glock stopped firing. Hands and knees and elbows were the principal weapons. The three-way fight made no sense. In the scrum, John felt a hard kneecap jolt his groin with shattering force and found himself wondering where his jockstrap was, just a little bit of protection would be nice, and he brought his knees up and legs together in a perfect sideways fetal crouch before someone's hand was on his face, the fingers inside his mouth trying to tear his head off.

His head torqued sideways and sudden pain exploded in his neck, and the probing hand was trying to gouge his eyes, and he pushed it away, desperate, and then the fingers were back in his mouth, pulling the inside of his cheek as if it were the handle of his own demise. And since, if he wanted to live, there was nothing left for him to do but bite down as hard as he could on the invading fingers, he did just that.

He felt the crunch of breaking bone. He could feel it vibrate through his jaw and then another scream split the night. With enormous feral power he bit down even harder and the scream soared impossibly higher.

Then Shanahan wrenched himself free. John felt a pounding in his temple and thought he was going to have a heart attack. But he also sensed the animal's will to keep fighting had broken. Shanahan struggled to his feet and staggered away from the bruised arena of the struggle, holding his maimed paws to his chest. The man broke into a run away from the clubhouse.

Kerdigan sat up in his bloody, dirty trench coat, sat up, fished for a fresh clip in his front pocket, and rammed it into the Glock. He tried to get a firm grip on the slippery weapon and while still sitting, propped his elbows on his knees to steady himself. He took aim at the retreating figure. He was in no shape to give pursuit.

One shot, two. Both misses. He was pulling the trigger a third time when it was John's turn to say, quietly, "No, let him go, he's an animal, don't kill him!" and Kerdigan tried to comprehend as the smaller man, still clothed in nothing but his boxer shorts, leaned over and pushed the barrel of the gun down and away.

"What are you doing?" Kerdigan said in disbelief.

"Let him go, Bill. Let him go." John took the pistol from Kerdigan's hand, and extended his other hand to help the old detective to his feet.

Kerdigan stood up. "Give me that," he said. Then he smacked John across the face with the open palm of his hand. The slap seemed to correct the crick in John's neck. "You stupid fuck, I had him in my sights."

"He's done," John said, "he's finished. He's a wounded animal. Let him go. Call it in."

Kerdigan attempted to slap him again, and John stopped the hand this time with his own. "Let it go, Bill. Just stop."

"You piece of shit, I had him, what the fuck is wrong with you? Why did you call me in the first place if you didn't want to finish the job?"

John didn't answer. Shivering, he began to put on his clothes. The big man, breathing hoarsely, walked a few yards away and brought back the knife. Holding it by its tip, he gave it to John. "Here," he said. "It's yours. Take it."

John shook his head. "I want nothing to do with it."

"Take it," Kerdigan said. "It's a Vaari. It's one of the finest made." Then he continued, "You saved my life, John. It's the least I can offer you. Consider it a small token of my respect and gratitude. Seriously."

"Well, actually, I think you saved mine. So thank you. Now let's go before we get sentimental."

They gathered up the remaining shells and casings and looked for pieces of Shanahan's fingers and then they walked back to Kerdigan's police cruiser, where he got on the radio.

Kerdigan was all business. He called in the coordinates and the identity of the suspect and then there was a pause. He listened for a bit and said, "Yeah, that's correct. Shanahan. Mark Shanahan. Yes, what about Reimer?" He glanced over at John who sat in the passenger seat of the cruiser, testing to see if he could still open and close his jaw without too much pain.

"Yeah," Kerdigan said. "Reimer was correct. Ten-four." He clicked out. Then he turned and looked at John again, and he was fierce when he spoke. "I'm sorry I hit you. But why did you call me if you didn't want my help?"

John rolled down the window and spit some blood and part of what seemed to be someone's pinky out the window. One of his molars was slightly loose. He tested it with his tongue, and looked at Bill.

"I called you because I didn't know who else to trust. You didn't bring the SWAT team. Why not?"

"Because you told me not to, you prick," Kerdigan said. "I trusted you, too. Did that ever cross your mind?"

John zipped up his windbreaker and spit more blood out the window. He put on his black stocking cap. Kerdigan leaned over and ran his big thumb across John's eyebrow. "He nearly popped your skin open right there. That's gonna be a doozy in the morning."

"Bill, thank you. I don't know how to say it. You put yourself on the line for me."

Kerdigan couldn't handle the moment. He said, "It was for you, John. And it was . . . for my brother. Louis said if anything happened to you . . . he would never forgive me." Then Bill looked away and pretended to take some grit out of his eye.

They drove on Lake Shore Drive. The sound of the sparse traffic ebbing and flowing around them made a gentle shushing noise.

"Will they find him?" John said.

"Yeah," said Kerdigan, after a moment. "Probably. I doubt if he's going to be alive. But still, you didn't let me do what I needed to do."

"I don't believe in that."

"John, I'm puzzled. I agree with you that he's an animal. But what kind of hunting ethics did your daddy teach you?"

"What do you mean?"

"In my world if you have a mad dog, if you have a wounded animal, there is only one thing to do." Kerdigan paused. "You put him down. It's called mercy."

Chapter 39

MONDAY MORNING. JOHN TOOK a back booth at the Melrose and contemplated a short stack of whole-wheat pancakes about to receive an anointing of butter and syrup. He would have preferred sitting outdoors, as he had just over a week earlier, when a young woman from Ohio came to him with her tale of woe.

He pushed the papers aside at his elbow. He tried not to think about yesterday's wretched sermon, the odd looks of his parishioners as they shook his hand on the way out.

Outside the rain was turning heavy. The drops formed rivulets that wormed their way in shifting patterns down the glass. John looked up. Alex refilled his coffee.

"Kerdigan was in here this morning at six," she said. "He had his arm in a sling."

"What happened?"

Alex smiled. "You mean you don't know? He said he hurt it playing racquetball with you. Said you have become a tougher competitor. Who would have guessed that's what you preachers do on weekends?"

John drank some coffee. "Kerdigan is an old man. I tell him he needs to slow down, but you know how well he listens."

Alex gave an eye roll. She looked more closely at John's face and said, "Must have been a really rough game."

John said, "He brings out the competitor. By the way, is Annie in this morning?"

"I wanted to tell you. She started calling in sick, not explaining. Two days in a row. The boss lost patience. I'm sorry, but she doesn't work here anymore."

"She still in Chicago?"

"I think so," Alex said. "But she was talking about moving back home."

John put the blueberry syrup over the pancakes and ate a little. He turned to the Metro section of the *Tribune* and saw the lead story:

DETECTIVE SLAIN IN SOUTH SIDE SHOOT-OUT

One of Chicago's "very finest" is how colleagues of slain detective Mark Shanahan describe the 49-year-old officer killed in a hail of automatic gunfire yesterday morning on the 7000 block of South Bell.

Shanahan, a twenty-five-year veteran with the Chicago Police Department, is the first officer killed in the line of duty this year.

Several suspects are being held for questioning about the shooting, which left two other persons dead and three wounded, including several individuals described as drug lords by the Police Department.

"Shanahan was one of the very best, always a stand-out cop," said Sergeant William Kerdigan of the Violent Crimes division after the incident yesterday. "He was not the kind of guy who wrote memos or asked his superiors for help or avoided the hard assignments. Mark always wanted to go out and take care of business himself."

That is apparently what happened in the early hours of yesterday morning, around 5 a.m., when Shanahan walked alone into a meeting of drug kingpins, which erupted in violence moments later. Residents of the area described the noise of weapons fire as "deafening" and said it lasted intermittently for almost ten minutes before police cruisers from Area 2 headquarters arrived on the scene.

Officers found three bodies, one of them Shanahan's, inside the two-story frame house. "The gunfire inside was what we would call torrential," is how Detective Kenny Trujillo described the scene. "He didn't stand a chance."

Shanahan began his career in the Chicago Police Department after serving two tours of duty as a Green Beret in Vietnam. His promotion within the department was swift, beginning with work on the Vice Squad and then the last 15 years in the Area 3 Violent Crimes division.

A firearms specialist, he had a reputation for extraordinary integrity and courage. At the time of his death, he was serving as part of the special task force investigating the spree killings that began in Chicago's Lakeview and Lincoln Park neighborhoods last fall.

"You felt safer around Mark," one of his friends said. "He was the kind of leader who always inspired confidence, who liked to say, 'We can do this thing, and do it right.' He was a cop's cop."

A funeral at City Hall with full honor guard is scheduled for Wednesday of this week.

John looked at Mark Shanahan's picture.

Alex came back and surveyed the untouched pancakes. "Is everything all right?"

"Just taking my time. Speaking of old men, I'm feeling a little achy myself. A man can overdo the workouts, you know." John pointed to the picture. "Ever see this man in here?"

"I have to admit," Alex said, "these cops start to look alike to me." She looked at the picture again. "This one's very handsome, though. Sad story."

"Very," John said.

"He might have been a hot date for a middle-aged girl like me."

"I think that is quite possible," John said. "And did you notice the alderman is twenty points ahead in the race?"

"I don't read that fast." Alex straightened the napkins, ketchup, and hot sauce, the salt and pepper, in the table's stainless-steel cozy rack.

John drank some coffee and looked Alex straight in the eyes. She said to him, "John, did you find out everything Annie wanted you to?"

"I did, yes."

"Good," Alex said. "I had confidence you would."

He toyed with the pancakes for a while then left some bills on the table and walked home through the rain. His umbrella was crumpling and he was wet by the time he arrived at the apartment, but he didn't care. He dialed Annie's number. Someone else answered.

"Annie?"

"No, this is Ruth Ann. Annie doesn't live here anymore."

"She moved?"

"Yeah, she went home. Who is this, anyway?"

"A friend. John Reimer. Did she leave an address?"

"No. All I know is it's in Fly, Ohio. Sorry."

"You don't have a number, anything?"

The woman on the line hesitated. "She mentioned a place called the Seven and Eight Tavern. You might call information."

"Thanks for your help. Tell her if she calls that I'd like to hear from her."

"Okay, I will."

"Goodbye."

198 DAVID SAUL BERGMAN

He hadn't been making things up when he told Alex about an ache. He knew he would have to see a dentist. He might have gone to bed yesterday after the morning church service, slept for four hours, and then chased the nap with some hot chicken broth. That would have been the wise course of action.

He needed to take better care of himself, as Nancy would say.

He had to sort out what, and what not, to tell Nancy. That was going to get interesting.

Chapter 40

He felt restless, or maybe even agitated and slightly sick. Breakfast at the Melrose, the *Tribune* story about Shanahan, the news about Annie—it was all too much. He could not face the week, toiling through the notes on his desk, the vain, half-baked scribblings about the unpardonable sin that lay there on torn sheets of legal pad, all of it unfinished, awaiting further revelation.

He had not felt a Monday this heavy in some time. Then he went into his church office to sort through Saturday's unread mail.

There was a letter from Meadows nursing home. He opened it up.

It was about Vi. The hospice care unit needed a consultation with the spouse, the medical power of attorney. Vi had been choking consistently at mealtimes and had stopped eating for several days. "As you know, Reverend Reimer, this is a common trajectory for the disease in its late phase," the letter continued.

That would have been since Monday or Tuesday, John estimated. He wondered why on earth they hadn't called. Perhaps they didn't want to leave a message. He hadn't exactly been available around the clock, either. All that time spent at Nancy's place. Twinge of guilt. The letter said they preferred to speak with him in person before he made any decision but attached to the letter was a medical release form: fine print, and two boxes, one of which needed to be checked, the line for his signature, the official addressed return envelope.

He put the letter down on the desk and couldn't look at it. He walked around his apartment and circled back to his study and picked the letter up again and dialed the number for hospice. He got Vi's supervising nurse on the line.

"I'm surprised I didn't receive a call," he said. He listened patiently to the response, and then asked, "What are the options at this point?"

He listened some more.

"No, not a feeding tube," he said. "I think that is already in your paper-work. No. She didn't want that. Say again?"

Then he said, "Yes, if that is your recommendation. Of course, order the morphine."

"She will be comfortable," the nurse said.

"Make it a healthy dose," John replied, "there is no longer any point in prolonging this." And yes, he said, he would fax the forms with his signature from the machine in the church office, and in a few hours he would get in his car and drive south through the fields of corn and soybeans and clover to be with her by sundown.

"Days?" he asked the nurse.

"Days into weeks," the nurse explained. "Maybe months." She said it was impossible to predict these things and then told him in her trained, therapeutic voice that no one, not even the medical professionals, can con-trol the final narrative.

John nodded and smiled. He knew that all right, but it was good at the moment to hear it from someone else. "Thank you for those words," he said.

After he hung up, he signed the forms and put an X in all the right boxes and went down to the church office and faxed the paperwork over. He walked heavily upstairs and dressed in his running clothes. He told himself he was not going to fall apart.

He walked to the lakefront.

Then he ran, stopwatch in hand, harder than he had ever run before in his life. Passing the thunderbird totem, he thought it appeared to float vertically, a compass in the landscape, and he took comfort in its fierce painted eye.

The eye of the thunderbird sees clearly, John thought, *almost as clearly as the boy from Meade.* With vision this good, he felt he could see to the other side of Lake Michigan. He turned south and looked once at the watch.

The sound of his shoes on the wet path beat a rhythm. By the time he sprinted in a finishing rush past the rocks at Fullerton, the merging of sky and water and the jagged outline of the city's massed concrete shoulders made him forget temporarily who he was, which was fine, because a man in his condition needed respite from the unrelenting workings of the brain.

It was spring on Lake Michigan, with a hint of sun. A single red-winged blackbird trilled in the trees, calling out for a mate.

John's chest heaved with effort. He remembered to look at the watch.

He looked, and then he looked again. It would be difficult to improve on that time. Walking up Fullerton Avenue, gripping the stopwatch, he wished there were someone he could tell.

About the Author

DAVID SAUL BERGMAN is the pen name for the literary collaboration of Daniel Born and Dale Suderman. Born, who teaches literature at Northwestern University's School of Professional Studies, is the author of *The Birth of Liberal Guilt in the English Novel: Charles Dickens to H. G. Wells*. His essays and fiction have appeared in *Fiction*, *Sojourners*, *Novel*, the *New York Times*, and the *Chronicle of Higher Education*. He is a former vice president at the Great Books Foundation and was editor of *The Common Review*, the Foundation's quarterly, from 2001 until 2010. Suderman (1944–2020) was a Vietnam veteran and a graduate of Anabaptist Mennonite Biblical Seminary. Over the course of his career he served as an administrator for Mennonite Voluntary Service, as owner and operator of an independent bookstore, and as an addictions counselor for the Salvation Army. He also wrote a regular column for the Kansas newspaper *Hillsboro Free Press*. His publication credits include *Books & Culture*, *The Common Review*, and *Mennonite World Review*.

Made in the USA
Monee, IL
06 March 2021

62065522R00118